BAYOU

Wendy Mae Mansell

Ormond Beach, FL

BAYOU

This is a work of fiction. All of the characters, names, incidents, organizations, and dialogue in this novel are either the products of the author's imagination or are used fictitiously.

Wirty Dord Book Co. books may be ordered through booksellers.

The views expressed in this work are solely those of the author and do not necessarily reflect the views of the publisher, and the publisher hereby disclaims any responsibility for them.

Front cover artwork by Leraynne S.
Interior Design by Laura Kreitzer Morgan

Library of Congress Control Number: in progress

ISBN:
979-8-9954503-0-6 (sc)
979-8-9954503-1-3 (digital)

I dedicate this book to my mama, because she'll whoop me if I don't. Thanks for always holding our world together, no matter how badly the men kept breaking things.

ACKNOWLEDGMENTS

I'd like to start by acknowledging my dear friend, amazing editor, impressive writer, and all around life-saver Laura Kreitzer Morgan, for her countless hours spent combing through my manuscript, booping my typos, and demanding I make it more VISCERAL. Without her, I wouldn't be half the writer I am today.

Datona, my beautiful boy, who brainstormed what a talking alligator might say, and believed his mom could do things like write a book.

My Wattpad readers, my OGs, who loved this book and its characters first. Without you, I doubt I would have ever finished any of my stories. You gave me the confidence to grow, and you will forever hold a special place in my heart.

Last but not least, I want to acknowledge my husband and my amazing babies Dixie and Scarlette, for allowing me time to write, even though we all know I'm the fun one.

I see the world slowly transformed into a wilderness; I hear the approaching thunder that, one day, will destroy us too. I feel the suffering of millions. And yet, when I look up at the sky, I somehow feel that everything will change for the better, that this cruelty too shall end, that peace and tranquility will return once more.

Anne Frank

BAYOU

1 NECESSARY

Danny stuck the needle in my arm, and the pinch was nothing compared to the burn. He was always apologetic while he killed me, like a doctor administering a vaccine to a child. *Listen, kid, this hurts me more than you.* But it wasn't a vaccine, and it didn't hurt him. He was the scientist. He had position and power; pumping poison into me and countless others secured that for him.

Danny hung the bag, connected the tube, and the fun began. *Drip. Drip. Drip.* My hands fisted; muscles twisted, as neon green snaked its way into my system. We didn't know what it was. We didn't know where it came from, or why the government wanted it tested. We just knew it hurt like hell: boiling blood, torching organs, devouring us like liquid gangrene. I'd done two bags the day before and barely made it home. It was only half full today, a kindness I'd pay for later.

Six more women made up my group, all at various stages of deterioration. I'd been around longer than any of them. Danny kept me whole. The rest weren't so lucky. I watched them come and go, one after the other, healthy to half dead to replaced.

Lita, the girl in the next chair, was close to the final stage, and she'd noticed the favoritism I received. I avoided her gaze.

I was an enemy, a traitor. I'd found a loophole and sold my soul to jump through it.

"Why does Willow only get half a bag?" It would be a miracle if she made it through the week. Festering sores coated her arms, her neck, her face. They filled the spaces where no hair covered her scalp. Angry, oozing craters marred her near translucent skin as if her body were a war zone. A war already finished. A war she'd lost. The fight should've been gone from her, but her question stole the moisture from my mouth. We didn't get to ask questions. We didn't get to say anything. I knew her rage. How it built over time, pressurized by the knowledge our world was fucked beyond repair. It was a dangerous mindset we all avoided. It didn't help. It only sped up the process.

The atmosphere charged as Danny stopped to stare at her.

Lita took a slow, rattling breath. "I have two kids who need me. I'm doing three bags. I'll barely be able to fill the ration tickets you give for this, let alone make it home and get them fed." Her voice broke and lifted. "They go to bed every night alone, with their mother passed out. I hear them trying to wake me, but I'm too weak to open my eyes. If I'm doing more, aren't I more necessary? Shouldn't I at least receive more tickets than she does?"

Danny shook his head. "These are trials. You knew that when you signed on. The amount we need to administer will vary, and the payment isn't based upon changes in the research."

"Bullshit!" She yanked against the straps binding her wrists. "Does this look like a choice? This is just to survive another day!"

"Stop it," I hissed.

Her gaze met mine, wide and wild. She scanned the other women locked to identical chairs, their faces, their doses, as if it were her first time seeing. She shouldn't have opened her eyes. She shouldn't have let it sink in. Her heaving breaths quickened. "This isn't right." She scrutinized the group again, pleading to the wrong people.

Heads lowered. Eyes averted. She was already dead, buried too deep to be heard.

"You just sit there," she said, shaking her head in disbelief. "We all just sit here!" Her gaze centered on Danny. "Undo my straps. I want to leave."

"For safety reasons, I cannot—"

"I want to leave!" Realization slackened her jaw, crumbled her features, because she knew it was over. She'd collapsed beneath the weight. Now the world would crush her, and the rubble would bury her children. She'd never make it home. She'd never get them fed. They'd never need to wake her again. "I want to leave. I want to leave." She seemed hypothermic. The way she shook. The way she stuttered.

Danny lifted a hand and rattled off handbook jargon, policies and procedures, scripted and meaningless nothings meant to keep the cattle from stampeding.

When he continued to talk over her, Lita threw her head back and screamed. Then, she kept screaming, as if someone really might help. Like it would make a difference. Perhaps wake the rest of us. Lita wasn't the only one too weak to open their eyes.

Her shrieking sucked the oxygen from the room. I couldn't breathe. I couldn't cope. I sat frozen, doing what we all did, waiting for an end. Softer cries mingled with the noise. The newest girl sniffled and shook, and the woman next to her murmured a sharp command to be quiet. Like me, the rest were wiser. Lita made us invisible. All Danny saw was her. All anyone watching would see was her, but any move or noise could break the spell. Any reaction at all and we would become her: defiant, defective, in need of disposal.

Lita wrenched and roared, bucking hard against the straps. The brackets holding the chair down rattled, and the pole her dosage hung from tipped.

Danny lunged and caught it before it hit the ground.

"Danny," I urged. For what, I didn't know. To save her? To make a deal?

He righted the pole and spoke from the side of his mouth. "They already saw."

To prove his words, three officials rushed into the room.

Wait! The sound locked at the base of my throat. One word. A humane word. An insane word. A word that would have sealed my fate with hers.

"There is no 'greater good'!" Lita wailed. "There's no humanity left to save!"

The men unbuckled Lita's flailing limbs, ignored her haunting screams, and dragged her away with no remorse. No pause. She'd committed the crime of being human. Human responses got you noticed. Being noticed got you listed. Being listed meant you were unworthy of inhabiting Earth.

A poster of Josef Arogander hung on the inside of the door, and the moment it swung shut behind them, he smiled at us. Approving. Blasting his message even there, even then. Deplete the population. Keep the balance between humanity and nature. Save the planet.

For the greater good.

I pushed through the front door and dropped two grocery bags into Merle's recliner. "Julia!"

She stepped into view, drying her hands with a dish towel too cheery for my mood; bright yellow baby chicks, smiling cows, and big, red barns. Old. Normal.

"They stopped taking ration tickets for produce." I motioned toward the bags. "All we can get is that god-awful gelatin shit they're always pushing." I kicked off my shoes and hurried for the sofa. The room spun, and my stomach churned, but it could have been worse. Danny had gone easy on me, and guilt about Lita gnawed at my insides. She'd been right. It hadn't been fair, and if she'd known the truth about Danny and me, she'd have been even more outraged. Her kids were alone now, and, tomorrow morning, they'd be no more.

I'd carry the blame.

Julia dropped the towel onto the counter, then stepped over to Merle's chair and peeked inside the bags. She grimaced. "I can't cook this shit."

Despite my thoughts, my mouth quirked up at one side. She always managed to draw a smile from me when I had no smiles left to give. Then again, you didn't see too many sixty-five year-old women who sported hot pink skinny jeans, lime green tank tops, and spoke like Julia. "It's a good thing you don't have to cook it. It's ready to eat. I hear the ham flavor is to die for." Literally.

Her jaw clenched. "Yeah? Well, then, we'll just let the supreme leader have at it, because there ain't no way in hell I'm going to eat ham-flavored fucking jello!" She kicked the chair and turned back to the kitchen. "You tell Josef Arogander that my squash grew in just fine, and if he wants a plate, he can meet me over on Kiss-my-wrinkled-ass Blvd."

I grinned. "Where's Merle?"

"Where the hell do you think?" She banged pots and pans as she worked to prepare a meal that had nothing to do with what I'd brought home.

I stood, and the neon green was a raging sea with waves large enough to sink me. I waded through the swells and found Merle in his usual spot inside the shed, working in secret. Gas-powered vehicles had been outlawed for years, but they'd have to kill Merle before he gave up his Camaro. Cherry red on the outside, chrome and love on the inside. He'd swapped the vin number with one on a junker when they started the round up, and low and behold, his baby had been hidden away, safe and secure for years.

When I stepped inside, he lifted his head. "Come here, Little Bit."

Little Bit. He'd been calling me that since the first day we met, and I'd hated it in the beginning. Men always started off with a little bit, then a little more, and more still. I'd have sooner expected to be struck by lightning than meet a man who wanted nothing from me. But then there was Merle, rare as rocking-horse shit, and treating me like his long-lost daughter. I'd been eighteen, just aged out of the system, when I stepped into him and Julia's diner, asking for a job. They'd given me that and so much more. They'd given me a home, a family, and proof that not all men were the same. So, when the diner shut down with all the others deemed menaces to

Mother Nature, producers of too much waste, I made my deal with Danny to keep them alive. And I'd do it again because they were worth more than the entirety of The Greater Good.

I peeked inside the trunk: duffel bags, a hand saw, a box of nails, a hammer, a flashlight. "What's this?"

"A plan." He pulled the lid shut and turned to face me. "An old buddy of mine told me about a couple of uninhabitable spots marked by the government."

I stared at him. "And?"

"We should go there."

I snorted. He was joking. Of course he was joking, but the longer I stood waiting for him to laugh, the more apparent it became he was, in fact, not joking at all. "You know we can't actually do that, right? If it's uninhabitable, that means you can't inhabit it."

"That's the thing." He pulled a folded map from his jean pocket and smoothed it out onto the rear of the car. "There's two of them that they know of." He pointed to the first spot, circled in red grease pencil, then followed a line drawn down the river and into the canals where another circle had been marked. "Him and his gang are already living in this one," he said, thumping the page.

I raised an eyebrow. It was no secret Merle had been involved in some less than wholesome activities in his past. Hell, even now, he looked ready to hop on a Harley and live free or die.

"They saw the same signs marking this other while scavenging for supplies. It's not that far from us."

"It's not close either," I said. "How do you propose we get there? Get in our flying machine? We can't drive this car.

They'd stop us within five minutes and take us all to the recycling bin."

Now he laughed. "With what? Those little fucking electric soapboxes they beep around in? Only way they'll stop me is if I choose to stop. No. We just go, haul fucking ass. From what Tex tells me—"

"Tex?"

He chuffed a breath, then glanced over with a stern jaw and crinkled eyes. "Yeah, his name's Tex. What's wrong with that?"

"We're taking advice about a place that may or may not exist, that apparently isn't inhabitable, from a man named Tex?"

"Look here, Little Bit. Men with names like Tex will be the only motherfuckers alive after this shit show is over. Now—" he turned back to the map "—from what Tex tells me, all we have to do is make it inside, and the officials won't follow. They're dumping shit in these remote locations, and whatever it is, they're scared to death of it. Won't even go in with a hazmat suit on."

Men like Tex were probably already lying dead in a puddle of neon green. "What does that tell you?"

Merle turned and gripped my shoulder. "It tells me we've got a chance there. You think we'll last here? What about when your teeth fall out like all the other lab rats? They call you necessary, but they aren't skipping this house during the raids because they need you alive. They skip this house because you're already letting them kill you."

I swallowed hard, my argument dead in the face of his honesty. They were killing me. I could feel it. I'd seen it happen to the other girls. It had happened today. My thoughts drifted back to Lita. I thought about her children, orphaned. I knew how that felt. Home alone. Waiting. Already condemned to be rounded up and executed. Unworthy. Unnecessary.

Unless…

I could save them, make it right, fix one thing about this ugly world. "One condition," I said, heart accelerating even at the thought of such a massive decision. It was absurd. It was suicide. But there were worse fates than death on my terms. My choice, not theirs. Then at least I wouldn't be dragged away, thrown onto some inhuman heap, and forgotten. At least I'd die having done something. "We'd have to leave tonight."

Merle's lips thinned; one eye squinted. The expression he made anytime there was bad news. "Why the sudden rush? Did something happen?"

"They took a woman from the lab today. She has two kids somewhere." I paused. My fault. My deal with Danny pushed her over the edge. She'd pleaded for an ally, and I'd said nothing. I'd watched, unblinking, as she was carted away to slaughter. Her kids were alone because of me. They would die because of me. "We bring them with us."

Merle barked a laugh. "There's that fuck-the-government attitude I was looking for!" He ruffled my hair and pulled me into a tight hug. "Can you find them?"

I sighed and nodded slowly. "I think so. I can ask Danny to check her chart and give me the address."

His smile faded, eyes dulled. Reality was a shadow even Merle's light couldn't survive. "Be careful. Don't trust anyone who works for them. If at any point it feels like things are off, you hightail it out of there and get your ass home. I'll get Julia tied up to make it easier to leave." He winked.

I laughed, but it was hollow. I had a bad feeling. It was risky, and risky equaled stupid, but I didn't have a choice. I had to do something. Something human. I had to do something sane before I lost what little sanity I had left.

My time was running out.

2
PAYMENT

The hallway was all creams and whites, smooth like velvet and immaculate. Vases of fresh flowers sat upon stone pillars, and paintings of peaceful landscapes hung perfectly spaced along the walls. Hell wasn't supposed to be beautiful, but it was. It didn't stink of sulfur or death. Little air fresheners, tucked discreetly into corners, misted the atmosphere with fresh rain. Murderer wasn't sprawled in blood across the last door. Instead, a gold plate engraved in pristine script read Dr. Daniel Clyde, Head of Chemical Therapy.

Therapy. Another ridiculous word to cover up another. The world was shaded in antonyms. Hot was cold. Up was down, and therapy was purgatory. Who were they lying to? Us or themselves? Perhaps it was simply an illusion to draw the holy into the fire. Regardless, I walked the hall each week, and tonight, I walked it again, dangerously unannounced. Most people didn't know the devil required an appointment, but he did, and showing up without one was a good way to die. I knocked twice and ignored the instinctive urge to turn back.

Danny wrenched the door open, saw me standing there, and scanned the hallway. His pallor reddened, a glimpse of his true form, then he pulled me inside and shoved the door shut. "Are you insane?"

"I know."

He pivoted and strode over to the window, checked the lot below, then twisted the blinds closed.

I stood silent, choosing my words. It had to be tonight. There was no time to wait, and I couldn't let those children die. Things like that happened all the time, and just like everyone else, I didn't look. I stepped back, sinking deeper inside the bubble we all kept around ourselves, focusing only on the survival of myself and those closest to me. I couldn't look away this time. I'd never even seen their faces, yet they dominated my focus. I saw myself, a child without a family, begging any who would listen for love and protection. I'd orphaned them. If that was the person I needed to be to survive, I didn't want to live. Not anymore. I'd had enough. "I wanted to ask for a favor."

"A favor?" He turned, posture rigid. "I just did you a favor this morning. You think it's easy to explain why I'm giving you a quarter of the dosage?"

The urge to laugh brewed, but my chest was blessedly too tight to oblige. What difference did one more lie make? Compared to all the others, this one was easy. But I didn't say that, because that would have been too honest, and honesty would have clashed with the carpet. "This isn't about treatment. The woman who was taken—"

He waved me off. "She's already gone."

He said it so casually, as if she were a bag of trash already disposed. A spark formed in the pit of my stomach and flared before I could snub it out. "I know that, Danny. I watched them drag her away."

His attention dropped to the cellphone on his desk. I

tensed. He wouldn't make the call unless he absolutely had to. He knew, if he did, he'd risk having his own dealings questioned.

"You aren't losing it on me, are you, Willow?" His voice was another lie, low and calm.

"No." The sunlight filtering through the cracks in the blinds dulled, gray mixing into gold. I was taking too long. This was taking too much time, and we hadn't even started yet. I stepped forward, closer to him, arms loose, face relaxed, pliant and obedient, just like they wanted us. "I need her address."

"Her address…" He looked me over, from my worn shoes to my plain, white T-shirt, and one corner of his mouth twitched. "You want to loot her house?"

"I want to check on her kids."

"Ah, I see." He grinned as if I'd told a joke. "They'll be gone tonight. You know that."

"I want to get them out."

His head shook.

He didn't say what I already knew, but I heard him as if he had. They were already listed. The minute she was taken in, their fate was sealed. It wasn't like the government would just give up when they weren't there. They'd come looking, and anyone with a connection would be searched. Me and everyone in the same clinical group would be suspected.

He tutted and collected a stray chunk of my hair between his fingers. "It's noble of you, truly, but impossible."

Impossible. Didn't he know? Impossible was our reality. One central government was impossible, until it wasn't. Mass killing people based off criminal record, class, financial status, education, was impossible, until it wasn't. Impossible was just another illusion, the worst one of all. "I understand the risk." I held his gaze levelly and swallowed all the words I wanted to say. "I'm willing to pay, the same as always."

His interest drifted to my lips. It was the deal we'd made. Favor for a favor. He'd allow me to keep my body whole if I allowed him to use that body at his request. It kept Merle and Julia alive, and it was all I had to trade for the lives of two more.

He sucked in a breath, mulling over the risks. It didn't take him long. He ran his fingers deeper into my hair. "What do I get?"

Bile rose, but I swallowed it. "Same as always."

"No. This is different. I need more from you."

A shiver raced down my spine, freezing me until I was cold and solid, impenetrable. Ice formed into blocks and piled high inside my mind, building a wall for me to hide behind. He wanted more, and my cup was drained. I'd already given him all I had, all that was left. "How much more?"

"Whatever I want."

Back on the empty street, back to reality, where the roads were coated in dirt. The trash twisted and twirled as a smoggy breeze carried it off to nowhere. That was me: trash on the road, used and discarded, left to decompose until someone made me disappear. Each move I made was accompanied by a sharp ache, like salt on a burn or sweat in a cut. My legs wobbled, stretched too far. Knots throbbed on my arms where his fingers had dug in and searched for bone. He'd burned me with his touch, left me charred, and I could smell him on my skin. Heady and thick, the putrid scent of smoke masked by men's cologne. I'd missed curfew, and the officials were already silently working their way around the city. That was probably Danny's intention. I get caught. I get killed. He doesn't have to worry about me just showing up at his office again.

He'd kept me too long and demanded everything. He'd taken and done until each step I took was a shadow of his torture. Still, I pushed on. The address he'd given me wasn't far from home. If I moved quickly, I had a chance.

I cut through yards and in between houses, ducking into the shadows each time a set of headlights shone on the street. The dull hum of electric trucks, the jangling clatter of their bulk rumbling over the potholes, the squeal of breaks. They sounded how the school buses used to, back before public schools had been considered unnecessary. But they weren't school buses. They were death. A distant cry echoed into the night, followed by a jumble of words spoken through haunting sobs. A scuffle. Shouts. Whoever they were taking was putting up a fight. I hurried to the next yard and toward my destination, away from the sound, praying they'd be able to hold them up long enough for me to accomplish my task.

Lita's house was small and dilapidated. The remains of once-white paint coated the worn wood in splotches, and the roof to a small porch hung low to one side, ready to collapse. The steps groaned at my weight. "Hello?" I tapped on the door. "Kids? If you're in there, I need you to open up."

Silence. I wasn't surprised. No doubt Lita had taught her children to hide, to stay quiet, to never open the door for anyone but her. But when the officials arrived, there'd be no hiding, and the flimsy lock wasn't enough to keep the flies from coming inside. I pulled out my ID, wedged it into the crack of the doorframe, then jerked on the handle. It gave a click, then swung open to reveal the dark squalor within. Toys and clothes were strewn around the room, trash and soiled dishes left to lay wherever they'd landed. A mixture of spoiled milk and mildew singed my nostrils, and I tripped over a bowl, the remains of whatever was inside spilling out onto my shoe.

"Kids?" I hissed, creeping through the living space. "Your mother sent me. We have to get out of here before the bad people come."

A soft thud sounded from the next room, and I rushed toward it, stepping over and around obstacles, heart pounding in my ears, until everything froze. I stared, dazed. Both children were there, huddled together, little mice amongst the filth, and for a moment, I had no idea what to do. I'd been so focused on saving them but seeing them changed everything. It made them real. It gave them life, and I was the only thing standing between them and their deaths. I couldn't fuck it up. I couldn't fail.

My gaze locked with the wide, frightened eyes of a girl no older than six. She looked like a ghost, lit up by a rising moon, her eyes inky black and alert. Behind her back, she shielded a boy even smaller than herself. He gripped something small and square with chubby, cherub fists as if whatever it was would grant them invisibility.

"It's okay," I whispered as serene as I could manage. "I'm not here to hurt you. I'm here to help."

She searched the room as if planning an escape, but she didn't move. My heart cracked at the sight of them, lost, abandoned, scared enough to know something was wrong but too young to know what to do.

"I know you're scared, but—"

Voices drifted toward us from the front door. I didn't think. I gripped their wrists and hoisted one onto each arm, tight against my sore hips as I tilted and stumbled in an unbalanced sprint for the back. They didn't cry, didn't scream or beg to be put down. They remained frozen solid against my sides, matching the cold leftover from Danny. Only they were different. Innocent. Deserving. Precious ice sculptures who would shatter if I let them fall.

The kitchen was in the rear of the house, and the back-door stood off to one side. The voices swelled as I fought to turn the knob without relinquishing my grip, and the conversation drew nearer.

"I hate taking the kids," a man rumbled.

"They're better off. Look at this place." Something clanged as if kicked or tossed.

I flinched and gripped the door harder, but my fingers had liquefied, and they slipped and rolled like drops of rain on a windowpane.

"Besides," the same one continued, "they kill the young ones different. They give them a cup of juice that just puts them to sleep. They even let them pick a toy to keep until it's over. At least, that's what I heard."

I held my breath, eyes burning, shaking so hard I could barely keep my grip on the two kids, let alone manage the door. Each boot step in our direction was like the ticking of an old clock. At any moment, its hands would align, and the bell signaling our final hour would sound.

The little girl reached out and quietly turned the handle

for me. I wanted to praise her, give her a shake and whoop until the fear left her face.

But I didn't. I couldn't, and as the door swung inwards, and footsteps echoed back from where we'd been, I stumbled into the night and broke into a full sprint across the back yard. Sore limbs and battered muscles burned in protest. My stomach churned with neon green, but I refused to stop. Refused to slow. The children hung on for dear life, their fingers too small and delicate for the force in which they used.

A break in the fence was too narrow for us to fit through together, so I released them and directed them forward, following behind with a grunt as splintered wood ripped clothes and tore skin. "It's okay," I reassured, gathering them back up with quivering arms.

The voices grew distant as I cut down the next street toward home.

3 HOT ROD

I ran through a vortex. My brain couldn't focus on anything other than the smallest actions. I was hyper aware each time my shoe hit the pavement, the thud, the cracks and dips embedded in the road. The neon green still burned through my veins, hollowing me out. Without time to rest and heal, I had nothing left to give. I was out of sorts, out of fuel, but filled to the max with basic animal instinct.

Run. Run. Run to stay alive.

It wasn't enough. I stumbled and collapsed, smashing my knees against the hard cement. My stomach rolled, and sharp pain ricocheted from my head to my toes.

Tiny cherub fingers curled against the back of my neck and tangled with the hair that'd broken free from my ponytail. I looked over in surprise, having forgotten the two children still locked within my arms. They were secure against me, held up by a strength I didn't know I possessed.

The little boy met my gaze. Somber. Solemn. Too aware for his age. I heaved a wheezing breath that broke apart inside my chest.

"I think I can," he whispered.

My brow furrowed.

"I think I can." He held up the block he still gripped in

his hand. It wasn't a block, but a small, thick book. I peered at it, straining to read the cover. A brightly smiling train chugged up a hill, fluffy smoke billowing out behind it. *The Little Engine That Could.* "I think I can," the boy repeated louder. "I think I can. I think I can!"

"The train," his sister said, gripping tighter to my opposite side.

My eyes widened, mouth opened, and I could have laughed—could have cried—at the beautiful innocence trapped within such an ugly moment.

"I think I can," I said back, pushing through the pain and back to my feet. I hoisted them up, re-secured my grip, then chanted the phrase beneath my breath as I pushed the final stretch. "I think I can. I think I can." Tiny voices echoed at either side, forming a strange, chaotic harmony.

When we reached the backyard to Julia and Merle's home, an almost insane laugh bubbled out of my throat. "We made it." I squeezed them both. "We made it."

A gunshot fired.

I jolted and stared wide eyed at the light shining through Julia's cheery, yellow curtains. For that split second, it was the loudest sound I'd ever heard, but the quiet that followed was deafening. "No," I whispered, lowering the children to their feet as I stared unblinking at the windows. "No."

The back door flew open with a bang, and Julia rushed out. Something dark coated the front of her shirt, and her arms shook uncontrollably as she stumbled across the porch and down the stairs.

Her gaze caught onto the sight of me, frozen in the yard, two small children at my sides, and her shaking stopped. "The shed!" Her steps quickened.

"Merle—"

"The shed!" She pointed toward it, already only a few feet from reaching us.

I grabbed the hands of both kids and tugged them toward the structure.

Once inside, Julia didn't explain. She moved like a woman half her age. She acted like she'd rehearsed this moment a thousand times before. "Get them in the backseat." She rummaged through the shelves of Merle's work area.

I did as she asked, stealing glances as she manically moved about the room. My fingers fumbled on the seatbelt; eyes burned with unshed tears. It couldn't be real. They couldn't have suspected me so soon. I'd escaped one level of hell only to emerge deeper into the pits. The blood on Julia's shirt turned her lime green a foreboding burnt, red orange, and I blinked hard, wishing I'd wake up and find all of it a nightmare.

By the time I'd fastened both belts, Julia was jumping into the driver's seat. "Get in!"

I faced the house, even though I couldn't see it through the walls of the shed. Merle.

"Dammit, Willow! Get in the fucking car!"

I slid inside, breathing hard against the sobs so ready to steal my last bit of strength. My brain rejected the obvious. It wasn't true. Merle was okay. We'd pull the car out, and he'd be ready to go. Julia would climb into the back, and we'd drive out of there together.

But she didn't stop. She didn't slow. When Julia revved the engine to life, it roared with an intensity that drowned out the world, and she tore from the shed without bothering to open the doors. They splintered and broke away, and the car teetered and bounced as we drove over their remains.

We sped down the driveway in reverse, and as we made it to the street, I saw him. Merle. He stood beneath the glow of the porch light, covered in blood, a shotgun clutched in both hands, and a man bleeding out at his feet.

I sobbed as Julia stopped, and he started in our direction.

The high-pitched blaring of sirens sounded in the distance. Too close. The next street over at most.

"Hurry!" I shouted.

Merle ran the short distance and jerked my door open, but when I moved to climb into the back, he stopped me. His expression was fierce, a glimpse of the man he'd once been. "I'll find a way," he said, sole focus fixed on Julia.

I shook my head. "No! Get in! We can go together."

"They'll be more focused on a man with a gun than two women in a car." He laid his big hand on my head, eyes never leaving his wife's. "I love you, old lady."

"I love you too, you dirty old bastard." Her voice shook.

The sirens intensified. They were almost there. Flashing yellow lights preceded the two cars that whipped onto the street.

Merle's jaw tensed. "Drive the hell out of it!" Then he stormed toward the approaching vehicles and fired both shells into the windshield of the first car.

I didn't see the rest. The car roared as Julia tore backwards onto the road and pulled the gear into drive. Tires squealed, rubber burned, and Merle disappeared into a cloud of smoke behind us.

Merle was right about the Camaro. The little electric cars the officials used didn't stand a chance against catching us. Julia drove full speed until we made it onto the abandoned highway, then she slowed to a steady eighty miles an hour and stared blankly out the windshield.

Darkness filled the car, even after the sun rose to chase the night away. My mind spun, envisioning him, imagining how it had all gone down, clinging to the scenarios that left him alive.

We drove for hours before Julia reached into her pocket and pulled out the folded map. She held it out to me and shook it. "Navigate." Her tone was hollow.

I took it and unfolded the square, smoothing it across my lap with lethargic motions. "We're on Interstate ten, now," I said. "We can take this all the way to Interstate fifty-five. That will lead us almost straight to where he marked."

She took a deep breath. "Good." She glanced in the rear view and studied the children sitting stoically in the back. "If Merle said he'd find a way, he will."

I nodded, though I couldn't quite find it in myself to believe the dream. How could he? We took the car. We took the escape. Merle was in decent shape for his years, but he was still an old man. Sixty-eight year olds couldn't walk all the way across states, let alone with an entire government working against them.

Julia reached over and poked me one time, hard, in the shoulder. "If he said he'd find a way, he will. Us mourning a man who isn't dead won't do us any good. Merle wasn't always the papa figure you know. He'll be okay." She shook her head and squared her shoulders. "Right now, we need to focus on getting ourselves and those kids to that marker. That's it. You hear me?" Her head turned, allowing me the full effect of her stern argue-and-I'll-slap-you look.

I nodded again. Perhaps she was right. Merle had seemed to have it pretty well under control, at least, for the fraction of a second I had seen him.

"Willow?"

I looked back at her.

"Everything's gonna be fine," she said. "I can feel it. Things will get better now."

4
UNINHABITABLE

The car jostled, jarring me awake just in time to stop myself from colliding with the dash. I clutched my head and grimaced. My mouth was dry, my throat burned, and my stomach rolled, angry about its emptiness. I needed to purge. My body knew, and it warred for its own survival. But the neon green had soaked in, flooded every cell, and there was no way to expel it.

It was a part of me.

"This is it." Julia motioned to the thick trees blocking our view.

I sat up, looked around, and twisted in my seat in an attempt to place our location. "Where…where's the road?"

Julia shrugged. "You passed out. The road ended. I took a scenic route."

I turned back, checking the children. They sat like little statues, staring innocently at the two of us as we spoke.

"You can't just drive through a…" I looked around again. "A muddy field."

"Why?" She snorted. "You worried about a fucking ticket?"

"How do you even know this is the spot?" I raised both brows at her and mentally kicked myself for falling asleep.

"I followed the signs."

"In a field?!"

She snatched my chin between her perfectly manicured fingers and jerked my head to the opposite side. Yellow signs lined the trees, dozens of them. They went on for as far as my eyes could follow, every ten feet. *Biohazard.*

"Oh." I pulled away from her and swallowed hard. For the second time, I questioned Merle's judgement. "Are we sure it's safe?"

"No. But I'm sure it's not safe anywhere else." She opened her door. "Now, get out and help me hide the car."

"Hide it?" I scrambled out after her.

Julia dipped down and gathered two globbing handfuls of mud, then with a wicked smile and dancing eyes, she smacked them onto the hood of Merle's Camaro and spread them around.

I stared at her grinning face.

She caught my ogling. "What? This car has been the other woman in Merle's life for decades. I can't wait to see his face when he gets a look at how I—" she paused to study her progress "—improved it."

My heart gave a lurch, aching with the knowledge Merle would probably never see what Julia had done, but I smiled despite it. I didn't get to do that to her. I didn't get to mourn and assume the worst while she needed me to be positive. The mud was thick and compacted, and it gave a plop as I dug my hands into it. I smacked it on the windshield then lifted a brow at Julia as I spread.

Julia pulled the back door open, smiling wide at the two children still huddled together like scared kittens. "C'mon, babies! What are you waiting for? I ain't ever met a kid who didn't wanna play in the mud!"

It was the girl who acted first. She moved slowly, scooting across the seat as she worked hard to pull her brother along to keep him close. When she made it to the edge, Julia bent down to her level. "What's your name, darlin'?"

She hesitated. "Eve."

"And your little brother?" Julia peeked around at the boy ducked behind his sister.

Eve answered for him. "That's Eric."

"Well, Eve and Eric, I'm Julia." She held out her hand.

I bit back a laugh. Julia's hand was coated. Globs of mud gathered between her fingers and clumped under her nails. If the little girl wasn't reluctant before, I couldn't imagine her wanting to take the offering now.

Seconds ticked by, becoming a minute before Eve finally reached out and complied, and the moment she did, Julia pulled her from the car with a continuous nod that made her look like a happy bobble head. "That's the spirit." She reached down, grabbed a handful of mud, and smeared it into Eve's empty palm. "Now, throw that sucker!"

Eve's hesitation didn't last long. My eyes widened as her gaze moved to mine…seeking permission? Guidance? Was that my role, now? Had our late-night escape deemed me the hero? Official stand-in guardian?

Julia waited, knowing gaze fixed on me.

I shook my head, released a breath, then shrugged. "Throw that sucker!"

Both children were coated in filth and exhausted. As soon as the car was covered, Julia parked it amidst the trees and loaded us down with what we could carry from the trunk. She led the way past the signs and toward whatever fate awaited us.

I had a pack on my back, a duffle in each hand, and the weight was more than I could bare. Julia had the same, only hers wasn't quite as heavy as mine. I didn't complain; even if I were ready to collapse, I wouldn't. Despite my body's deteriorated state, I was better off than Julia. She should have been living the retired dream. She should have been sewing in a circle of old women or playing bridge at some club house. She shouldn't have been walking along a murky bank, absorbing god-knows-how-many toxins into her aging body.

The children filled the gap between us, following Julia as I kept a close pace behind. Eric was so small. He often stumbled and fell, and Eve was the perfect big sister, always quick to lift him back up and help him as he struggled. Patches of fog clung to the air, disappearing just before we could catch up to them. They reminded me of ghosts, there one minute, gone the next, a shadow in my peripheral I could never be sure was there. Perhaps they were people who'd come before and died, or people who hadn't come and wished they had. Here too late, part of the chemicals that'd killed them.

When we'd been walking for hours with little change in scenery, Julia dropped her bags and flopped down against the trunk of a giant cypress tree. "This place is uninhabitable," she said. Her shoulders slumped, back bowed, but the angle of her jaw was hard enough to compensate. "I've been waiting to see a break where we can make some sort of shelter, but the only place big enough to stand in is right beside the fucking water."

I motioned the kids to sit on either side of her and gratefully relinquished my own load to the dirt. "It has to open up at some point. Let's just rest here a little bit, then we can keep moving." I took the spot beside Eric and smiled reassuringly at the kids. "We'll find somewhere soon. Don't mind Julia. She gets cranky when she's tired."

Julia snorted but made no attempt to defend herself.

I rested my temple against the tree, sighing heavily as my muscles loosened and relaxed.

"Willow?" Julia hissed.

My eyes sprang open, expecting to see hazmat suits, flashing yellow lights, and a group of officials ready to haul us back to atone for our sins. Instead, I saw nothing. "What?"

"Look. In the water." She pointed. "What is that?"

I peered in the direction and scanned the murky surface. Three bumps blended in with the surrounding debris, rough, just like the broken limbs protruding all along the winding canal…but different. They moved, dipped beneath the surface only to pop back up a second later in a new spot a few feet closer.

Julia slowly stood, shaking her hand down at Eve to take hold. "That's an alligator," she whispered. "We need to keep our motions slow and steady and get the hell away from it."

I followed her lead, scooping Eric into my arms and positioning him on my hip. The bags stayed scattered on the ground behind me. As much as I knew we needed them, I couldn't hold Eric and them at the same time.

"Just move slow." Julia took a measured step forward.

"How fast do alligators run?" I hissed back.

The water stirred, a head floating up. A set of jaws opened

wide, revealing rows of discolored teeth big enough to remove a limb. Then, a high guttural voice called, “Oh, I can run fast! Real fast!”

For the tiniest fraction of a second, the world froze. Us, it, the water, the breeze. Every sound stopped. The alligator had spoken. Then, in the next instant, the world exploded into action.

“Fuck that!” Julia abandoned caution for a full sprint. She dragged poor Eve behind her, leaving me to stumble after with a bouncy toddler on my hip.

“Wait!” the gator called from behind us. “I wasn’t ready! That’s cheating!”

Julia looked back with wide, panicked eyes, then seeing me so far behind, turned around to meet my side and push me ahead of her. “Dammit, girl! Go!”

I pushed ahead, gripping Eve’s hand and leaving Julia to follow alone. My body protested, once again asked to perform beyond its capabilities. Eve stumbled to keep up, her little legs too short, but I didn’t pause long enough to lift her onto my opposite side. I didn’t think it would speed us up. The added weight would likely cause my legs to break.

“Hey! Where you going?” it called again. “You dropped your old lady!”

I glanced back and stumbled to a stop. Julia was on the ground, backing away from the massive gator looming over her. It matched each inch she gained.

I sat Eric back down and pulled him and Eve together behind my back. There were only three choices. Protect the children, save Julia, or find some impossible way to do both.

I couldn’t leave the last person I had. Merle had forced

me. He'd forced us both to leave him behind, and I refused to do it again. I would not be alone out here, and I would not mourn them both. I'd rather be eaten.

I led the children behind me, both of their wrists gripped in my left hand as I reluctantly closed the gap between us and Julia.

"It's about time!" the gator said. "You can't be leaving this old lady lying around like this. Don't you know there's gators out here?"

I stared at it. Careful. Ready and waiting for the moment I'd be forced to fight. I had a plan. Kick it in the head. It wouldn't kill it, but it would at least buy me a few moments for Julia to flee. Or, maybe, I could wrestle it, jump on its back and hold its jaws shut like those men in khaki hats always did. *Crickey, you're a live one, ya' are. I've lost my mind.*

It flopped onto its stomach and panted. "Woo, that was exhilarating! I haven't ran that hard since Croc and I used to race. He always won, but at least he didn't cheat." He side-eyed both of us. "You're supposed to say, 'ready, set, go' *then* run."

"It's talking," I hissed toward Julia. "How the hell…?"

The gator tilted its head at us. "I'm sitting right here, and my name is Gator, not It." He lifted his chin and huffed.

Julia nodded shakily. "Yes. Well…it's nice to meet you… Gator." She cleared her throat and pushed me back an inch as she stood. "We're new here, and…I guess we were just a bit startled, is all." She pushed me again, hard.

He bobbed his head up and down, and his jaws parted into a toothy grin. "Well, that's alright then! I should have known you were new. We don't get too many humans around here. Only the ones that come by to dump the sludge, but they're always wearing those white suits with the spaceman helmets."

He hopped back to his feet, and I squeaked, scuffling out of instinct and almost falling backward.

The gator ducked his head low and fixed his gaze with mine. "Don't be scared. I won't eat you. My best friend is a human."

For a nano second, a glimmer of hope surfaced. A human, in this swamp, alive. But I couldn't quite hang onto the feeling, not when the good news came from the jaws of the unbelievably bad news.

"There are more humans out here?" Julia asked.

"Just Croc," he answered, smiling widely up at her.

How was she so calm? How was she able to talk to that *thing* like it was any normal day and we just needed directions?

Oh, by the way, do you know the way to the survivable parts of this place?

Of course! You just make a left at the tree that looks like all the other trees.

Why, thank you, talking-thing-that-isn't-supposed-to-be-talking!

My breaths were ragged as my focus bounced between the two of them. It was the final straw. I was a half-broken camel. A psychotic laugh fought to bubble free of my lungs. This couldn't be real. This wasn't real. I was laid out on the road. I'd never made it home. Merle and Julia were sitting in the living room, watching the news and worried about where I was.

"He's got a big ol' house. Real fancy. I can take you ladies there if you'd like. Your kids, too. My oh my, you are a fertile one, ain'tcha'? You gotta be careful with little ones, and Croc's place is safer than out here. Critters would just love to gobble the lot of you right up."

Julia dusted off her hot pink pants. For what reason, I didn't know. All she managed to do was smear mud, and something told me the gator didn't give two shits about how put together she was.

"We'd be much obliged," she said.

"We would?" I said.

"We would." She turned with both brows lifted and lowered her tone to an angry whisper. "We don't have many options, and I'd rather not piss off the talking alligator."

I clenched my jaw and nodded. The kids were huddled together, watching with wide, excited eyes and open smiles. It surprised me. While they'd grown to trust Julia and I a bit more, they were always cautious, scared. But now, with a gator large enough to turn them into muddy appetizers, they were…enamored. I supposed it would make sense. He was straight out of a cartoon, and if I weren't too busy visualizing my feet sticking from his mouth, I'd have been just as amazed.

We gathered our things and followed him, and it was the oddest thing I'd ever done. I stared at it, feeling more hysterical by the second. His tail swished back and forth, legs bowed wide, sashaying across the mud and roots.

The sun fell its final few feet beneath the horizon, and lightning bugs emerged. Brightest neon green. They glittered around us, forming clusters and waltzing across the air, breaking apart, disappearing, then lighting up one by one to dance again.

"It's just ahead. Big place. *Nice* place. And Croc, he's a real nice guy. He'll be more than happy to help you ladies out."

The trees spread out and formed a canopy above a large circular yard. The fireflies lingered in clusters around the doorway and light glowed from two small windows across the front. It was a shack, barely big enough for two rooms, and the way it fit into the surroundings seemed as if it'd sprung from the very swamp itself. A dock extended at least twenty feet out, reaching from the front door to hover above the murky depths of the canal.

"Croc!" Gator picked up his pace as we drew closer. "Croc!" His head swished over toward us. "He's gonna be real happy. Croc don't ever get to see people, especially super fertile lady people."

My hesitation magnified. "If that alligator calls me fertile one more time, we're leaving."

Julia shushed me.

The front door creaked open, and a massive shadow stepped into the light. Long, matted dreadlocks hung heavily against his bare chest and shoulders. A beard, braided into two, filled the space between each side and dangled to his stomach. All that covered the rest of him was a pair of torn jean shorts and dried mud.

He froze at the sight of us, hands hung limp at his sides, mouth agape.

Gator rumbled a laugh. "I found these *fertile lady humans*, and they need a place to stay," he teased.

Croc jolted back to life. "Hello." He paused and scratched his beard, still gaping. "Croc has a house." He motioned behind him as if we wouldn't have noticed. "Croc can share it with you and provide food and water." He stepped over to the edge of the dock and pulled a cage from the depths. It was full of fish, flopping back and forth and barely distinguishable in the inky night atmosphere. "Croc is a good hunter." He straightened and dropped the cage. "Croc is strong." He flexed.

"Julia? What the hell is going on?" I spoke through barely parted lips.

Croc stopped talking and watched.

Julia was quiet a long moment. "I think…he's trying to impress you."

There it was. Another deal. Another hurtle for me to throw my soul over. There were a million Dannys, and it didn't matter where I went, I'd find another: A foster home, a group home, an after-school program, and now, a chemical swamp. It was the story of my life, and I fought the urge to throw up my hands and venture off alone. Nobody knew about that part of my life, not even Julia and Merle. It was my shame to carry. My burden to hold, and I didn't want them to look at me different or feel guilty about what I'd had to do to keep us safe. It was the same reason I wouldn't walk away now. That wasn't who I was. I didn't abandon, and I'd especially never abandon Julia. "Why me?" It was a question for the universe.

Julia answered all the same. "I'm old, and it's you he's staring at."

He was. He watched our conversation with an acute awareness, a studying, a determination that was far too sudden and more than a little off putting. When we stopped talking and focused back on him, he said, "Croc would make equally strong children."

My lips pursed.

Julia snorted.

Gator spoke up again. "He ain't lying. He's real strong. Faster than me, even in the water."

I took a step back.

Croc's expression tightened, and he matched the motion, extending a hand as if at any moment he'd jump off the dock and drag me away by my hair.

Julia eyed him up, from his feet to his head. "There'll be no babies. We already have those." She motioned to the children, then fell silent another long moment, studying him in return. She didn't seem worried or upset. She didn't seem reluctant in the least. Her expression held the same warmth she'd offered me when I stepped into Merle's Diner all those years ago. "You haven't been around humans much, have you, hon?"

My attention shifted between the two of them, and I tried to see whatever it was Julia did.

He shuffled his feet, scratched the back of his neck. Almost bashful? Ashamed? Embarrassed? It was an odd look for a man his size, especially given his appearance. "No, but—"

She cut him off. "Alright then. That's not how it works. No babies—"

"But—"

She pointed and gave him *the look.* The I'm-old-and-will-beat-you-to-death-if-you-disrespect-me look. I'd felt the force of it a thousand times since I'd met her, but I didn't see how it could work on a man who looked like he'd just returned from a war zone.

"No babies," she snapped. "That's the rules. You don't make babies with humans you just met."

His jaw worked as if an argument were bouncing around

inside his mouth, but whatever magic Julia possessed was more powerful than I realized.

He motioned toward his door. "Do people offer shelter to humans they just met? Because it's dark, and Croc doesn't want the other gators to eat you."

Julia nodded and smiled. "What a nice young man. We'd love some shelter."

I gaped as she walked ahead, and both children quickly moved to follow. Croc didn't move or look away as he waited for me to join her.

I swallowed hard and reassured myself that Julia had it under control. I wouldn't need to make a deal. We could get by without one this time. Regardless, the children were no doubt hungry. They'd been walking for hours, and the longer I stood still, the more my own fatigue fought to knock me over.

There was no other choice. Julia was already on the porch. The kids were right behind her. I hoisted the packs and sighed, vowing this time would be different even though I knew…

I'd do whatever I needed to keep us safe.

5
PROVIDE

Stepping into the shack was like stepping through a time portal. Relics of a time when people were free, and the world made some sense. A couch, boxy and outdated, sat coated in filth under a large window on the back wall. A lamp, finely made with iron-style lace and ornate stained glass fought to be noticed beneath a blanket of cobwebs. Altogether, the house was only big enough for three rooms. A kitchen, one great room, and a small bedroom that protruded off the back like an afterthought. The door to it stood wide open, revealing a twin-sized mattress on the floor and a massive array of boxes lining the back wall. To my left was a wooden ladder that led to a loft space just big enough for a person to lay flat in.

No need for a tour; I barely needed to turn my head to see it all. A kerosene lantern illuminated a round wooden table dead center of the kitchen, but whatever burned inside the glass wasn't kerosene. I paused; eyes narrowed at the neon green sludge resting in the bottom. "What's in that lantern?" I walked toward it, already knowing the answer. I knew nothing about the chemical they'd pumped into me every day for the past few months, but I knew this was it. I knew every face I'd watched wither and fade away. I knew how long each woman lasted; whether she'd cried and begged or sat stoic and resigned. I'd known it was toxic. I'd known it was deadly, but flammable? The flame was brighter than average, a slight lilac hue to its edges. They'd injected that into us. Into human beings. What I really wanted to know was where the hell this man got it from, and how he'd discovered it would burn.

He motioned toward the light. "That's sludge," he said. "Sludge makes fire. Croc provides that."

Julia laughed beneath her breath. She was bent down a few feet behind me, rummaging through the bags in search of food for the children.

Croc held his beard, pulling it in a way that made me think it was a nervous habit.

"I've had enough sludge. Thank you."

For a long moment, our gazes held. His eyes were intense, shimmering around the edges with the same neon green, probably a reflection.

He tilted his head, watching me study him, then gently pulled a chair from the table. "Croc provides food."

I opened my mouth to decline.

Julia interjected. "I have something for the kids to eat. They're exhausted. Would you mind if I laid them down somewhere?"

He jolted like an eager dog trying to earn a treat. "Croc has bed."

Julia leaned back and winked at me as he gently took her arm and led her toward the open doorway. I followed at a distance.

The bedroom was carpeted at least, though the color was uncertain. Julia took the top two blankets off the twin mattress and popped them into the air, forming a cloud of dust that made Eric sneeze.

Croc jumped at the sound, then stared down at the boy with wide eyes. Before I could think to be worried, he dropped down onto his knees, leveling himself with the child.

Julia spread the blankets back over the mattress.

Eric stayed with him, looking back with matching curiosity. Child-like, both of them. But Croc wasn't a child, and when he lifted his massive hand and touched the downy brown curls, I took an instinctive step forward.

"It's fine, Willow," Julia said, still focused on her task.

I chewed my lip and watched as Eve stepped closer as well. Neither of them had looked at me like that when I'd found them hidden among the filth. Neither had seemed so relaxed, not even in the car after we made it away. What was it about this place, this man, that put them so at ease? A part of me wanted to scoop them up and keep running until we reached the end of the world. Another part wanted to join in, allow myself a blissful reprieve from warranted fear and constant survival. The privilege of naivety, of blind faith. I couldn't remember the last time I'd experienced something so valuable.

Croc smoothed the hair between his fingers, marveled at the texture, then let go and grasped Eric's hand, pulling the tiny fingers up to study one by one. "Small," he whispered.

My brows lifted as Eric reached his free hand up and tangled it into the man's matted locks.

Julia finished her task but didn't move from her place on the floor. She watched the two, lips softly curved.

Eve stepped closer and followed her brother's lead. She took a different clump of the wild man's hair and pulled it toward her until they looked like two children at a petting zoo.

A wide smile broke across Croc's face, giving a glimpse of surprisingly white teeth.

"Alright, kids. Come and eat what Papa Merle packed for you."

I inwardly flinched at his name, but Julia was too busy opening wrappers and cans to notice.

Eve released his hair and moved toward the mattress, but Eric lingered. He stared into Croc's eyes, the same way he'd done mine when I collapsed in the road. "Safe?" he asked, the -f a little too pronounced.

Croc stiffened, and his attention centered and ran over the little boy's face, the downy hair, his chubby arms, as if checking for injuries. "Croc protect." His tone was deeper than before. "Croc is strong."

Eric smiled and lunged forward, wrapping his tiny arms around Croc's neck and burrowing his face into his hair.

My vision swam, eyes burned, and I turned away, blinking rapidly as I made an escape. Too afraid to go outside, I ended up in the kitchen and sat in the chair he'd pulled out for me. It wasn't right. How fucked was the world when this was the answer? How messed up was it that two small kids would find comfort in a situation that should have been traumatizing? Normal was dead. It wasn't going to come back. They'd never know it. I'd never have it again.

Julia stepped into the room, and I heard the front door open and shut a second later.

"Are you sure we're safe here?" I asked.

She pursed her lips. "So far so good." She took the chair beside mine.

I leaned closer, my mind battling between what I'd just witnessed and the frequent mention of my fertility. "I don't know." I glanced toward the opening. "Where did he go?"

"To *provide* us food." She snickered. "You need to look on the bright side. We found shelter. We found food. There's a person who has managed to survive out here." She took my hand in hers and squeezed. "We're free. We're alive. We're safe. That's a lot more than the rest will get."

I flinched. It was more than Merle might get, and I was an asshole for forgetting. She was right. It could be worse. We could have been rounded up like the countless others and sent to die. I sucked in a deep breath and focused on the fact I was still able to. "You're right. Okay."

The front door opened and closed again, and Croc flopped three giant fish onto the tabletop.

"What the fuck!" I jerked away, so hard my back cracked. Fish. Not fillets or chunks. Whole fish, so big their tails hung off the edge. They gasped for air, snarling at us with hundreds of tiny sharp fangs. I pulled my hands inward; curled my fingers. "What the fuck is that?"

Croc tilted his head. "Fish." He sat on the other side of Julia, across from me, then seeming to have read my mood, focused more on her. "Food." He motioned at the wiggling, not-dead fish.

Even Julia couldn't manage to hide her reluctance. "It's food, Willow."

Croc beamed then looked at me expectantly. "Croc catches the biggest fish. Never small ones." He stared, eyes roaming my face, my hair.

"Yeah! Croc catches big fish. Some fish bigger than me!"

Gator called from somewhere outside, and the sound drifted in through the opened window behind us.

Croc nodded and dipped his chin toward the flopping creatures.

"I don't eat fish," I lied. I did eat fish, just not those fish, not live fish, and never a fish that could eat me back.

Thankfully, Julia had the same opinion. "We were thinking, you've provided so much already, how about you let us provide the food."

She stood, ever the diplomat, and left the room only to return a moment later with one of the duffle bags.

Croc's face fell, but his curiosity over what she had seemed to outweigh his need to be the dominant-alpha-whatever.

Julia eyed the table. "Perhaps we can put the fish back and eat them later."

He stared at them a moment then nodded, gathering them back up and moving straight for the door.

Julia snorted as soon as he'd gone. "That was interesting."

"Have you ever even seen a fish like that?" I asked.

"No. But I've never seen a talking alligator either, so I'm rolling with it." She grabbed an old towel from a pile of junk in the corner, used it to wipe off the table, then pulled some of the food from the duffle bag.

Protein bars, canned wieners, saltine crackers, and…

"You brought the Jelly foods?"

She grimaced. "Merle made me. He said I wouldn't have my garden right away, and I'd just need to suck it up."

Croc returned and dropped back into his seat, studying everything Julia had set out as if it were a puzzle.

"Here," Julia said, opening a can of sausages and a pack

of crackers.

He looked at it how I'd looked at the fish.

"What animal?" He pulled one of the wieners out and jiggled it. His eyes widened in horror. "What part?"

Julia cackled, loud and hoarse, and despite the situation, I couldn't help but join her.

Croc shifted uncomfortably.

"Don't worry, boy," Julia said, forcing her laughter to fade. "If I'd been hunting for those, they'd be a hell of a lot bigger than that."

I choked and spluttered, then fell into a coughing fit.

"Water," Croc said, retrieving a large bottle from the counter behind him and two glasses from the cabinet. The glasses were old, straight from another era. He poured a portion into each one, then sat back and fixed his eyes on me.

I took a deep drink, grateful to find it clean and not the green murk outside. My coughing slowed, then ceased. I hadn't realized how parched I was until the moisture hit my tongue, and the moment it did, I chugged the glass empty.

Croc smiled and lifted back up to refill it as if he'd found the answer to all the world's problems. "Croc provides."

My brow furrowed as I looked from him then back to Julia.

Her eyes danced. "He provides."

"I'm happy you're enjoying yourself," I grumbled, not caring that the wild man could hear me. "Must be easy to be so relaxed when you're not the one trying to be impregnated."

"You're called Willow," Croc said, either not caring about what I'd just said or unaware of any type of social cue. I was betting on both.

I ate a few of the crackers, avoiding having to answer, or acknowledge, or have any interaction with my new Jungle Danny. Eventually, however, when Julia cleared her throat louder than Merle's engine, I looked up at him. "Yes."

"You have hair the color of mud, and your eyes look like swamp sludge."

My jaw clenched. Well, then. That was nice. "Thanks." The word came out flat.

Julia snorted.

"Croc likes the mud and the sludge."

"That's very sweet, Croc," Julia said, laughter clear in the undertone of her voice.

My mouth fell open.

Croc beamed. "We can make babies now?"

"No." Julia gave him a stern look.

Croc's smile fell. "But you said—"

"You can't make babies unless Willow wants to. That's how it works."

His face whipped in my direction, and his mouth opened around the words.

"No," I said.

His lips pursed. "Why? Croc has shelter. Croc has water." He picked up the sausage and wiggled it. "Croc has—"

"Nope!" I covered my ears and looked at Julia in exasperation.

She laughed. "I don't doubt it."

"You're not helping!"

"Doesn't seem like I need to." She laughed again.

He motioned to my half-full glass as if it were all the answer needed. "Croc can provide for other babies, too."

I bit back a snide remark. He was like a child. How long had he been out here? It was as if he were one of those people who had been left to go feral. But he wasn't feral. He could speak well enough. He didn't maneuver like he'd been raised by the talking gator outside.

"I don't know you."

"I'm Croc."

I groaned. "Yes. I know. But I don't *know* you, and I don't want children." I paused for emphasis. "Ever."

His expression fell. "You have two."

"I didn't make those." I pointed toward the room where we'd left them. "And I don't plan to make any." Another pause. "Ever."

Croc mulled over my words for a moment, digesting them, his gaze shifting from the open doorway and back again more than once. "Never?"

"Never-ever-ever-ever-ever." I pushed my chair back and crossed my legs to drive the point home.

Croc turned forlorn eyes onto Julia.

She laughed. "Don't look at me. My baby maker stopped working decades ago."

The atmosphere around the table fell silent for one breath, then two, then another as seconds turned to minutes and tension grew.

Julia was the one to finally ask the crucial question. "Would you like for us to leave?"

"No." It was instant and rough. His entire body tensed. His eyes widened. "Please," he said. "Croc won't make babies. Croc will provide." He grabbed the water and hurried to refill both our glasses. "Don't go." He sat back down. "Croc will even—" he paused and grimaced at the sausages "—Croc will eat the…" His Adam's apple bobbed.

Julia snorted and gripped his hand. "Calm, boy. It's alright. We won't leave."

My mouth parted on a breath. He didn't want a deal. He didn't require… My eyes lingered across the table, mind spinning. I still didn't want to agree with Julia, but with little options and his reaction, I couldn't help but nod. "We won't leave." I chewed the inside of my cheek. "Not now, anyway."

His shoulders fell. "Croc likes you here." He glanced up at me, then over to Julia. "Croc doesn't want to be alone."

6
PROTECT

Croc gave Julia and I the loft, and while I didn't feel comfortable leaving the children alone, Julia pointed out how small the shack was; we were practically in the same room. She thought Croc was harmless. I wasn't so sure. He confused me. Hell, the whole place would confuse anyone. Croc had the social skills of a caveman. I'd expect something like him to sooner feast upon our flesh than offer us a place to sleep. But, so far, that wasn't the case. He didn't need a deal. He didn't require it—not yet, anyway. He'd watched us climb the ladder with the saddest expression I'd ever seen on a grown man's face, and as much as I hated to admit it, I was beginning to agree with Julia.

I twisted in the tight space. A thin mattress offered little cushion, but the sleeping bags Merle had packed helped. We'd found three tightly rolled inside one of the duffle bags, and I'd stared at the third, chest tight and eyes watering, until Julia took it from me and draped it over the children.

I looked over at her, lying stiff and flat beside me. Every part of her was parallel to the ceiling, her arms at her sides, legs straight and toes pointed up.

"Julia," I whispered.

"Yes, Willow."

I bit my lip. A woman her age must be exhausted after the

hell of a day we'd had, but I had to pee, she was on the outside, and I hadn't remembered seeing a bathroom anywhere since we'd arrived.

"I gotta pee."

"Of course, you do." She heaved a sigh. "If I climb back down that ladder, I'm not going to make it back up here." She cracked an eye open at me. "You've gotta crawl over me."

"But where? Did you see a bathroom?"

She was quiet a moment. "No. Just…look for one, and if worse comes to worse, ask Croc."

"Oh, that's a great idea. I'll just ask the man who wants to knock me up where I can go to drop my pants. Brilliant."

"I'll admit, the man doesn't know proper etiquette for shit, but I don't think it means he'd try to force anything on you." She tilted her head, pondering her own words. "It's like he's…"

"A kid?"

"Yeah, but…no. He's definitely a man." Her brows furrowed. "Think about it. I provide. I hunt. I'm strong. It's like he's going off what he's learned from animals. Hell, if that man had feathers, he'd have probably spread them out and did a chicken dance across the front porch."

I snorted at the image. "It does seem kind of sad. The way he reacted when you mentioned us leaving…"

Julia nodded. "I'm not sure what led to him being out here, but I've got a feeling he needs us just as bad as we need him." She patted my cheek, then flattened herself as best she could and motioned me over. "Go pee. I'm exhausted, and it's not like we've got anywhere else to go. We'll ask questions and figure it out tomorrow."

I scrambled across her, ignoring the bundle of nerves in my stomach. Julia was the wisest person I knew. She'd always, since the day I'd met her, known the right thing to do. I trusted her judgment more than my own. The woman was a matriarch, old enough to have seen it all and tough enough to have survived it. Even now, tonight, she didn't weep. Tight lipped, she held it in, refusing to grant herself the privilege of worrying about her husband. It kept me from breaking down. Who was I to cry over Merle when Julia couldn't? No. She was being strong for us, and in turn, I needed to be strong for her.

The ladder rungs creaked as I made my way down, and I sighed when I found the living space empty. I'd expected him to be laying on the worn-out couch, but even in the dark, it was clearly empty.

There were only four doors in the room, and I already knew one led out front. I tiptoed and peeked in on the children. They slept soundly, huddled together, drawing comfort from each other. The other two doors were catty-cornered side by side and, thankfully, wouldn't require me to have to walk around anymore than needed. The last thing I wanted was to be heard and approached, alone, vulnerable, and too exhausted to think straight.

I opened the first and gagged. It was a bathroom alright, but every surface was covered in a grime so thick, the white porcelain looked black. I pushed it closed and pressed my forehead to the door, swallowing convulsively until my stomach calmed.

The second door gave way to something far more beautiful. I stepped out and peered around. A patch of ground spread out fifteen feet before the water cut it off. The cypress trees looked silver as the moon lit them up and painted ripples in the canal. Fireflies blinked in and out of focus, swarming like magical spells being cast by some invisible wizard. In the daylight, it'd just looked like muck, but at night…

I studied the area for a private place to go. It was just like camping. I'd get it over with quick and go right back inside. No harm. No foul.

I headed toward one of the trees, then—with one final glance around—lowered my pants and squatted.

The water stirred.

"Shit." I jolted and lost balance, and with it went the control I had over the steady stream of piss I'd already begun. It sprayed my legs, my jeans, my shoes. "Shit!" I hissed again, trying to right myself, or at the very least, stop the flow, but a dam had been opened, and I was trapped on the other side of it.

Another splash, and I didn't care. I scanned the darkness, heart still, breath held, and ears primed for sound.

Glowing green eyes raised up from the water, first one set, then two, then more.

Time slowed, an unearthly quiet settled, and a small voice whispered urgent warnings. I tried to keep my eyes glued to the threat, but there were too many of them. Slowly, I lifted myself up, pulled my piss-soaked jeans back into place, and took several cautious steps backwards. The house wasn't that far, and the last gator hadn't necessarily been threatening.

But these gators were different.

As if choreographed, they all sped forward. Faster than the last had. Faster than any damn thing I'd ever seen. It made no sense. Alligators didn't hunt in packs, but that's what they were doing. Like scaly lionesses, they flew up the bank from every direction.

I panicked, screeched, then flailed until I lost balance and landed on my back.

Something flew past me. Not a gator. It came from the opposite direction, so fast all I could make out was a blurred shadow. Then it stopped, and it was clear. Croc gripped one of the gators by its tail and jerked it high into the air. Like a living baseball bat, he swung it hard into another, then pounced higher and farther than any normal man ever could to tackle the next.

"Oh shit!" one of the gators screamed. "He's got Jo-Jo!"

"Nu-uh!" another bellowed. "She's too damn bony for all this." It turned and scrambled back into the murk, and not a second later, the remaining few scattered and bolted after him.

Croc knelt by the earth; gaze fixed in the direction they'd retreated. Each breath he took shifted his back and shoulders, and each exhale chuffed as if he really were a beast.

He was.

No normal man could move that fast. No human could lift a creature that size and swing it around, and no amount of training could allow someone to jump the way he had.

"How did you do that?" I rasped, throat raw from the beating it'd received by my pounding heart.

He tilted his head, giving me a view of his profile before he slowly stood and turned to face me. He seemed more massive than before, probably because of what I'd just witnessed him do. "Croc protects," he said, voice deeper, rougher.

I nodded slowly, then held my breath as he closed the gap

between us and stretched a hand out.

"Th-thank you." I took it and allowed him to lift me from the ground.

Croc stood close, his chest level with my face and chin tilted down. His nose brushed the hair at the top of my head. "Your scent is stronger now," he rumbled. "It drew them."

My body froze. I said the only thing I could think of. "I pissed all over myself."

He hummed, as if that were something attractive. "Your scent is nice." He leaned closer, pressed his nose to the side of my head and sniffed. "Croc noticed it right away."

I cleared my throat and stepped back. "That's not weird at all."

He tilted his head, eyes searching my face as if he didn't understand what I meant. "You shouldn't come out here alone. Croc will protect."

"I had to pee."

"Next time, Croc will watch you pee."

My mouth fell open. "Uh…no, Croc will not watch me pee."

"Croc protect."

"If Croc tries to watch Willow pee, who will protect Croc?"

His chest puffed up. "Croc is strong."

I ground my teeth. "You're not allowed to watch me pee. I said so. It's a rule."

Croc stared at me a long moment. "I don't think I like rules." He bowed his head and kicked the ground, pouting like a little boy who'd been denied a toy.

My annoyance dulled a fraction, and when I spoke again,

my voice was less harsh. "How long have you been alone, Croc?"

His head whipped back up. "Croc lost count."

"Since you were small?"

He nodded once, expression somber.

My thoughts veered. They'd been doing that a lot. We'd only been there a day, not even, yet I couldn't seem to keep my judgment on a straight line. How damn small had he been? How the hell could he have even survived? I'd have thought it wasn't possible, but after spending time with Eve and Eric, I knew that wasn't true. They were wise beyond their years, careful, alert. Had he adapted the same way they had? Had he laid awake at night, frightened and silent? "Who was here before?"

"Pappy." He shuffled again, one foot to the other.

He said it how I imagined he did when he was a child, and his grown man's voice sounding so lost and heartbroken made my own heart forget how to beat. Each thud was punctuated by remorse for a boy I'd never met, and a man I didn't understand. "What happened to him?"

"He got too old and tired to wake up."

My chest constricted. "I'm sorry."

His brow furrowed again. "Why?"

I shook my head. "I'm sorry that it happened—is what I meant."

Croc studied me another long moment. "Okay. Croc forgives you."

I snorted and rolled my eyes. This was impossible. Outside this place, the world had gone insane. Yet, somehow, we'd managed to find a place even stranger. "Goodnight, Croc." I turned away, then stopped. I ground my teeth, and shook my head, hating the way he played on my emotions. His situation was too close to home. No family. No parents. All alone. An orphan, just like I'd been. Only, his had been worse. I couldn't imagine it. He'd had absolutely no one.

I turned back around and offered him a tight smile. "Thank you," I said. "You're a…you're a very good protector."

He beamed.

7 CLEAN

Julia awoke refreshed, renewed, and on a mission. Every feminine, grandmotherly bone in her body activated. She opened windows, organized, and beat the dirty life out of curtains and couches.

Both kids sat in the middle of the living room, munching on dry cereal and watching her zoom around the space.

I had none of Julia's energy, but I'd changed my clothes, my nausea had gone, my muscles felt stronger, and my head blessedly didn't pound. The chemicals were finally fading, and it was a relief to see myself healing versus the alternative. I had no idea how my body would react without it.

I sat at the kitchen table with a cup of room-temperature instant coffee gripped between my hands. Merle had packed three jars of it. I'd found them while searching the bags that morning, and the gold mine I'd sifted through made me wonder how long Merle had been planning this. I was most excited about the large bottle of whiskey hidden in a side pocket. If I'd ever needed a drink before, I needed one now. Merle had always known what I needed, even when I hadn't known it myself. His carefully formulated plan had succeeded, without him, because it had never been about himself. It had always been about me and Julia.

Croc was sitting across from me, curiosity shifting

between where Julia moved about and my glass.

"Croc?" Julia flew into the kitchen like a hummingbird, hands on hips, buzzing with momentum. "Do you have any cleaning supplies at all? Some soap? A rag?"

His forehead crinkled, creating lines in the caked mud. Something told me cleanliness wasn't on the extensive list of things Croc could *provide*.

"What about under the sink?" She pointed to the cabinet doors.

Croc shook his head. "Pappy locked it." He paused, thoughtful. "That's a rule." He smiled, then, as if proud to have one of his own.

Julia inspected it then looked at me. "It has a child lock on it."

Julia fingered the latch for a second, and the doors popped open to reveal the bounty within. "Jackpot!" She pulled out the bottles, one after the other, stacking them all onto the counter above her. They tipped over into the sink, too many to fit on the counter.

Croc seemed indignant that she had the nerve to break his rule, but instead of protesting, he shook his head and blew out a breath. I wanted to laugh. Already, Julia had become the boss of this place, swamp man included. I pictured Merle sitting next to us, rolling his eyes and giving me a knowing look, and my chest ached in a way that wasn't all sadness.

"Willow," she said when she finally reached an end. She tossed a pair of yellow gloves at me. "Finish up that coffee, girl. We're gonna scrub this place from top to bottom."

I blew out a breath and sent up a silent prayer that she wouldn't assign me the bathroom.

Croc watched with avid curiosity as Julia delegated, and we both sprayed and scrubbed and soaked and scraped. He wasn't idle long, however, not with Julia around. That is, once she convinced him he was allowed to touch the chemicals.

She utilized his height, setting him to work on everything above our heads, then his strength when no amount of elbow grease was enough to remove a particular spot of grime. Each time he'd finish up, she'd praise him, and that beaming smile would fill his face once again.

I got the piles. Mountain upon mountain of stuff filled every empty corner, and it was my job to give it a place or mark it as junk. The kitchen had mostly garbage, discarded bottles with labels too faded to tell what they'd once held. Fish bones with rotted heads and deteriorated fins, and other things I couldn't name and didn't try to. I pushed through the task, eager to finish before my brain figured out I was blocking its signals to my stomach.

When I made it to the bedroom, things got easier. Everything was boxed, stacked high against the back wall. I pulled them all down, one by one, and sat on my knees as I inspected the contents.

Knickknacks and odds and ends. Scraps of material, spare blankets, old shoes. I paused. Books. Children's books. ABCs and 123s. Rhyming words and silly stories. A stuffed bear, one eye loose and dangling down its face by a thread. I sat it off to the side, fighting to ignore the visual of the little boy the man had once been. Had he packed it away? Had his Pappy?

I pulled down another. Photos. I sucked in a breath. Pappy was older, just as tall and three times as clean as the man currently helping Julia. In every picture, he wore a dress shirt and slacks, leather shoes and a tweed cap. His face was clean shaven, jaw square, and I could find no resemblance between him and who I could only assume was his grandson. He was too old to be his father. What had happened to his parents?

I pulled out another. A tiny boy, no bigger than Eric, smiled cheekily at the camera. He held a less worn version of the bear I'd found in the other box. *Jesus.* He was precious. So fucking precious and innocent. I rubbed my chest, pushing hard against the sharp pain that echoed behind my rib cage. More photos followed. Pappy holding him. Pappy laughing. Croc with cake smeared all over his face. Him standing on the edge of the dock, pointing out a gator in the canal.

I couldn't handle it. I couldn't see. My chest ached in a way that wasn't natural, and my eyes burned with unnecessary moisture. I pushed the photos back inside and picked the box up, carrying it with purpose to the living room. "There's pictures here." I placed it by Julia's feet. "If you…want to do something with them." I turned before she could question me.

I needed a break, a distraction, so instead of tackling the rest, I grabbed the other box and brought it into the living room as well. "I found this, too," I said, opening the flaps so Eve and Eric could peek inside.

Julia turned. "Oh, thank god! I was wondering what I was going to do about these kids having some toys."

Suddenly, a large arm shot past me, and I flinched back. Croc gripped the bear and pulled it up to his face. He felt its ear then stroked the side of its head with gentle fingers. "Bear

bear," he whispered.

My fingers curled into fists, nails digging into my palms as I fought against the insane urge to hug him. I had no reason to do that. It wouldn't benefit me at all. But he needed a hug. He deserved a damn hug, but it wouldn't be from me, not when he'd made it perfectly clear he wanted much more than that. A hug would only confuse him, lead him on, and that wouldn't do any good for anyone.

If Danny had taught me anything, it was what a man would do if given permission, and I loathed him. I hated Danny. Croc was different, and the more I learned about him, the more impossible it became to feel anything other than pity.

I stood and turned away. "I'll let y'all finish those boxes. I'm going to clean the bathroom."

By the time we finished, the bathroom was white, the couch was floral instead of brown, and the wood-burning stove was not only clean but blessedly operational. Pictures lined the walls, a sad story laid out for me to see everywhere I looked. More toys had filled the other boxes until the kids were overflowing with trucks and blocks, crayons and half-used coloring books.

And they were happy. They were kids. Their giggling laughter brightened the house more than any cleaning ever could. They ran across the living room, bouncing on the couch and grabbing one toy after the next.

"Croc, can you catch us some fish?" Julia asked as she hung the towel she'd been using over the oven handle. "I'm thinking I should work us up a feast to reward our hard work."

He squared his shoulders and puffed out his chest, eager to be of service. "Croc provides."

I rolled my eyes at Julia as he rushed outside. "Fish? Really?"

"They won't be so bad if I cook them," Julia said.

She'd better hope they aren't as sentient as the gators. They were liable to fight back, and I wasn't going to have any part of those teeth. Still, I'd seen worse. "I suppose it's better than ham jello."

"You're damn straight its better than ham jello!" She grabbed a large frying pan and set it on the stove. "I miss my garden."

The front door opened and shut, and before I could glance over, a fish was held out in front of me.

"Fuck!" I reared back and clutched my chest.

Croc snatched it back away from me and scrunched his whole face.

"I'm sorry," I breathed, lifting a hand, palm outstretched in his direction. "I like the fish better when they aren't in my face."

Julia snorted. "Croc, hon, you think I could have you do me one more favor?"

He squinted at me another moment as if trying to solve a puzzle, then turned the expression on Julia as if she knew the answer.

"Could you cut off their heads?"

Croc looked down at the fish for a long moment as new questions formed in the lines of his forehead, the set of his mouth, the angle of his jaw, but he never voiced them. He left them there, poorly kept secrets written on a bulletin board, and when he shrugged one shoulder, it was as if we were the ones that made no sense. "Croc will cut off the heads." He stepped back outside.

Julia followed. "I'll teach him how to clean them up. You kids want to learn, too?" she called over her shoulder into the living room.

Both raced after her, and I was amazed by their excitement. Like little rubber bands, they'd been stretched but hadn't broken. They'd just…snapped back.

I watched them go then flopped down at the table with a huff. All around me, the shack looked like a home. It was amazing how different it was. The kitchen was white with yellow trim, and the curtains, still damp from Julia's scrubbing, had a pattern of corn stalks that added to the cheery colors. It was perfect for her. Like it had been decorated with her in mind.

A layer of sweat plastered my hair to my forehead and soaked my shirt. All day, it had dripped into my eyes, and now that the sun had begun to set, they burned with a mix of irritation and exhaustion. I laid my head across my arms and closed them for a blissful moment, only to drift off the second I did.

Sizzling woke me, and I opened my eyes to find Croc's face mere inches from mine. He'd taken the chair to my right and matched my position, laying his head across his arm, and who knew how long he'd been staring at me.

I shot upright and blinked until my vision adjusted. "Julia?"

She stood in front of the stove, back to us, but she turned

to watch Croc rise, then winked at me. "Good news," she said. "Pappy had a garden! I asked Croc if there were any edible plants, and low and behold, he took me to the motherload. It's glorious! We've got corn, raspberries, cranberries, asparagus, mint, and rice. Gigantic vegetables!" She held her hands out, indicating the size. "It's all a little unkept and overgrown, but Pappy didn't play around." She stepped to the side and motioned to the four burning eyes on the stove. "We're gonna eat good today."

I ran a hand across my face as if I could wipe away my lingering fatigue. "See? You've got your garden after all." I yawned, then glanced at Croc as he sat upright. "But do you think it's safe? Wouldn't it be contaminated?"

Julia shrugged. "I don't know what the hell they've been dumping here, but it's not killing anything; it's enhancing it." She clasped an ear of corn in a set of tongs and heaved it out of the water with both hands. It was huge, as long as her forearm, and when she put it back, the top half stuck out of the pot. "Who knows, maybe it'll help an old woman out." She did a little shimmy, wiggling her brows in time with her shoulders and…other things.

Just like that. Shelter. Safety. Food. The place was the complete opposite of what we'd left behind. Julia had ventured out one time and found an ear of corn large enough to feed a small army.

Nothing like outside. Not since the changes started. The lines to get inside our local grocery store used to reach the stop sign on Fifth Street. Hundreds of people would stand hours, desperate to prepare for a danger they couldn't see. None of them knew they'd never get to finish using the supplies. None of them realized the lines would get shorter, and shorter, then nonexistent. That's when the looting started, because no matter how many people vanished, the food grew less and less abundant.

Money lost its value as the government started issuing tickets based on necessity. The more a person contributed, the more they received. Crime escalated, clearing the neighborhood even more.

The worst was the families. Mothers stood with their children, alone after their husbands were caught stealing or fighting in the long-extinguished militias. Their kids, bone thin and silent. Well, not always silent.

My mind flashed with memory. Walking with my bags toward the exit, gaze fixed and vision tunneled to only see the misty world beyond the sliding glass doors. The path home. Until a crash sounded loud enough to corrupt my focus, and I broke my biggest rule: don't look, don't watch. I stared.

The mother was bent, face ashen, her toddler gripped tight by one arm while the other worked furiously to pick up the shattered glass. A pickle jar. That's all it had been. Store brand dill slices. When heavy steps echoed into my right ear, I'd turned away, toward the exit, fighting not to hear her wailing cries, her begging, the screams of her innocent child.

"Willow," Julia said as if she were calling me in from the next room.

I blinked, and the images receded.

"Are you listening? Croc said pumpkins grow in the fall." Julia leaned forward and pinched Croc's cheek, giving it a jiggle as if he were one of the kids. "Pappy provides."

His lips curved, but his eyes didn't match. He ran his

finger across the table, tracing an old crack in its surface as if remembering how it'd gotten there. "Croc filled the tub with water for you," he said, voice quiet. "Julia said you'd like that."

Julia turned back to the stove and began whistling the intro to an old commercial I used to hate. I glared at her back, not missing the slight shake to her shoulders. She knew exactly what she was doing, and I was overjoyed that in these challenging times she'd managed to find a serious topic to treat lightly. Not really. Not at all. Of all the things she had to make a joke about, the talking gators, the razor-toothed fish, the flaming sludge, she'd chosen my impregnation.

Croc cleared his throat. "You don't like it?"

Dammit. He sounded so innocent, so unsure. After the day of watching him reminisce over photos, cuddle old bears, and going through image after image of him as a child, it was hard to be brutal. "No. That's great. Thank you."

"You've got time to wash up before this is done." Julia stoked the fire beneath one of the pans, then shook it rapidly as she added a splash of water and leaned away from the steam billowing into the air.

I pushed myself up from the chair and shoved the hair off my forehead. I'd seen shampoo and soap, even a razor, and I grabbed them all and stared at them how a person lost at sea would stare at fresh water. Once they were gone, that was it. I wondered if Julia knew how to make soap. Something told me we wouldn't find a massive bar laying around somewhere outside.

I paused in the living room. Eve and Eric played quietly, rubbing crayons against the same page of a coloring book. I lingered for a moment, watching them, huddled together, murmuring, smiling, damp heads and too big clothes. Julia had bathed them. They looked newer. It swelled my heart and frightened me at the same time. I was glad they were adjusting but terrified someone would rip it all away. Would it make it worse? Would it make it harder for them?

I shut myself inside the bathroom before my morbid thoughts could ruin the moment, then eyed the tub. The fact it was the same room I'd seen the night before was astounding. More cheery colors, white and yellow, a hint of turquoise in the tiles. For as small as the place was, Pappy had obviously taken pride in the details of his home.

The water was cool but nice after the sweltering day, and I took my time washing, allowing it to soothe my battered muscles. I finished and dressed just in time to emerge as Julia was setting the table.

Croc's attention was honed on the meal like a pirate who'd discovered gold, but the moment I entered the room, he lifted his head and sniffed the air hard. He hummed, low and deep. "Croc likes that smell."

Julia scooped an extra piece of fish onto his plate. "It's better cooked, isn't it? I'm so hungry, I could devour this whole table."

Croc's eyes locked on me and roamed, darker, intent. He sucked another breath in through his nose and blew it out slowly through parted lips. "Croc wants to devour."

8
NO SNIFFING

Julia made a sauce from the raspberries, drizzled it across filets of steamed fish, then laid it all over a bed of rice. She used a knife to scrape kernels off the massive corn directly onto each plate and chopped up one stalk of asparagus, which was enough for everyone to have a serving.

Eve got the remaining chair at the table, while Eric sat in Julia's lap. I could hardly believe they were the same kids from the day before. They played with their food in between bites. Eve stuck two pieces of corn over her two front teeth and smiled goofily at Eric, who laughed hysterically at his sister and tried to mimic her. Julia didn't reprimand them. She laughed along, praising them as clever and applauding their ingenuity. Her word choice made me have to bite back my own laughter.

Croc didn't make a sound, but he looked ready to develop a twitch. His focus jumped about like a boxer with three opponents: cooked food, bathed Willow, giggling children. He'd dig into the fish and rice, then stare at Julia as if she'd conjured a miracle. He'd study the children, smiling wide at each thing they did. That didn't bother me. I even found him endearing in a sense. It was sweet when he admired the food. It was even sweeter when he admired the children. But when he focused on me…

As if on cue, Croc leaned over, and it wasn't the first time. He'd been doing it since we sat down. He feigned interest in Julia, shifted his body toward mine, and sniffed.

My teeth clenched, eyes narrowed at my plate. I could have ignored him. I'd have been more than willing to even make excuses for him. He's never smelled strawberry shampoo. He only knows the smell of muck. This is just as new to him as everything else. I even went so far as to pretend he had a cold.

Eric managed to get the corn over his teeth and giggled manically.

We laughed along, my attention distracted for that blessed second, before Croc leaned close again. This time, he was sneakier yet bolder. Perhaps convinced I was too preoccupied to notice. He dropped his fork on the floor between us, bent down to pick it up, then took a long sniff as he languidly lifted himself back up. He hummed low in his throat.

I gripped my near-empty plate and jumped from the table. "Thank you, Julia. I'll clean up."

Julia stood from her own chair and plopped Eric into her spot. "Good. I've got one last thing to clean before this day is over." She walked around to Croc, lifting a long dreadlock into the air by two fingers. "How do you feel about cutting some of this off?"

Croc's eyes widened and shot to the leftover fish. "Croc likes his head attached."

Julia barked a laugh. "No! Not your head!" The kids broke into giggles.

I focused on rinsing my plate, needing to distance myself. Sure, it was cute. It was more of his endearing side. But nothing about that hum had been cute. Nothing about that sound had been innocent. It was sinful, intriguing, off-putting, and more than the smell of shampoo deserved.

It took Julia a moment to compose herself. "Your hair, son. Just the hair."

Against my better judgment, I glanced at him.

Croc's eyebrows lifted. "My hair?" He fingered a dread and stretched it down the length of his nose, going cross-eyed. After a moment, he shrugged. "Okay."

Julia clapped her hands. "Good answer. Now, come with me, and we'll leave Willow to do the dishes."

They wandered to the bathroom as I focused on the massive task of cleaning up the mess. It was more difficult, doing dishes without running water, but I managed to work out a system, pouring from a jug as needed while trying to be frugal with the soap. I scrubbed the pans, then the plates, then dried them all with a clean towel and put them back where Julia had placed them earlier in the day. Eve and Eric darted off to the bedroom, and I listened to their continued fun as I finished wiping down the kitchen.

When I was done, Julia and Croc still hadn't re-emerged.

I stepped into the living room, eyeing the closed bathroom door. I could hear them inside—Julia's murmured words, splashing, a grunt. I grinned, already convinced the poor man was being tortured. My attention wandered around the room as I took a seat on the sofa. Julia had performed a miracle with soap and water. I traced the floral pattern on the cushion, running my finger from the big white flower to the vine, then the little yellow flower to the cluster of tiny blue petals. The carpet was still brown, but it seemed as if it'd always been.

It looked like a home. Nothing extravagant, but good all the same. It reminded me of Julia and Merle's place. Just enough. I'd lived in beautiful homes before. I'd been placed with foster families that had endless money and little time, and their houses had been modern and bare. They'd been white and sterile. At Julia and Merle's, I'd had an immediate feeling of comfort and safety. That was why the children were so at ease. They could feel that here the same way I'd felt it there.

Julia stepped out of the bathroom and closed the door behind her. "He's gotta do the rest on his own. An old woman's heart can only take so much." She gripped her chest, smiling wickedly. "Woo, girl," she said as she stepped over and flopped down beside me. "You could do worse with impregnators."

"*Really*, Julia!"

She rolled her eyes. "*Sor-ry!* No need to get your panties in a bunch. He's a good-looking man. That's all I'm saying."

I stared at her, more than a little worried about what she'd found underneath all that grime and fur. "What do you mean?"

She winked, then turned as Eve sprinted into the room. "So, what are you two up to?"

"Eric thinks he's a gator man!" Eve said, laughing.

Eric scooted from the bedroom on his stomach, then popped up onto his hands and knees and crawled as quickly as he could to Julia's side. "I'm fast," he said, once again pronouncing his -f a little too much.

Julia snorted, then whooped a laugh and fell back into the cushion.

I bit back a grin. "You're enjoying yourself way too much."

She sobered and sat up. "And? You're being way too miserable." She shook her head. "Don't get pissy with me just because you desperately want to find faults in a good thing and can't. C'mon, kids. Let Julia get y'all tucked in."

Damn. How could she be totally in the wrong and still make me feel guilty? It wasn't a joke. It wasn't funny. Yet, denying her a bit of fun, knowing what she'd lost and how hard she must be trying to cope, felt like the ultimate crime. She wasn't hurting anyone, and I didn't have to agree with her. "Julia, I didn't mean it like that," I said.

"Don't worry about it." She waved, not bothering to look back. "Something tells me you'll find something to be happy about in about two seconds." She snickered. "That man makes others look like off-brand versions."

The moment she disappeared inside the bedroom, a feeling of dread coursed into my stomach. I'd just started to stand, determined to make an escape before I was caught alone with the unknown, when the bathroom door flung open.

My jaw unhinged, lips parted. Holy hell. Holy…hell. He's not possible. That's not possible. This isn't the same person.

His hair was gone, cropped to the scalp, and the beard, while still present, was clean and short. He wore a pair of dress slacks and a button-down black shirt, something Julia must have found while rummaging through the boxes of Pappy's things.

I stared at the angles of his face, the strong line of his jaw, the long, straight nose, then the eyes…darkest green, almost black. They shimmered, catching every ounce of light within the room. Wait. It hadn't been a reflection before? No, they were glittering with neon green, just as unreal as the rest of him.

He sat beside me, and I was too awestruck to move away. His scent filled my senses, a mix of Julia's soap and something more earthy. Natural. Masculine.

I met his gaze and couldn't deny it. He was gorgeous, hands down the most attractive man I'd ever seen. I cleared my throat. "Uhm…hi." *Nice.* I clenched my teeth. "You look…different."

Croc stared directly into my eyes the entire time I spoke, and it was so much more intense when he looked the way he did. He rubbed his head, then his jaw. "Croc feels different. See?"

Before I could stop him, he gripped my hand and placed it on his head, running it down the side of his face, then to the smooth skin of his neck. The whole time, his eyes held mine, locking me in place. "Spikes," he said, describing the way the short hair felt.

I swallowed hard and nodded. "Yeah, it is." I pulled my hand away and choked out a wheezing laugh. "You…you look nice."

His lips curved. "Croc isn't mean."

I shook my head. "I know. I meant…never mind. I meant, yeah, Croc is nice."

He suddenly grabbed my wrist, then flopped back into the cushion, pulling me with him.

I gasped in surprise. "What are you doing?"

He shifted his weight, leveling his face with mine. "You want to run. Croc wants to keep you longer."

For a moment, I couldn't respond. He was too close, and

any conversation between us would inevitably lead back to me salivating over how fucking good he looked. "How do you know I want to run?"

He lifted one brow, and it was the most human expression I'd seen him make. Was it just his appearance making him seem more normal, or had his previous look made me imagine him differently?

"Croc can smell fear." He let go of my wrist and placed his hand on his lap. "Julia likes Croc. Babies like Croc." He fell quiet a moment. "Willow doesn't like Croc."

"That bothers you?"

"Willow is Croc's favorite."

My heart beat a little too fast, and I couldn't for the life of me understand why I was still sitting there. It didn't make sense. Nothing made sense. It was Julia's fault. She'd called me out on my attitude, rightfully so. I was trying to find something wrong, and the only reason for that was this man. He hadn't done anything. He was nothing like the others. Even his interest could be explained away by the fact he'd never encountered a woman before. Of course, he'd be intrigued. It was unreasonable for me to write him off based on that, regardless of my previous experiences.

"It's not that I don't like you," I said, battling to find the words that would make him feel better without leading him down the wrong path of thinking. "I like you just fine, but as a friend."

"Friend?" He was too damn innocent, and it made it impossible to be mad at him.

"Yes. As a friend. That means stop sniffing me."

His lips parted then closed, and he looked as if he were

ready to argue but thought better of it. "You smell good."

I bit my tongue, then sighed. "So do you."

He beamed.

"But that doesn't mean I'm going to walk around sniffing you." I never thought I'd have to explain that. It was one thing, even considering setting boundaries with a man. Men didn't give a shit about boundaries. At least, none of the ones I'd encountered. But none of them had treated me like a bottle of nasal spray, either.

"You can." He moved closer.

I pushed him back. "Friends don't sniff friends."

He grimaced. "Is that a rule?"

"Yes. A very important rule."

He leaned back, and a low, frustrated groan rumbled through his chest. "Alright, Willow," he said. "No sniffing."

9
JAMBALAYA

The sound of Julia's laughter seeped through the walls and pulled me from a dead sleep. I pushed away the blankets, head clouded with fog and eyes crusted at the corners. For a moment, I just sat, like a corpse waiting to be reanimated. Then the sound rang out again, and I climbed down the ladder to follow it.

A chunk of wood held the front door open, and outside, the yard was a bustle of activity. Julia sat in a kitchen chair she'd taken out onto the deck, her feet propped up on another chunk of wood, watching Croc wrestle Gator across the dirt.

Eve stood on the sidelines, cheering them on like a little gambler, fists shaking, hands clapping, shouting out to Croc as if she'd placed her bet on him.

Unlike the previous day, the wildlife was abundant. Toads hopped in and out of the water, herons meandered across the yard, and a group of baby alligators laid along the sidelines, taking in the spectacle.

"Good morning," I said to Julia, forcing myself to accept everything and question nothing. To question would be to add logic into an atmosphere totally illogical. I'd left one world, painted in falsities, only to enter a new one painted in hysteria. I knew the last one was fake, and I couldn't accept that this one was real.

Gator clamped his jaws around Croc's leg and rolled, but when his bright yellow eyes centered in my direction, he froze.

"Well, good morning! I was beginning to wonder if you were ever going to get up," Julia said, pulling my attention back to her.

Eve gave a cheer, and I looked back to find the odds completely shifted. Croc slammed Gator onto his back, sprawled across his white belly, and pinned him with one flat hand against his neck.

"Uncle! Uncle!" Gator cried. "You're way too strong for me, Croc! I'm no match. No match at all! Willow! Are you watching? Do you see how strong he is!"

Julia snorted, and I rolled my eyes when Croc cut a not-so-subtle glance over his shoulder. "Yes, I'm watching. Croc is very strong."

I caught the curve of Croc's lip across his profile.

Dammit, he was cute. But he wasn't cute. Not in the least. He was downright sinful. He'd abandoned the button down. His body was stretched out, every inch of the sinewy lines along his back exposed, naked but for the dress slacks that hugged him far too well…

"Your mouth is hanging open, Willow," Julia said.

"Stop encouraging this."

"Encouraging what?" She uncrossed her feet, then crossed them again, taking a long dramatic sip from the glass of instant coffee in her hand.

I grunted.

"He likes you," she said.

"No shit? That's not saying much, considering I'm the

only woman of childbearing age he's ever encountered." It was bad enough he looked the way he did. I didn't need Julia egging it on.

She dismissed me with a wave. "Don't sell yourself short." Her lips quirked. "With that mud hair, and those sludge eyes, you could have any swamp man you wanted."

I picked up a twig and tossed it at her but couldn't stop a laugh from bubbling out. "Where'd all the animals come from?" I asked to change the subject.

"I feel like I've walked into a fantasy novel. I'll tell you; I haven't had this much excitement in my entire life. All of them can talk. Just like Gator."

My eyes roamed, taking in the moving beaks, the cacophony of croaking murmurs.

"It's like a damn fairy tale," she added.

"Are you sure we're not still in the car, heads cracked against the dashboard?" It would make more sense. Hell, anything would make more sense.

"Trust me. The thought crossed my mind."

The match ended between Croc and Gator, and Croc took off on hands and knees toward a squealing Eric. He caught him easily and held him shielded and secure as he rolled them both across the grass. Gator cheered for the "Tiny Man," and Eve giggled as her brother fought back. Croc landed on his side, then allowed Eric to push him backward, pinning him to the earth with what little weight he had to use.

Croc let out a deep, hearty laugh and feigned distress. He slapped the ground, begging for mercy.

My heart swelled, and Julia nudged my calf with her foot, pulling my attention back to her knowing smile. "Ignore how he looks all you want, but there's nothing more attractive than a man who's good with kids."

"He basically is one." I sat on the edge of the dock opposite her.

No sooner did Eric roll off his chest, Eve ran forward and body slammed Croc with the full force of her small frame.

A breath of air whooshed out of him, and Gator roared with high-pitched laughter. "I guess you ain't so strong after all!" he cried, jaws open wide and head bobbing. The baby gators snickered in time, but Croc didn't seem upset by the taunting. He allowed Eve to bend his arms, pretending to struggle against her strength, and I couldn't deny Julia's assessment. It was attractive, and it had nothing to do with his bare arms and perfectly formed physique. It had nothing to do with the deep baritone of his laugh, or how masculine he sounded when he did it. I could ignore those things, but watching him like this…

I shook my head.

When the wrestling stopped, Croc hopped onto the dock, pulling the little ones up one by one behind him, then hurried them toward where the planks stretched out over the water. "Stay," he said, as if they were two puppies still in training.

He dove into the water and came back up a second later with a massive fish in his hand.

This, like everything else, amazed Eve and Eric, and before he could offer, they were begging for a turn.

To my relief, Croc didn't try to teach them how to fish. Instead, he took turns carrying them on his back as he did laps up and down the canal. He swam unlike any human I'd ever seen. He didn't splash, barely kicked. He glided, body waving in time with the water, shooting him impossibly fast and making the children screech with laughter and beg for him to go faster.

Julia watched it all as if Croc were her son, the kids were her grandchildren, and this was just a normal family picnic that'd occurred a thousand times before.

They all loved him, and it was becoming increasingly hard to view him in any negative light.

The day drew on like that. Sun and activity and laughter. When the twilight closed around us, and the fireflies arrived to join in on the festivities, Croc showed the children how to build a fire using old wood and Spanish moss, and the flames grew so high, the embers seemed to mingle among the stars. Croc took a seat on the ground a few feet from me and Julia, and the others—animals and children alike—joined to form a circle. A hush settled over us until the only sound was the fizz and pop of wood being turned into ash.

I'd never known serenity. I'd never had a perfect day. But this was. The day had been outrageous and otherworldly but perfect. The crackling fire, the dancing lights, the soft burble of water, all of it. I relaxed in ways I didn't know were possible, and a calming warmth, a smooth comfort, lulled me into a sense of total security. I didn't want it to end, and it seemed neither did Croc.

He cleared his throat and broke the stillness with his deep baritone, lifting and lilting, perfectly pitched and eerie in its beauty. Unlike when he spoke, Croc didn't miss a word as he enunciated the lyrics to a song that sounded exactly how the day had felt. His gaze shifted around, landing for a moment on each tiny face staring sleepily up at him, dreamy eyed and smiling.

I couldn't look away. Had his grandfather played it? Had he sung it for him so many times he'd memorized each rise and fall and note?

There were no instruments, but chirps and croaks and night sounds gradually drifted forward to aid him. Magical. Hypnotic.

Then, with a glance around the group and a wicked grin, he picked up tempo, slapped his thigh, hopped to his feet, and danced. Wild and carefree, tone unhindered by the exertion. Beaming. The children's fatigue was sucked away as they jumped up to mimic his gyrating. Eric twisted from side to side, rocking his knees and waving his arms.

Then, Croc found me across the fire and paused, one heartbeat, then two, then three, before he rushed forward and yanked me from my seat.

I gasped in surprise as he spun us around, carrying me with him in the dance that had no rules.

Gator crowed, and Julia laughed. The children circled us, and the animalistic music grew louder.

There was no room for thought in the spaces where fear had resided. The world spun too fast, when before, it had barely spun at all. My lips curved, laughter escaped, and I couldn't worry about the world, or deals, or consequences when I was too busy holding on. Only, this time, it was different. I wasn't holding on for life. I was living. This was living.

He finished and stopped, breaths heavy as he held me close and smiled at me.

Julia gave a round of applause fit for a proud mother.

I remained still, another heartbeat, another. The warmth

in my chest spread to my belly and made the air stifled and hot.

It was perfect. *He* was perfect. With the children, with... *me*.

Croc's smile faded, eyes roaming across my face, searching, searing, and the sounds of laughter seemed to warble away. A bubble formed, enclosing us, and for the briefest of moments, I forgot how to breathe.

He leaned in and pressed his mouth to my ear. "Croc is glad Willow is here," he murmured. "With Croc."

His beard scratched my cheek, his breath warm against my skin. I couldn't answer him right away. The truth was, I was glad, too. It was impossible not to be. "Thanks for the dance." I drew away and softened the action with a pat on his shoulder.

He pulled me back and spun us again. "Croc provides."

10
TEACHER

In the days that followed, Julia transformed the living room into a schoolhouse. She organized the children's books from easiest to hardest within the windowsill, then added her own personal books to the opposite side. Her romances. I should have known she'd bring them and could imagine that'd been what she was desperately scavenging through the shed for on the night we ran. Shirtless men and barely clad women filled most of the covers, and I rolled my eyes, praying she didn't intend to include them in her lesson.

Each morning after breakfast, she'd pull the kitchen table into the center of the living room and take on the role of educator. Eve and Eric quickly grew accustomed to the routine, partly because they had an example to follow. Croc took his lessons from Julia as seriously as any man ever could. He followed her every word and absorbed everything like a sponge. Whatever chemicals the government dumped here had made him impossibly fast, strong, and, from what I could tell, smart.

I picked a spot on the arm of the couch, where I observed more than participated.

"We know the alphabet contains all the letters, and all the letters make a sound," Julia said. She'd broken down one of the boxes and nailed it to the wall below the loft, creating her best version of a one-use black board. The alphabet filled the top in big black letters, and Julia opened her marker, ready to add more. "The sounds work together to form words." She wrote the word dog, then made each letter sound. "D-o-g. Dog."

The children listened, but not to the extent Croc did. He was entranced by everything Julia showed him, and no sooner did she finish explaining, he jumped up from his seat, crossed the room, and took the marker from her hand. He scanned the alphabet a second before he set to work writing the letters C-r-o-c.

Julia patted him on the back. "Very good!"

He beamed, then pressed the marker back to the board and spelled W-i-l-o.

Julia shook her head. "Not quite. Some words are a bit more complicated than others, and some have silent letters. Believe me, honey, whoever came up with the English language had a huge stick up their—"

"Julia!" I coughed and pointed toward the little ears in full-blown learning mode.

She shrugged. "What? I was going to say T-shirt." She wrinkled her nose. "Doesn't that sound annoying? No wonder he was such an asshole."

Eve and Eric giggled as I smacked my forehead and collapsed sideways onto the couch.

Within the span of a couple weeks, Croc could read and write. He had better handwriting than Julia, and he'd devoured every book on the windowsill, romance included. Nothing was too hard or complicated. All it took was one explanation, and the knowledge was a part of him. He started helping Julia teach the little ones and was better at it than she was. He whooped and cheered for any little thing they did, and his patience and praise made them learn faster than I'd have thought possible.

They all loved him.

I'd been dormant throughout the learning experience. I helped prepare meals, clean up messes, and fetch materials whenever Julia needed a particular book or something from the garden. I volunteered to do anything that didn't require me to interact with him. The night we'd danced, I'd lost myself. For that moment, he was a man, the world was right, and I'd been interested. I'd never been interested in a man before. Apart from Merle, men were just things I had to deal with.

Croc had too many appealing qualities. He hadn't been tarnished. He was innocent, and while he'd made it clear he didn't like the rules, he followed them to a fault, which was more than I could say for the others.

The weeks watching him learn had made one thing perfectly clear. No matter how attractive he was. No matter how good with children, how conscientious, how polite, or how sweet, it didn't change the fact he wasn't an adult. Not really. He'd never been outside the swamp. He'd never met another woman. His interest in me was just like his interest in everything else. He wanted to learn. He wanted to study, and as appealing as the thought was, I'd been experimented on enough.

Julia, however, wasn't on the same page.

"It's your turn," she said one morning as I was finishing up washing the breakfast dishes.

I turned to face her, one brow lifted, slowly drying my hands as if it would somehow stall whatever awful thing I knew was coming. She had the look, the tone, the I've-had-enough-of-your-shit expression.

"To teach Croc."

I tossed the towel onto the sink. "Pretty sure he already knows more than me."

"He don't know shit about the world," she said. "I taught him how to speak properly, read, write, and as much math as I could. The boy already knew about nature and animals." She stepped into my path, blocking an escape I hadn't even started yet. "You're the expert on the bullshit going on outside this place. They had you in their facility. You saw firsthand what happens more than I ever did, and he has a right to know."

"Why me? It isn't like I know their secrets!"

"Why not you?" She lifted both brows, challenging me, daring me to give my reasons so she could explain them all away as bullshit excuses. She'd rip them from me, simplify and stupefy my carefully formulated thoughts. I needed them. Without them, I'd…

"Fine," I hissed. "I'll tell him all about it."

"Outside," she said. "Somewhere private."

I glared at her, and she lifted her hands in mock innocence. "I don't want the little ones to hear and get upset."

"Sure you don't." I pushed past her.

She snickered.

Croc was in the living room, leaning over Eric and pointing out the words in a book about farm animals.

"C'mon," I snapped at him. "Julia says it's my turn to teach you."

Croc straightened, then faster than my mind could follow, he rushed forward to stand less than an inch from my back.

I gripped the door handle tight, then shouldered him back so I could open it. The day was warm, surprisingly clear given the cloudy gray skies we'd had for over a week. I walked to the edge of the dock, took off my shoes, then sat to dip my feet into the cool, murky depths.

Croc took the spot beside me and matched my position. "I'm ready."

I bet you are. "I'm supposed to tell you about what it's like outside of here."

He shifted. "Is that all?"

I looked over at him. "What else were you expecting?"

He examined my face, before he gave up whatever fantasy he'd had and shook his head. "Nothing."

"Good." I lifted one leg from the water and bent it at the knee, turning toward him.

Once again, Croc mimicked me.

"Outside of here is…different from here." *Excellent job, Willow. Really insightful.* "What I mean is, there are roads and buildings and other people."

He stopped me. "Like in Julia's books."

"Yeah," I said. Duh. He'd probably read enough to explain it to me. "So, you know about towns and businesses? Doctors and lawyers?"

He smiled and nodded. "I learned a lot from Julia's books."

"Did you?" I paused. No doubt anything he'd learned from Julia's books couldn't be good for me. Why did she even let him read those? I had the answer to my own question the moment it entered my mind. She probably laughed herself to sleep thinking of how this would alter my situation.

Croc shifted closer. "Did I ever tell you," he started, voice smooth and low. "Your eyes are so deep, they remind me of the ocean, and when you look at me, it's as if the tide has just rushed forward, and I'm suddenly lost at sea."

For fuck's sake. I pulled back and furrowed my brow, my suspicions solidified. This was too much…and funny and annoying and ridiculous, and I had no damn idea how to even begin to deal with it. "You said my eyes look like swamp sludge."

He opened his mouth, closed it, then opened it again. "I was wrong. They're like the ocean…and your hair is like the sun setting on the horizon—"

I stared at him for a long time, unspeaking. I knew it. This wasn't helpful, but then again, Julia never was when it came to this problem. "Croc, my hair is brown. How can a sunset be brown?"

He reached forward and fingered a piece of it. "Only the best ones. The best sunsets are always brown."

Despite myself, one very persistent giggle rose to kick the inside of my throat. I choked a bit and forced it back down. "Have you ever even seen the ocean?"

Gears turned across his expression. "I love your dress."

I looked down at my worn-out jeans and torn tank top and lost it. All the laughter flew out of me, and my body doubled in half as if deflated by the release. I lifted a hand and took several deep breaths. "I see," I started, "I should have known. You don't need to explain any more of that." My cheeks burned. "Julia's books aren't exactly learning material."

Croc shook his head. "I learned a lot about—"

"Nope! No doubt you did, but that's not what we're

talking about."

His mouth shut, forming a straight, disappointed line across his face.

I gave him a minute to digest and accept that he wouldn't learn any of that from me. "I'm not going to teach you that. Those books aren't realistic at all. That's not how the world is, especially now."

A rumbling groan vibrated from his chest, but he didn't argue. He waited, expectant, gaze open and attention centered.

Good. Now that I'd made that clear. "Humans make a lot of trash," I began. "We produce a lot of pollution, smoke and gases and shit that hurts the planet."

Croc leaned forward and focused on my words.

"A couple of decades ago, things got really bad. People were scared, and they got behind a man who said he could fix it. A new government formed, new leaders put in charge, with that same man leading all of it. They came up with a plan to help repair the damage and save the Earth, and ever since, that's what they've been doing. It's changed everything, so Julia's books likely don't reflect the way things are now."

"Like when Julia fixed my house up? They wanted to clean the trash and make it nicer?"

"Kinda." My tone was dry. "Only, she didn't need to kill a bunch of people to do that, but you're getting the idea."

He stiffened but didn't comment. He waited for me to continue, but it was obvious I'd captured his full interest.

"It started like that. Just cleaning up the trash. But soon after, it extended into having less people to create it. That's when the killings began. First violent criminals: men and women who'd been convicted of murder or some other act that hurt people." I paused a moment, giving him a second to process. "Then, they moved on to minor offenders, from the common thief who stole a candy bar to someone who just couldn't afford to pay their car insurance. The more people they got rid of, the lesser the offense needed to be. They shut down all the schools, businesses, and social programs. They limited resources like food and clean water. They kept track of how much trash people made, how much they consumed versus what they contributed to society. Everything is monitored and tracked."

I picked at a loose strand on my jeans. "If you want to live, you have to give more than you use. I took a job doing chemical therapy. It labeled me necessary and provided us with food tickets. Necessary addresses get passed over when they round people up at night, so it kept Julia and Merle safe, too."

"Merle is Julia's man," Croc said. It was a statement, not a question, and I ignored the ache in my chest hearing his name brought.

"Yes, he…is." I ripped the strand off and tossed it into the murk. "The chemical therapy made me sick. It made everyone who did it sick. They'd stick needles in our arms and inject us full of this neon green liquid. I think it's the same shit they're dumping out here." I met his gaze then. "I think it's what's made you so…different."

"The men in the suits." Croc nodded. "They come every week and dump the sludge where the big water pours into the canal." He pointed behind him, off to some distant point I couldn't see and had never been. "Gator watches them to make sure they don't head this way. They never do."

"They won't. Whatever they're dumping isn't safe. That's why Merle made the plan to come out here, to escape them."

"The kids?"

The image of Lita kicking and screaming as they drug her away flashed in my mind, then the house, the squalor, the little arms clinging to my neck as I ran. It felt unfair they'd recovered so well. It felt wrong to have gone this long without mentioning her, reminding them, but I didn't want to. I didn't want to tarnish this new life they'd found. I didn't want to dampen their lights when they'd only just begun to shine. "I knew their mother," I said, looking away. "She was taken. I went and got them just before we left."

"You protected them." There was a reverence to his tone I didn't deserve.

"No, Merle gets the credit for that. If it weren't for him, we never would have made it out of the driveway."

"Merle sounds very strong," he said.

I smiled at that. "Yeah, he is."

Croc laid his hand over mine, then waited a minute to be sure I wouldn't pull away. When I didn't, his lips twitched. "Can I show you something?"

I took in the weight of his hand, the roughness of his palm, and the zing of sensation that shot up my arm at the contact. "What is it?"

"A surprise."

Oh no. Bad idea. There were enough surprises to last me a lifetime without him making up new ones. "It isn't anything from one of Julia's books, is it?"

"No." He gripped my hand, imploring, begging like a child asking for a piece of candy.

Dammit. He was impossible to be mean to, and I'd never had an issue with being mean before. Something about him, though, was different. It would be like snubbing the children, drowning a kitten, or running around touching baby birds in their nests. "Alright, then," I grumbled. "I guess."

"Good." He released my hand and stood. "Later, after dark. I can't show you when the sun is out."

"What? Wait, I—"

He rushed off before I could have a chance to change my mind.

11
GLOW

When dinner was done, the dishes were clean, and Julia was tucking the children into bed, Croc walked up behind me and gently cupped my elbow.

"You already agreed," he said in way of greeting, as if he knew I would change my mind.

I turned, one brow lifted, but the expectant, puppy-eyed expression on his face was more than the strongest woman could stand. I sighed and shook my head. "Fine."

He beamed and pulled me along, only to stop right outside the front door and bend down. "Climb on my back."

I took a step back. He was shirtless, which wasn't surprising. He usually was, and the idea of that kind of contact, let alone spreading myself against him, felt far too dangerous. And intimate. "Why?"

"I need to climb." He looked over his shoulder. "If you want, I can carry you in front of me." He stood and turned, opening his arms wide. "You'll need to," he paused and did a slow appraisal, all the way down and back up again, "You'll need to wrap your legs around me, and hug my neck." His voice lowered, Adam's apple bobbed.

The man looked ready to have a heart attack. "Oh, is that all? I bet you'd like that, huh?"

Croc nodded. "Very much."

I scoffed and twisted a finger at him. "Not happening. Turn back around."

He grimaced but didn't argue. He did as told, pouting. His shoulders stiffened when I linked my arms over them, and I felt him shiver as I stretched across his back. He gripped my legs on either side, securing them into place across his abdomen, then took a deep, shuddering breath.

"You okay there, Tarzan?"

"I don't know who that is, but I don't think I've ever been better." He stood and held me with one arm while his other scaled the side of the house. Gravity didn't care about my hormones or how uncomfortable I was. The minute it pulled at me, I instinctively locked my legs and gripped him tighter.

Croc made short work of the climb, and as he sat me down on the roof, my attention immediately narrowed to a pile of blankets and pillows arranged in its center. They were situated under a lean-to built out of sticks and moss.

"You made a bed for this?" I took a step backward.

He grabbed my hand and pulled me forward, preventing what would have been a very nasty fall.

I looked back at the place I'd been about to go over.

"Careful," Croc said, letting go of my hand. "That's my bed. It's always here."

"Oh." I stepped forward. "You sleep on the roof?"

"For almost as long as I can remember," he said. "After Pappy was gone, I got scared at night. Too many shadows in the house. Too exposed. Anything could get in, and my imagination made it hard to sleep." He shrugged one shoulder. "I thought being high up was safer."

"And now?"

He studied my face, from hairline to temple, lingering on my mouth before meeting my eyes again. "Now, I stay for the view." He extended his hand and waited patiently for me to take it.

I hesitated, chewing the inside of my lip.

"You're safe with me, Willow. I'd never do anything you didn't want to do." He paused. "Do you want me to take you back down?"

Dammit. He didn't make it easy. Didn't he understand? I wasn't worried about what he wanted or didn't want. I was worried about myself. I was worried I'd forget our situation and agree to things I shouldn't. Every day it was harder to remember what he was. He wasn't feral anymore. Wasn't wild. He spoke, acted, and carried himself better than men who hadn't grown up under these conditions.

As if he could read my thoughts, he lowered his hand. "How about I walk ahead, and you follow me at whatever distance you want?" He tilted his head, then pivoted. "It isn't far." He started toward the end of the shack and climbed onto where the roof rose over the loft, then took a seat along the edge and glanced back at me.

I took a deep breath in through my nose and didn't release it until I'd closed the space between us.

Croc's lips curved when I sat without leaving a huge gap between us, then he pointed toward the winding water stretching off into the distance.

My breath caught. The trees opened, clearing the view for miles, and glowing; neon-green glitter shimmered in time with the current, illuminating the canals. It looked like a painting, some surreal landscape that only existed by imagination. But it did exist. It was tangible. It was real, and I was surrounded by it.

"The sludge isn't as bad as they think it is," Croc murmured. "It doesn't hurt the animals. It doesn't hurt me. It makes the fish and the garden grow bigger. It burns for ages, giving us light without having to gather wood." He turned his face toward mine. "And it brought you."

My heart skipped, and I cleared my throat as if it would send a message for it to keep its shit together. "And Julia and the kids." Not just me. I was nothing special, and I didn't like that he thought I was.

He smiled. "And Julia and the kids."

A breeze blew over us and made the trees sway. So much beauty created out of pain. How many people had died from that same green? This initiative had destroyed how many lives? Yet, looking at it then, in that form, a new part of nature, it was the most wondrous thing I'd ever seen. "It's weird to see it this way, but you're right. It's beautiful."

Croc hummed his agreement, still focused on the view. "When you told me your story earlier, I knew I needed to show you. That way, you could see yourself the way I see you."

I forced my face to remain forward. Looking at him was a bad idea. Sitting there was a bad idea. How had he gotten so good at talking? When had he learned the perfect thing to say? "Oh yeah?" I kicked my legs back and forth and watched my feet move. "How is that?"

"You're upset by the things you did."

My eyes widened and shot to his. He couldn't know. Could he? Had he somehow been able to use my scent to hear the parts I didn't say? "What part of my story made you think that?" I swallowed hard. "I didn't do anything. I'm not the one—"

"I agree. What you did was brave. You were strong. You let them do things to you to protect your family. But when you told me about it, your scent changed." He tapped his nose. "You're ashamed of it."

I couldn't answer him. He had sensed it, just not the details. In one statement, he'd managed to tell me something I barely admitted to myself. I was ashamed, but not of my decision to be in the trials. My shame had nothing to do with injections and everything to do with all the deals I'd made in life. The prices I'd paid. My deals with Danny. The fact I was alive when others were long gone, all because I'd always been the girl willing to…

"I feel shame, too," he said, interrupting my thoughts. "About the way I acted when you first arrived. I hadn't known as much as I do now, and I'm sorry if I scared you." His voice grew rough. "Even now, it's—" He paused. "Your scent makes me think about…it makes me…it's hard to think straight sometimes." He offered me a grim smile. "I'm working on it."

Men were stronger, and more often than not, they held all the power. They wielded weapons of privilege and the ability to do as they pleased. Croc was different. He attacked with sweet words and kindness, and I wasn't sure how to combat him. They were the perfect thing to say, especially when I knew, without a doubt, how much he meant them. He made me want to shake him, hug him, scream my frustration, and cry with gratitude. He tore me in two, one half determined to keep what little soul I had from being taken, the other ready to hand it over. He could have it, just so I would know it would never end up with the next asshole at the next stop along my timeline.

That was ridiculous. It wouldn't be giving. With Croc, I'd be taking, and no matter how I tried to spin it, I was in charge here. I was the one with the advantage, the leverage. I would be the asshole. "Can you please stop?"

He shifted, and a look of pure guilt creased his brow. "What did I do?" he asked. "I'm sorry. I didn't mean to—"

"No!" I growled. "Stop being so damn perfect. Can't you see I'm trying to do what's best for you? Can't you see I'm the *only* woman you've ever met? I'm damaged goods. I only seem so great because you have *nothing* to compare me to." I sucked in a breath and ground my teeth. "You think I'm not tempted? You are fucking gorgeous! You think I'm immune to how fucking inhumanly perfect you are?"

His lips curved into a wide smile.

"No!" I scolded again. "No smiling! That's the point. I'm doing the right thing for both of us. Don't make it harder. Can't you just burp or fart or act like a dick? Do something wrong for once in your damn life!"

In an instant, he turned and pushed me backward, locking me in place with the upper half of his body.

I gasped, stunned silent for a long moment before my words finally had the courage to resurface. "What are you doing?"

"Something wrong." His gaze was fixed on my mouth, and before I could say another word, he slowly leaned forward and feathered his lips against mine.

A shiver rushed across my skin, tingling from my scalp to my toes. I should have pushed him away. I should have told him to stop. He wasn't aggressive. He didn't make it where I couldn't break the contact. One word, one sound of distress, one press of my hand against his chest, and I knew he'd move away. But my brain betrayed me. It wouldn't send the signals. Instead, it focused on the sensation of his lips against mine, the smell of his skin, the heat of his body.

He did it again, the lightest caress, then tentatively traced my bottom lip with the tip of his tongue. I gasped again, and he took the opening, deepening the kiss, tasting me. A low, rumbling groan shook his chest, and his free hand lifted to tangle into my hair. He was completely tuned into my every reaction. If I made a sound, he'd repeat whatever caused it. If I shifted closer, he'd mimic the move. Just like with everything else, he studied, learned, then mastered until I was putty in his hands, and he molded me like an artist.

"I like this idea," he said.

I nodded, too overcome with sensations to do anything other than agree with the person causing them.

"Much better than rules." He pressed his nose to the side of my neck, took a deep inhale, then pressed opened mouth kisses down to my collar bone.

I arched my back and whimpered, and every reason I had to stay away from him didn't matter. I'd never felt like this. *It* had never felt like this, and the shock of just how different it was, made me rationalize why I couldn't possibly stop him. It was only now. It was only one time. I could do this. It was okay. It felt way too good to stop.

But I didn't need my reasons, because I had Gator.

"Croc!" His high-pitched cry rose from below. "Croc! Are you up there? Please be up there! There's a man down here, and I don't know whether to eat him or not!"

Croc stiffened and shot upright, and I followed him with the same urgency as one name echoed through my mind.

Merle.

Gator was in the front yard, a disheveled and disoriented man barely standing at his side. It was too dark to tell, and I shook Croc's shoulder. "Get me down! Hurry!"

He scooped me up, this time in front, and I was too anxious to find out who had arrived to argue. We dropped rather than climbed down. Croc landed easily on his feet but refused to release me once we were on the ground. "Stay behind me," he said, tone sharp.

It was the first time I'd ever heard him sound mean, and it was enough to make me obey, hands on his back, peeking around as we drew closer and…the man's face grew clear.

Ice filled my veins, bile flooded my throat, and my stomach churned as if a new dose of chemicals were already connected to my arm. "Danny," I breathed.

His gaze shot to mine at the sound of his name, then widened as he got a glimpse of my face. "Oh, thank god. Willow."

12 HEARTBEAT

All the shadows I'd pushed aside rushed back at the sight of Danny's face. The last time I'd seen him, his hands gripping, his body against mine. I'd selfishly given into my own desires and conjured the fate I deserved.

"Why are you here?" I asked as a hundred bad answers ushered through my mind. He'd brought them here. He came looking for us. He was a doctor. A scientist. They'd sent him in first to inspect, and now, he'd report back. My hands shook. He'd report back, and they'd come. Each breath was hollow, and the world was suddenly out of focus.

"Someone tipped them off," Danny said. "About the doses I was giving. They showed up unannounced and audited my files, checking them with the subjects I had in therapy at the time." He paused. "One didn't match up."

My lips parted around a breath. He'd replaced me. There'd been more than one. Hell, there'd probably been dozens, a hundred. "You got caught."

Danny grimaced and nodded.

Croc hadn't said a word. He stood stock still, like an impenetrable wall between me and the man I'd once relied on for protection. Only, with Croc, his protection was unconditional and absolute. There were no half measures, slight adjustments, or just-enough-so-I-can-lives. No price. No expectations. There was just me, Julia, the kids, and god help any asshole who wanted to harm us.

Acknowledging that made me relax, and I pressed a hand to the center of Croc's back in silent gratitude.

Danny couldn't hurt me, not in the present moment. But he was here, and I had no idea what to do about it. I'd escaped purgatory. I'd found a way into whatever heaven this was, but the Devil was tricky, and it hadn't taken him long to track me down. "Are you hurt?" I didn't care, but seeing him brought back the urge to lie, to pretend, and like riding a bike, I slipped right into that familiar rhythm.

"I'm just worn." He exhaled heavily to punctuate his statement. "I had no warning. No time to prepare. I grabbed the only bag I keep with me," he held up a boxy, leather case. "I took a government vehicle as far as I could, then walked the rest of the way here."

"You knew about the dumping? This place?" My suspicion grew. What were the odds? How likely was it for him to come to this exact spot, finding us?

"Of course, Willow," he said. "I know everything that has to do with my work. They have half a dozen of these sites."

"Good," Croc finally spoke. "Go to another one."

Danny paled, suddenly more aware of the massive monster towering over him. He tilted his head back, inspecting him how he would a chart full of vitals. "The next site isn't anywhere near here…"

"Good," Croc said again.

Danny stammered, mouth opening but no sound brave enough to emerge. For a moment, he looked lost. He was alone, in a strange place with no advantage. He was at our mercy, and he knew this. It was written on his face. He didn't say the words, but his expression made it clear. He was pleading, begging *me* to help *him*.

It was nice. "What is it, Danny?" I asked in mock innocence.

Annoyance pinched the corners of his eyes and mouth, but a glance at Croc kept him from reacting how I knew he would were the situation different. "Please. Willow." His voice tightened. "Let's not forget I kept you alive. I helped you. You'd have died a long time ago had it not been for me."

"What are you willing to pay?" I crossed my arms and lifted a brow. "And be careful, Danny. Croc here is a bit sweet on me. Say the wrong thing, and I just don't know if I'll be able to save you." I sighed. "You know how it is. There's only so much I control around here."

"You've made your point!" he snapped.

Croc took a large step forward, and Danny stumbled.

He loomed above him, at least a foot taller and twice as big. "I still haven't made mine." His voice was a low rumble, barely intelligible.

The tone shot a shiver down my spine, and I stared at him, stunned. It was a side I'd never seen before. Even when he'd saved my life from the alligators, he hadn't been frightening, not really. Impressive, yes. Awe-inspiring, yes. But this was different. This was the kind of threatening that resounded. It didn't matter that he was on my side. It didn't make a difference if it was directed at me or not. "Croc," I breathed, too afraid to call out any louder.

He stiffened a fraction, then took a step back and reached behind to grip my hand.

Danny lifted his hands in surrender, but his tight jaw told the truth. He was painting himself, just as he always had. The color of acceptance sloppily thrown over his irritation. Total submission in exchange for temporary time to plan. "Yes," he heaved instead of *no*, "I'm sorry. You're right, Willow. What do you want me to do?"

I'm not sorry. You're wrong, Willow. How can I gain control?

I clutched Croc's fingers, giving myself a moment to remember he was with me, then I smiled at the situation we had found ourselves in. Our roles had reversed. Danny had used every bit of his power to prey on the ones below him. He'd added to the suffering of those steadily walking toward their deaths. He'd humiliated me, degraded me, and I wanted him to feel that shame. I wanted him to feel small, but I couldn't think of any punishment worthy of his crimes. At least, not yet.

"You're a Doctor. You can start by checking to make sure everyone is healthy. Then, I want information. I want to know about the green. I want every piece of knowledge you have."

Danny nodded and shook his bag. "This is my medical kit. I have all of my basic supplies." He cut a glance at Croc. "I'm a doctor. Doctors are particularly useful things to have around."

Not in my experience.

Croc snorted, then gripped the back of Danny's neck and pushed his head down, forcing him into an awkward walk toward the house.

I followed behind in awe of him. It was like a dream. Could he sense how deeply I'd been destroyed by this man? Could he pick up on my desires, like he had up on the roof?

Did he know the man he held had hurt me in ways that could never be truly healed?

Did he know Danny was part of the reason for my shame?

Julia and the kids were fast asleep inside, and Croc made no move to expose them to his captive. When he made it on the porch, he shoved Danny hard, dropping the man as if he were another fish he'd pulled from the canal. "Gator," Croc said, and it was all he needed to.

Gator pulled his big body onto the dock and laid beside Danny, mouth split apart into a toothy grin that was anything but friendly.

Croc went inside, then emerged a second later with the lamp that'd been burning on the kitchen table. He hung it on a dock post, then looked at me.

Suddenly, he was my best friend. He was an ally. We had a common enemy, my enemy, and having this man on my side was like having an army. "Thank you, Croc."

His stoic expression broke a fraction, just a small crack that lifted the very corner of his mouth.

I focused back on Danny and swallowed a fresh wave of bile. The last thing I wanted was for him to touch me, but I also knew I'd be an idiot to pass up the chance to utilize his skill. The chemical therapy had taken a toll on me, and while I'd been feeling better, I had no idea what long term effects the green had. I didn't know what living in this strange environment would do. I sat beside him, then nodded toward his bag. "Just check me out and see if everything is okay."

"I can do a physical, but I have no way of determining any underlying—"

"No shit, Danny. I didn't expect you to have an MRI

machine in your bag."

His lips pursed. "Right." He shifted to his knees, opened the bag, then pulled out a stethoscope and positioned it into his ears.

When it came time to touch me, however, he paused and looked at Croc, whose hard stare would have made me take my chances with the gators.

"It's fine," I said. "Go ahead."

Danny cleared his throat and carefully took my wrist between his fingers, then slowly—painfully slow—pushed the stethoscope to the center of my chest. The minute he got close, I held my breath. I didn't want to move. I didn't want to create any more contact than was needed, and I didn't want to get a whiff of his scent. It would be too much.

I flinched as he pressed the cold equipment to my skin, then quickly lifted a hand toward Croc. "I'm fine."

"Take a deep breath in and hold it," Danny said, listening intently as I complied. "Blow it out slow," he continued. "Again. Deep breath in through your nose..." He fell silent, brows furrowed. After a few moments, he removed the stethoscope, tapped it, then put it back.

I continued to hold my breath, hating each gulp of his cologne he forced me to inhale, focusing on the night sounds, the fireflies, and Croc's unwavering presence.

"Let it out slow," Danny said. "Now, breathe normally." He listened, face blank and out of focus as he forgot all about Croc, his situation, and the danger. "Amazing."

"What's amazing?" I drew away.

Danny sat back. "Your heart. It sounded a bit off, then when you held your breath, it slowed."

"Is that not normal?"

"Not to this extent. The average heart rate is fifty to one hundred beats per minute. Yours slowed down to three." The words awakened something in him, some eager piece of his scientific mind.

A cold chill raced down my spine. "What does that mean?"

"For swimming," Croc said.

Danny opened his mouth, then closed it, choosing to focus on me. "I don't know yet. It could be the environment." He side-eyed Croc. "If I could check his, maybe…"

"Good," Croc said. "Check mine. Willow is done." He smacked his chest twice, then balled his hands into fists and let them hang ready at his sides.

Danny hesitated. "You're sure it's all right?" He lingered. "Maybe I shouldn't."

"You're done talking to her," Croc said. "I wasn't asking. Check mine."

He didn't need to say it again.

Danny looked ready to bolt as he felt Croc's pulse and listened to his heartbeat, and Croc didn't give him any reprieve. He glared at his face, jaw tight, eyes narrowed.

But something happened. Whatever Danny heard made him stand straighter, listen more intently, and lose himself in his work. He dropped the stethoscope and stepped back, appraising his finding like a prized horse at a market. "That's impossible."

"What is it?" I asked.

"It's for swimming," Croc said again.

"He all but stopped his heart, then sped it up, then

slowed it again. He controlled it!" Danny cupped his forehead and looked Croc over with a new intensity. Like a puzzle. An experiment.

I wanted to hide him. I wanted to shield him from view and protect him from all I knew a man like Danny would do. But I also had questions. I had questions that had been burning my mind since the first time I'd seen the neon green. I had questions about this place, about my heart, about what they wanted to achieve with their studies. I had so many questions and, for once, I could have them all answered. But I wouldn't. Not tonight, because as much as I needed those things, I needed to protect Croc more. "That's enough for now."

Croc rumbled agreement. "You sleep outside," he said. "Gator will protect you."

Gator snickered, and I gasped as Croc closed the gap and scooped me into his arms. I scrambled, clinging to his neck and fighting to regain balance as he scaled the house.

13 CHANGES

I was so focused on the shock of Danny's arrival, I didn't process the fact Croc was taking me back to where he slept until we were already on the roof. Thankfully, he didn't go for his bed. He led me to the backside, then released my hand and sat with his legs dangling over the backyard.

I should have asked to be taken back down. Even if I'd chosen to forget my million reasons to say no before, I remembered them now, vividly, and the thought of doing anything even remotely intimate with anyone, Croc included, made my skin crawl and stomach churn.

Still, I couldn't ask him to take me down. I knew I'd never fall asleep after what had just happened, and the thought of being without him while Danny was mere feet away was too daunting. I took the spot beside him, this time, leaving space between us.

Croc studied my profile. "I didn't bring you up here to break more rules, Willow. I did it so he'd think this is where you are. When you're ready, I'll take you down on this side, and you can go in through the back door."

My shoulders relaxed. There he went, being too perfect again. He kept doing that, smashing my perceptions, broadening my expectations. He'd even stood between me and one of the men I'd known, ready to defend with no reason to believe it would benefit him to do so. I sighed and relaxed. "Thank you."

"Do you want to go now?"

Our gazes held. I had a million questions, and no doubt, so did he. "Not yet."

"Good." He shifted to face me, pulling one leg up and holding his ankle with both hands. The position was so casual, it put me even further at ease. Croc wasn't worried about Danny.

"I'm still not sure if he's telling the truth," I said. "If he was sent, we're all dead already. If he wasn't, he may be tempted to use what he's found here to regain his position."

"He wasn't lying," he said, tapping his nose, then his ear. "I could tell when he lied, and he did, just not about that."

My eyes widened, then a broad smile stretched across my face. "That's…you are so fucking handy, Croc. You have no idea what it means to me that you can do that, right now." I took a deep breath and exhaled a huge chunk of the stress inside my chest. "What did he lie about?"

Croc held the stupidest grin. "Everything else. His behavior. The way he was with you was a lie." His expression darkened. "I can kill him, if you want, when you're ready." He rolled his shoulders then supported his weight onto one hand.

He'd said the words as if offering to drive me to work or help me move my furniture, not kill a man in cold blood and feed him to his alligator.

As if on cue with my thoughts, he added, "We could let the gators have most of him, then send him floating up to where they dump the sludge. That way, when they find him, it will make them even less likely to come in here."

It was a beautiful idea, but not one I was sure I could carry out. I shrugged. "Maybe later. Right now, I think it's best if we just keep him from leaving."

He nodded. "Gator won't let him wander."

We both fell silent, and the night grew impossibly still. But the silence wasn't heavy. No. It was easy, comfortable. It was the quiet I sometimes experienced in the morning, when the world was still asleep and fresh thoughts ran unhindered.

I leaned back on my elbows and stared up at the millions of stars. There was only one problem left to interfere with my somewhat peaceful existence, but the question wouldn't voice itself. I couldn't voice it. If I asked about what Danny had found, any answer would only solidify it as fact.

My heartbeat. Had I changed? Was I a mutant, just like everything else in this place? It made more sense than me staying the same, and the possibility disturbed me more than Danny ever could. It would bring a whole new level of death to the way things used to be. There'd be no going back, not for me, not ever.

My mind drifted, remembering the early days, when some of the countries still had different leaders, and the news constantly reported all the work being done in the space program. They'd tried to send people away, off to a distant Earth-like moon circling some distant planet. But the incubation didn't work, and everyone who tried never made it and didn't return. The thought had been terrifying. I'd been barely a teenager, and I'd had nightmares about being up in space, adrift, staring down at Earth and having no way to get back.

This felt like that. It felt like I was becoming something alien, and I'd never be myself again. "Croc?"

"What's wrong?" His voice was soft, tone all-knowing. No doubt he could tell I was on the verge of mental collapse.

I imagined he could, and in the quiet, surrounded by darkness and warm, night air, secrets didn't seem that important. "I'm scared."

The silence deepened, seconds becoming minutes, before he finally said, "I'll kill him in the morning."

I laughed. "Not Danny. He doesn't scare me, not with you here."

He hummed. "Willow?"

I turned to look at him. At some point, he'd laid back as well. His hands were clasped behind his head, face pointed toward the sky, eyes serenely shut. "Yeah?" I asked.

He cracked one eye open. "Say that again."

I stared at him. "Say what? That I'm not scared of Danny?" I laughed. "Yes, Croc. You are *so strong*. I've never felt as secure as I do in the circle of your raw, masculine protection."

He grinned as I continued, theatrically moving my hands and fawning over my salvation. At the end, I pressed the back of my hand to my forehead and swooned back down into my original position with tousled hair and heaving lungs.

Croc reached one hand over and gently pushed the hair out of my face.

I peeked over at him, grinning. "Was that good?"

He nodded but didn't speak. He had the most intent look on his face. Set mouth, tight jaw. After a moment's pause, he pulled his arm back, looked to the sky, and the knot on his throat bobbed twice. "What are you afraid of?" he asked, voice deeper than before.

For a moment, I'd forgotten all about it. "My heartbeat," I

said, and all at once, the seriousness collapsed back into place.

He rolled to his side and propped his head on his hand. "You don't have to be scared of that. It's for swimming. It won't hurt you."

"I know that. It's the change part I'm afraid of." I took a deep breath and laid my head down across my arm. "Everything I've ever known is different. The world is different. If I change, too, I'll have nothing left."

"The corn changed," he said. "But it's still corn. Just bigger." His tone seemed almost ancient in its simple wisdom. "When Julia taught me the right words to say, it didn't change who I was. It just made me better able to communicate—" he paused—"with you." His eyes shimmered a bit brighter. "You'll always be Willow. Now, you're just a Willow who won't drown."

I snorted. "I guess that's a good thing, then."

He smiled. "A very good thing."

The moonlight reflected off his face, adding depth to his angles and luminosity to his skin. Was he naturally beautiful or had that changed at some point, too? In one day, he'd managed to take himself from a person I avoided, to someone I confided in. I took note of our current position. How had this happened? I looked up at his face. No doubt he was thrilled, but I couldn't find it in myself to be angry. Not after everything he'd done and all the things he'd just said.

"You're a very sneaky wild man," I scolded. "I think it's time for me to go to bed."

His lips curved. "Alright, Willow." He pushed himself up to his feet and extended a hand to help me stand.

I took it and allowed him to carry me down, avoiding his

attention until we'd made it to the back porch.

When he started to open the backdoor, I stopped him. "Wait."

He turned back to me, then allowed his hand to slide off the doorknob. "Yeah?"

"One more thing."

"You want me to kill him now?"

I shook my head and bit back a laugh. "No. I'll let you know if I do."

His head tilted and brows furrowed as he waited for me to continue.

I bit the inside of my lip. Dammit, I'd lost my mind. That had to be it. I had to have gone completely insane somewhere between talking alligators and surprise Danny. Regardless, none of that dominated my thoughts. Not tonight. Not now. What Croc had given me was something I hadn't had in years. Security. Peace of mind. A moment of simply being, and an ear to lay all my burdens to rest on. I wanted to give him something in return, something I'd never given freely to another living soul.

"Bend down," I said before I could change my mind.

Croc did as asked, bending at the waist until his face was level with mine.

"Don't move," I warned.

He nodded, gaze intent and searching.

I cupped his face, holding his eyes with mine, then softly pressed my lips to his in a kiss far more innocent than the ones he'd given me. "Thank you," I said, stepping back.

Croc nodded again, frozen for a moment, before he regained his senses and straightened back to his full height.

“Goodnight, Willow,” he said, voice rough. Then, he turned and tripped, falling off the back steps.

I reached out, but I wasn’t fast enough. He sprawled across the ground below, then scrambled back to his feet and waved a hand up into the air. “I’m okay,” he said. “That didn’t hurt at all.”

I threw a hand over my mouth and watched him start back toward the side of the house.

I shouldn’t tease him. Should I? Oh hell, why not? “You sure you’re okay?” I called.

“I’m great,” he said, still refusing to look back.

I chewed my lip, biting back laughter, then reached behind myself to grip the doorknob. “Oh, okay. As long as you’re sure.”

“I’m sure.”

I twisted it and pulled it open a crack. “Well, then, if you don’t need me to kiss it better, I’ll just head on to bed.”

“Wait!”

He didn’t get a chance to finish before I slipped through the opening, shut the door, and fell into a heap of silent laughter against it.

14 GOOD CROC—DOWN BOY

The next morning, Danny examined Julia. She was the one I wanted to get checked out the most. Her age worried me. I'd barely been able to stand after a dose of neon green, and I was well over half her age. She was practically rolling in it, and I was afraid her immune system wouldn't be able to cope the same as everyone else's.

Croc towered over the pair with even more animosity than he'd shown the night before. Danny didn't do anything that seemed out of place. He followed the steps, checking her heart rate and blood pressure, listening to her lungs. But each new time he touched her, Croc rumbled low in his chest, a warning sound that caused the doctor to stop and explain what it was he planned to do.

Julia relished the attention, seeming to take pride and great humor in the fact she had a personal bodyguard.

I'd been too easy going about the prospect of murder. When it came to Danny, it wasn't the most horrible thing I could think of, but still, I couldn't really consider it. My answers the night before only seemed to encourage Croc into that way of thinking.

"You're perfectly healthy," Danny said, sounding disappointed. "No abnormalities." He turned, focusing on the children perched side by side on the couch. "How about you, young man?" He started toward them.

Croc moved sideways, blocking Eric from view. "You don't touch the babies."

Danny froze and took a step back, then looked to me for help. "I can't examine them if I don't have access. Tell him, Willow. You know me well enough; I wouldn't hurt a child."

I snorted. "Do I?"

His lips thinned. "That's hardly fair."

"The world isn't fair," I said, repeating the same words he'd said to me and countless others.

Croc shoved his shoulder, knocking him backward, and I almost laughed. He hadn't even done it aggressively. It was so sudden and leisurely, how a person would push aside a cat they didn't want to climb into their lap. *Down, boy*, it said. *Bad, bad.*

Danny caught his balance and glared. "I can't check them if I can't—"

Croc held out his hand. "Give me the equipment. I'll check them."

Danny scoffed. "I majored in biology at one of the best universities in the country, graduated top of my class in all my medical studies. These aren't normal physicals we're performing here. I'm checking for mutations. They could be so slight, even I may not notice it if I'm not careful. How can you expect to—"

"It can't be that hard if you can do it," Croc said.

Danny's cheeks flushed, and his mouth opened and closed several times before he said, "And what's that supposed to mean?"

"You're not that smart if you're still talking." His tone deepened, low enough to reach hell and bring the devil back up with it. "All morning, you've been lying to yourself, trying to pretend you have control." He leaned closer and shook his head slowly. "You don't. You won't. You're a grown man who needs protection from some very hungry friends of mine." He motioned with his chin toward the back window, then extended his hand again.

Danny paused a long moment, then pulled the stethoscope from his neck and placed it on Croc's palm.

It was the same as the night before. Whenever Croc got that way, some basic instinct flared in my chest, warning me to move away. The children felt the same. They sat perfectly silent, staring wide eyed at his back, and it wasn't until he turned and smiled at them that they finally relaxed.

Julia, however, wasn't afraid of anyone. Her eyes danced. She studied Danny's red face, his fisted hands and stiff posture, cackling like an old, evil witch.

"Julia," I hissed.

"What?" She laughed harder. "That was some scary shit. We should start a mafia. I always wanted to be a mob boss." Her eyes rested on Danny, and she didn't seem to care that he looked ready to spontaneously combust. "It's a good damn thing you wore brown pants, ain't it, hon?"

Croc grinned and put the stethoscope into his ears, mimicking what Danny had done. He gave Eric's side a tickle, smiling at the giggle it earned him, before he pressed the cool metal to the small boy's chest and listened. Danny didn't offer his knowledge, and Croc didn't ask for it. He did things differently. He didn't ask for deep breaths. He didn't hold Eric's wrist or ask to use Danny's watch. He took a deep breath in, puffed his cheeks out, then asked Eric, "Can you do that?"

Eric nodded eagerly, already used to learning from Croc and always ready to earn a new dose of the praise he frequently received.

Croc listened intently, expression softening on Eric's puffed face, then nodded. "Okay. You can breathe," he said, ruffling the boy's hair. "You have a strong heart! Very strong!" He glanced at me. "Perfect for swimming."

My eyes widened, then locked onto him as he repeated the test on Eve. Perfect for swimming. Mutated. How? Julia hadn't, and they were with her almost every second of the day. They ate the same things she did, drank the same water.

Danny observed with acute concentration, the confiscation of his equipment and pride forgotten. He was a scientist, after all, and I knew the look on his face. I'd seen the same fascinated stare the night before. He'd had it in treatment, anytime he reviewed our charts. Only, here, in this place, there was an almost manic gleam in his eyes, and I knew, this was what he'd been searching for. This was what they'd all wanted to happen.

Croc tossed the stethoscope back to Danny and knelt in front of both kids. "Do you feel sick?" he asked.

Both shook their heads.

"Are you hungry? Tired? In pain?"

Again, same answer.

He smiled. "Then, you're all done. Go play with your toys."

Danny reached out. "Wait! There could be more! I want to see just how much—"

Croc spun on him and bared his teeth. "You're done." He grabbed his shirt, and I had to scramble to stop him from hauling Danny back outside.

"Wait, I'm not done."

Croc paused and let him go.

"What is it?" I asked, knowing he'd know exactly what I was talking about.

Danny sat back like a petulant child, scooting to lean against the wall and loosely hanging his arms over his knees. He fiddled with something, a bit of string he'd acquired at some point, twisting it around his finger tight enough to turn it red, then unraveling it to start again. "It's a lot of things," he finally said, tone vague.

I ground my teeth. "You don't get to do that, Danny. You don't get secrets. Not here. What is it made of? Where did it come from? And why are you injecting it into people?"

He dropped the string and looked up at me. "Alright, Willow. I'll tell you." He sounded smug. "The original product is called chemical 426, an engineered variation of hydrochloric acid, much stronger than any corrosive ever manifested."

Corrosive. "You injected a corrosive into human beings?!" Not only that, but he spoke about it as if it was no big deal.

Danny ignored my outburst. "It had to be corrosive to melt down the garbage. All that trash isn't just disappearing. It's being consolidated. Anything and everything gets thrown in, melted down, but the result is a toxic cesspool. At first, they were able to contain it in specially made silos, but the workers kept dying, and eventually, they stopped showing up." He picked at his mud-stained khaki slacks, retrieving a new thread. "A lot of the people listed get sent there now, forced to work until they're gone. You've seen what it does to people, and what you received in treatment was nothing compared to how it is in its original state. If I'd injected you with its purest form, you wouldn't last the time it would take to scream."

Garbage. Trash. My stomach churned, and instead of neon green, I pictured the dumps, piled high, the stench that wafted for miles surrounding them. That was inside me. They'd put that into my blood.

Danny talked about it as if it meant nothing, because I was nothing. Another lab rat. A test. "They ran out of room years ago and started dumping. There are six sites like this, all remote locations picked by the heads at the capitol. I don't know what criteria they used. Probably just a lack of desire to inhabit. I can't imagine them ever wanting to visit here, and the others are just alike. Blocked off and out of the way." He glanced at Croc again, eyeing him like a puzzle. "We wanted to see if humans could adapt to it. We've been making slight variations, searching for a mix that isn't deadly. Now, it seems it only needed to be diluted. I thought a lot about what I found last night. The environment here, the natural wildlife in this ecosystem, and the traits you inherited. They all match up. The ability to slow one's heartrate mimics an alligator's. The way his eyes glow at night is another aspect I'd like to inspect further."

"You injected me with garbage." Didn't he feel even the least bit of guilt? How could a person dehumanize another so thoroughly? How could he live with himself, knowing what was in those bags? I wanted to vomit. I wanted to open myself up and bathe my organs.

Danny bowed his head and nodded, twisting the stupid string, not a care in the world about all those who died, all the suffering he'd helped inflict.

Croc gripped his arm and hauled him back to his feet. "That's enough."

I nodded, grateful for his ability to read me, and the minute they stepped outside, I turned to Julia. "Don't look so happy," I said. "It isn't good that he's here."

She shrugged. "Oh, I don't know. Picking his brain seems useful, and I don't see him causing too much damage with Croc snarling up his ass twenty-four seven." She wiggled in her seat, hands clasped together. "I think it's kind of fun."

"Yeah, I guess." She was right, but that wasn't my problem. My problem was that the man made me sick to my stomach. Just being in the same room with him made my brain sift through every second of our last encounter. Whenever his eyes met mine, a snapshot would flash, and I'd see one part he'd taken, then another, and another. He'd left me almost too broken to get away, and then he'd found me. If it hadn't been for the kids that night, I doubted I'd have survived. Now, I knew just how far his desecration had gone. I was grateful Croc wouldn't let him near Eve and Eric. As bad as I wanted to know they were healthy, I wasn't okay with those hands going anywhere near their innocence. He'd tarnish it.

Julia didn't know about the deals I'd made. If either her or Merle had suspected, they would've insisted I stop. They didn't know the lengths I went to keep us all alive, and I would never put that guilt on her, especially not now.

Croc stepped back inside a moment later. "Gator is guarding him. Would you like to try out your new skill?"

My brow furrowed. "Try out my…"

"Swimming," he said. "I swim every day around this time. I thought maybe you'd come with me."

"Go on ahead." Julia stood and ushered us both toward the back door. "You two will just be in my way here. It's Sunday. I'm going to play around in the kitchen and see if I can come up with something extra special for us to eat. Don't worry about the little ones. I'm sure they'll be happy to lick bowls and spoons until we get it right."

Croc wrapped his hand around mine and squeezed, then pulled me outside, down the steps, across the backyard, and to the water's edge. I followed, wanting to disappear yet desperate for something to distract me. I wanted to exist in this new plain and forget what had happened in the old one. I wanted to forget Danny. I wanted to go back in time and not ask him anything. The information I'd acquired was too dark to process. My mind blocked it, pushing it just below the surface of acceptance.

I focused on the present, on Croc, for the first time welcoming his ability to steal my attention. I looked down at my shorts and T-shirt. A bathing suit hadn't been deemed survival gear, and stripping to my undies felt like a far too slippery slope. "I don't have anything to swim in," I said.

Croc cocked his head. "We'll swim in the canal."

I snorted, but a familiar warmth spread over me. Once again, he'd managed to pull me a bit further from my nightmare without even trying. "I mean clothes. I don't have a bathing suit."

He peered down at me. "What's a bathing suit?"

I opened my mouth to explain, then thought better of it.

"Never mind. I'll just wear this."

He studied me a moment, then nodded. "Stay close to me, and nothing will bother you."

I hesitated, remembering how deadly the gators could be. They'd swarmed like a pack of hyenas the last time I'd come too close, and something told me they were even more agile in the water. "How close? Are you sure?"

Croc pulled me ahead. "Don't worry. I won't let you wander too far."

15
DOGGY STYLE

I'd never been a strong swimmer. When it came time to kick my legs and flap my arms, I always ended up looking like a drunk seal. But I was a solid doggy paddler, and when Croc started forward up the canal, that was my go-to.

After a few minutes of him getting too far ahead, he turned back and waited for me. He followed my motions, biting his bottom lip to stop it from quirking. "Why are you doing that?"

I stopped and just managed to tiptoe my chin above the water. "What's wrong with it? It's called a doggy paddle."

His lips broke free, and he lifted his hand to cover them. "A...doggy paddle?"

"Yes," I said. "It's a very popular form of swimming." *For children who don't know how to swim yet.* I ground my teeth, not liking his judgment but also grateful to have something to talk about. Doggy paddling seemed like the perfect thing to explore compared to everything else I could be thinking about. Still, he was being a bit insensitive. "Since when do you make fun of people, Croc? I've never seen you be anything but curious. Don't you want to know all about the doggy paddle?"

He rumbled a laugh and shook his head. "No. I don't think I do."

"Oh, I see. Well, then, if you don't like the way I swim..."

I struggled toward the bank, but one step across the uneven ground sent me plummeting below the surface.

Croc pulled me up by my arm and deposited me back where I could stand. "Do it again?"

I glared at him.

"What? I want to learn. I do. Show me again."

I stared at his sincere expression a few minutes. He was full of shit. He didn't want to learn. He wanted to laugh at me some more. Regardless, I begrudgingly swam forward a couple of feet.

Croc snorted, then chuckled, then exploded with deep, throaty laughter.

I stood again, and in my new spot, I was able to place my feet flat on the ground. "You're making fun of me."

He shook his head, but it didn't mean much when he was leaned back howling.

Once again, it was impossible to stay mad when he looked the way he did. Sure, the children made him laugh. Julia made him laugh, but not like this. This was different. The cadence and depth of each rumble of his chest caused a zing of warmth to course through my stomach. I ignored the feeling and crossed my arms, waiting for him to finish.

Croc took a deep breath and relaxed backward into the water. His floating felt like a brag. *Look what I can do!* it seemed to say. *Bet you can't do that*, is what I heard.

"I don't get it." He smiled despite my obvious annoyance. "Why do you scrunch your body up like that? Your legs are barely doing anything, and your hands…" He pulled his up to his chest and mimicked me, flapping them back and forth like a T-rex challenging someone to a slapping match. He laughed again. "It's like you're trying not to touch the water."

"Hardy-har-har. I get it, okay? You win. I'm not a good swimmer." Jerk. I hated braggers. So what if I couldn't swim? I'd never needed to. I didn't live in a swamp, and I'd been too busy surviving to participate in extracurricular activities.

He shifted back upright. "Really? So everyone doesn't swim like that where you're from?"

I crossed my arms. "Kids do, until they learn."

"Ah, I see. That makes a lot more sense." He dipped down, bending his knees until the water reached his chin, then slowly closed the space between us and pulled me down to his level. "Why didn't you learn?"

There it was. His curiosity, genuine this time. I pursed my lips and heaved a breath. "A lot of people don't. For most, going swimming just means being chest deep in water and playing Marco Polo."

"What's Marco Polo?"

My lips parted. I shouldn't have been surprised, yet I still was. It was easier to forget with his increased knowledge, but occasionally, I'd get a reminder of just how sheltered he'd been; how much he missed out on. Sure, I'd missed out too, but at least I knew what it was. "It's a game," I said. "One person closes their eyes and tries to tag the other. Every time the seeker calls out the word Marco, the hider has to answer with Polo and try not to get caught."

His brows lifted; interest peaked. "Let's play."

The water was murky, the perfect place for hungry little creatures to hide and steal my toes. It was bad enough being in it, I wasn't about to close my eyes and throw caution to the bank. "I don't know. What if something sneaks up on us?"

A wry, dismissive grin curved his mouth. "Have you seen anything yet?"

"Well, no, but you can't see anything."

"I can, but you won't. Like I said, they know better than to come near me. I hunt, Willow. Do you think the fish aren't smart enough to stay away?"

"It's not the fish I'm most worried about." Well, it was the fish. Them and everything else. I wouldn't come within five feet of a bunny juiced up on the green, not with what I'd seen it do so far.

"The gators, too. They won't mess with us." He stood to his full height and closed his eyes. "Me first. How do I start?"

I chewed my lip, searching the area one last time, before I gave in and moved quietly away from him.

"Willow?"

"Polo," I said, then shifted course, reverting to my doggy paddle when the water got too deep.

Croc stood a moment, head tilted, listening, then all at once he dipped down to disappear beneath the water.

My heart kickstarted as I searched for him. Should I remain still or hurry away? Why did it feel like I'd just signed up to box with a heavyweight? Oh, right, because he was a swamp thing, and I was a doggy paddler.

My scream ripped through the air as he emerged like a bullet and caged me against his chest.

"I caught you!" he boomed, laughing heartily.

"That's not fair!" I wriggled free. "It wasn't even a game. Your freaky mutant magic took all the fun out of it."

"I thought it was fun," he said. "Your turn."

I rolled my eyes and huffed. What I should have done was

swim to shore, get out, and head back. But Danny was there. Danny and all the things I didn't want to think about. Here, it was just Croc, boyishly excited to have learned a new game, even if it wasn't challenging in the least. "Fine," I grumbled, closing my eyes. "I'll give you a minute."

"Polo," he answered.

How the fuck? He sounded as if he'd swam a mile ahead of me, and I'd only just closed my eyes. "How did you get so far?" I waded toward the sound. "Don't go too far! I don't want to get eaten."

Silence answered, and I stopped to listen. The wind rustled through the trees, water burbled against stone, insects chirped, but no splash, no stirring in the water, no Croc.

"Marco!" I called.

"Polo," Croc whispered directly into my ear.

I squeaked and spun, reaching out to find nothing but water. "See? This isn't a fair game."

He didn't respond.

I ground my teeth. "Marco."

"Polo," he whispered again on the opposite side.

I tried to grab him, but he was too fast. I growled my frustration. "Marco!" I cried again, arms stretched wide to try and catch him in the act. He wasn't there.

"Polo," his voice rumbled right behind me.

I twisted, and lunged forward, falling under the water and spluttering back to the surface. Gravity took my hair and plastered it against my face, and I had to hold my nose and dip backwards to fix it.

I'd just lifted my body upright, using both hands to smooth my hair back, when his fingers grazed mine.

My eyes flew open, finding his as he cupped the back of my head and pressed his mouth to mine. No testing. No practice. Just like with everything else, he'd learned quickly, and his discovery the night before was nothing compared to this. He was urgent, desperate, devouring.

My body warred with my mind. One hand pushed him back, while the other pulled him closer. My brain sent a signal to tell him to stop, but my lungs propelled a moan instead. I shouldn't. It was wrong. It felt right. It wasn't fair to him. It wasn't good for me. He was perfect.

He settled me against him, supporting my weight and allowing the water to carry us both where it wanted to. His hands explored, running up my arms, gripping my shoulders, then running flat down the full expanse of my back.

"Ooh, whatcha' doin, Croc?" A croaking voice interrupted. "She got a bunch of flies in her mouth?"

I opened my eyes and screamed. There on the bark of a nearby tree was a frog the size of a fucking cat. Massive and slimy, with oversized black eyes and a wide toothless mouth. I screamed again.

Croc pulled back with a heavy sigh.

It stretched its head forward, peering into my opened mouth. "I don't see any. You must have got 'em all."

I scrambled backward out of Croc's lap and once again sunk beneath the surface. Murky brown and forest green clouded my vision, particles dancing with the rhythm of my desperation, until Croc pulled me back up and held me by the arm.

He shook his head at the unwanted visitor. "No flies here, Ribbit."

The frog leaned closer.

Croc waved him off. "I think I saw a swarm of flies down by my dock. Big ones. Some as big as you."

Ribbit tilted his head in the direction, then turned back to study me. "If there's no flies, why'd you have your tongue in her mouth?"

Croc didn't even pause. "I was just making sure."

"That's smart. You never know, I guess." He paused. "Wait—" He focused on me. "If you thought there were flies in your mouth, why didn't you just eat them?"

"Ribbit." Croc's voice tightened. "Go away."

The frog reared back. "Well, then, okay. There's no need to be rude." It gave us one last indignant look, then hopped off the tree to disappear into the bush.

Croc turned back to me. "I don't suppose you're going to be okay with us pretending that didn't happen?"

He wanted to continue the thing that shouldn't have even started. Things were getting out of hand. He was getting too comfortable, and I was letting him. I was encouraging him, and as easy as it would be to saddle the blame on his shoulders, he didn't know any better. I controlled this, and if I didn't get my head straight, I'd be no better than the men in my life. I shook my head. "It's probably better that it did." I cleared my throat. "We should head back."

His jaw tightened, but he nodded and helped me wade to the side and climb up the embankment. We walked back in silence, having never made it far to begin with, and we were almost home when Croc said, "I can teach you how to swim. No rule breaking or games next time, if you want."

No rule breaking. No games. A ping of guilt ricocheted

through my chest. I'd let things progress too far and made him feel like he'd done something wrong. I'd seen bad men. I'd encountered them time and time again. Croc wasn't that. He wasn't like them—like Danny. "We both broke the rules," I said. "But we need to follow them now. I'd like to learn, but we can't do that again. I need to know that you'll be good."

He grimaced. "I'll be good." We stepped up to the porch, and Croc took the lead to open the door. He turned back just as his hand gripped the handle. "I wonder if Julia knows how to cook frog."

16
PURE

That night, after an extra-large feast from Julia and a blessedly hot bath, the house was silent, and all the world was asleep apart from me.

I lay on the couch, staring at the grooves and marks that lined the wood beams above my head, thinking. Two days in a row I'd crossed the line I'd drawn between myself and Croc, and it was becoming harder to justify why I needed to stay on my side. He'd evolved, changed so much it was difficult to remember he was the same man we'd met upon arrival.

He'd gone from incomplete sentences to poetic wisdoms; caveman to Casanova, dirty to polished. My line had no chance against him. It was mere chalk on a sidewalk, and his touch was a torrential downpour, blurring the edges. If I didn't stop this soon, it'd wash away. I needed that line; for him, for myself. I didn't want to be a test. I didn't want my body used again in the name of knowledge. But then Croc stood next to Danny, and the line blurred more. They weren't the same. It wasn't the same.

I chewed my lip and focused on a specific point in the ceiling. He was like a boy when we'd arrived. He'd been left to fend for himself and miss out on all the experiences that came along with growing up. It would be unfair for me to take advantage of that. He was gorgeous, caring, great with kids, protective, funny.

What if a day came when we were forced to leave, and I'd allowed myself to pretend I deserved him? What if he meets others and sees the truth? I'm not extraordinary. I'm an orphan. I have the most basic education and no real talents. My hair is like mud, my eyes sludge. My hips are a little too wide. My breasts are a little too small. I'd soiled my virtue more than once, and I'd sold my soul to countless devils like Danny.

I was a used car, a junker, and I wasn't prepared to deal with being cast aside the minute Croc found out there were newer, shinier things for him to test drive.

There it was. The truth. It couldn't happen. I couldn't let it. Croc had done so much for us. Our protection came before anything, and if I ever wanted to look myself in the mirror again, I needed to do the same for him…and myself.

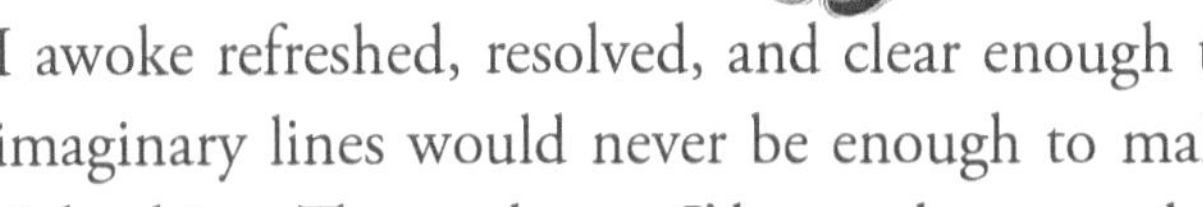

I awoke refreshed, resolved, and clear enough to realize that imaginary lines would never be enough to make me do the right thing. The truth was, I'd never been good. It didn't matter that they'd pumped me full of garbage. I'd been trash since I was cast aside as a baby, and there were only a few instances in which I was proud of myself: every night the raids had passed Merle and Julia's house, and the night I'd saved the children.

That was the answer. If I wanted to be a good person who did good things, I needed to stop keeping a distance and start focusing on the ones who needed me most. Eve and Eric.

They were better than any line I could draw. Not only could I rest assured I was having a positive impact on what little life I had to live, I also didn't have to worry about slipping down any forbidden rabbit holes with two tiny witnesses around to chaperone.

When Croc asked me if I was ready to learn to swim, I easily agreed and gathered the children to come with us. They had the same new skill, after all, and knowing how to use it could only help them should a situation arise where they needed to hide.

Of course, he agreed. He'd fallen even harder for them than I could ever imagine he had for me, and both kids squealed in excitement when we shared our plans with them.

We swam in the water out front, allowing Julia an opportunity to watch. This, unfortunately, gave Danny the same opportunity.

He sat against a tree, the same spot he was forced to eat and sleep, and his attention was fixated on the four of us.

I kept my back to him as much as I could and tried to forget he was there. Eric rested on my hip, laughing wildly as he smacked his chubby little hand into the water, splashing me in the process.

Croc held Eve outstretched in front of him by her arm pits and chanted, "Kick, kick, kick," as her legs worked hard beneath the surface.

"Work it, girl!" Julia cried. "Look at them little legs go! She's a natural!"

Eve beamed. "I'm good," she told Croc. "I'm almost as good as you!"

He rumbled a laugh. "I don't know. I don't think I can kick quite that fast."

Her eyes lit up. "Yeah, I think your right. I'm super fast.

That's my power. I can turn it on when I want to." Her face scrunched up, then she propelled her legs. The small, erratic kicks almost made Croc lose his grip.

"Whoa, now! Hold on! You kick any faster, you might just shoot up into the sky."

He spun her in a large circle, laughing at her excited screech, then stopped and loosened his hold. "Now, you're going to kick your legs just like that, but this time, extend your arms out on either side of you and move them in circles. Can you do that?"

She nodded, and tried, and Croc studied her movements for a long moment. "Kick a little harder. Don't forget to keep kicking. A little bigger circles." He smiled as she worked, then released his hold and allowed her to hold herself above the water.

She dipped down, water reaching her chin, and I jolted, ready to reach out and snatch her before she went under. I wanted them to learn, but the process made my muscles tense. They were alive. Alive and safe, and I wouldn't lose them, especially to something as stupid as water.

"Kick! Move your arms!" Croc said. "Keep going! Use the water to push yourself up. You've got it!"

She struggled, huffing, then after a moment managed to get her head all the way above the surface.

I relaxed.

"I'm doing it! Granny Julia, do you see me? I'm doing it!"

"I see!" Julia crooned. "You're doing fantastic!"

Eric imitated his sister, gripping me with one arm while the other moved in a big circle and kicking his legs in an uncoordinated rhythm.

Croc helped Eve over to grip the dock and stretched his hands out toward me. "You want to try, big man?"

Eric scrambled away from me, making it clear who his favorite was.

Croc repeated the lessen, but Eric was a bit too small and couldn't propel himself enough to tread water on his own. Croc flipped him over, laying him on his back. "Make pretend like you're going to sleep," he said.

Eric closed his eyes and snored.

Everyone laughed, including Danny, who up until then had faded into the background. I ground my teeth and tried to pretend it wasn't him, but my laughter died at the sound of his.

"Very good," Croc said. "Now, relax. If you relax your body all the way, you'll float."

Eric stopped snoring and opened his eyes. He looked serene, staring up at the sky, innocent and carefree, safe, and when Croc removed his hands, he stayed that way. It was a testament to the amount of trust these children had in Croc. He was both mentor and protector. He was a god in their eyes, and it occurred to me just how much they'd needed him.

Eve swam toward Croc, and without prompting, matched her brother's position. They floated together, gently carried by the water, and Croc watched them both with the softest expression on his face.

"I wish Merle was here to see this," Julia said.

I looked up at her, but she didn't meet my gaze. Her eyes were glassy, fixed on the simple beauty of the moment. "He would have loved it," she whispered. "We never knew how precious times like this were until they were gone. You're too young to really remember what it used to be like, but when I was a girl…" Her voice broke, and she let the words trail off, shaking her head. "Enjoy this, Willow. While you can."

I swallowed hard against the lump in my throat and nodded. "I wish he was here, too."

"I know you do." She looked at me then. "Don't write that old man off, yet. His hardheaded ass won't give up easily. If anyone can make it out, it's him."

I nodded again, but it'd been so long. Julia would never accept the inevitable. She'd keep holding out hope until she saw with her own eyes that he was gone. I'd seen her, when she didn't know I was watching, staring off into the distance, waiting for him to arrive. He was her childhood sweetheart, her knight in leather armor, and despite how they'd bickered and snarked at each other, she viewed Merle in the same way the children viewed Croc. Invincible. Unshakable. Capable of taking on an entire world.

I wanted to feel that way.

Croc lifted Eric onto the dock, and the soaking wet boy immediately ran for Julia's lap, drenching her clothes and returning her to her usual self. She cackled, tickling him for his sins against her, then pulled him into her arms and held him close.

Croc lifted Eve to sit with her feet in the water, then looked at me. "Your turn. Are you going to hold yourself up, float, or"—he grinned—"doggy paddle?"

I narrowed my eyes and stuck my tongue out, earning a laugh from Eve as I waded away from the dock and mimicked what I'd watched the kids learn. I could feel the water, the way it moved with my body, and after listening to Croc talk, it almost seemed easy. I flapped my arms like some regal bird, hands flat and pushing downward as my legs kicked my body up. "Ha! How's that for a doggy paddle?"

His grin widened. "Much better than the other one." He stretched out on his back, relaxing.

"The water has skin," he said. "You can see it if you look close enough."

I took a deep breath and leaned back, forcing my body to relax. My shoulders and top half stayed up, but my legs still dangled below, unlike Croc, who looked like he had a pool float beneath him.

I studied where the water met my arms and saw what he was talking about. A thin skin, barely noticeable. I took a deep breath in, blew it out slow, and focused harder on relaxing my entire body. I gently moved my arms and feet, propelling myself up the final bit, and did it. I was floating, arms outstretched, feet shoulder width apart, sun shining through the canopy above my head, sky clear blue, and day perfect.

Julia was right. It was simple. We were free, one with nature, human, and the moment was pure beauty. I made a silent vow to heed her advice and enjoy every second.

When our lessons ended with a promise from Julia for dinner, and everyone began heading toward the house, Danny cleared his throat. "Willow? Could we talk? Just for a minute?"

I frowned and bowed my head, noting the lines my wet feet made on the dock. Croc didn't leave, and I didn't think he would. He stood there, no doubt glaring at Danny, though I never lifted my gaze to check. I didn't want to talk to him, especially not alone, but I knew it was something I'd have to do sooner or later. I had to face the devil, look him in the eye and demand honest answers from his liar's tongue—answers about things I didn't want anyone else to know. I lifted my face. "It's fine, Croc. Give us a minute."

His brow was furrowed, and he looked away, staring at the boards I'd been so focused on before, as if my thoughts had ingrained into their surface.

"I'll be fine."

He nodded, then with a reluctant pause and a warning glare at Danny, he started for the front door. "I'll be right inside."

The water dripped, abandoning me. This new world was so different. It'd never occurred to me just how much until Danny arrived. Even he was different. No longer pristine but coated in mud with disheveled hair and rumpled clothes. This place had never been painted in the illusions. "You have something to say?"

"I want to...apologize."

I almost laughed. Of course he wanted to apologize. He needed forgiveness so he could find a way closer to his new findings. "Apologize?"

Danny shifted, pulling himself to his feet. "What I did to you was wrong. I let my personal desires interfere with my work. It was unprofessional and out of line, and I sincerely regret my actions."

Lovely. How clinical. "Was that your letter to HR? If so, I can see why you had to run." Is that what he thought? Never mind what he'd done to me. Never mind that he'd killed people. Never mind that he'd treated me like a body, a vessel, something without sentience or feeling or basic human rights. "Is that what I am? Is that what all those people were? Your work?"

His mask slipped, and his jaw worked, chewing the next lie so it would slide smoother from his lips. "We're saving humanity from extinction. What we've found here is the answer. I need to check those kids. I need to monitor and—"

"Absolutely fucking not. You're not a good person, Danny. You're pure fucking evil, and I'd rather a gator eat you than let you near those kids."

"I'm evil?" He took a step forward, coated in false calm. "For what? Am I supposed to let the entire species die to preserve a few like you?" His lip curled. "I gave you a gift, Willow. I kept you alive. I know you don't want to hear it, but you're a waste of space. You consume resources and contribute nothing. That was my mistake. The pretty ones, the girls like you. I would have been invisible to you before the initiative started, and I wanted to be seen. I took my own gratification as payment for something that wasn't mine to give. That wasn't what was best. That wasn't for the greater good."

The greater good. Unnecessary. Good for nothing but what my body could provide. The words slit me open and allowed my every insecurity to spill out, laid bare like a slaughtered animal hung suspended from a tree. I believed them. I agreed, but I wouldn't stand for judgment, especially not from Satan himself. "Is that what you tell yourself?" I sewed up the cracks he'd made in my armor, saving the wounds for another time. "That people like me are the ones that need to go?" I ate up the space until I was close enough to spit on him. "The truth is, people like me, people like the ones in your group, we're all that's left of humanity. You," I sneered, "are not human. Humans don't do what you did. There's nothing human about what you do. None of us believe that greater good bullshit you use to make yourself feel better. We all know you're the devil, and if you're not careful, I'll have you put back in the fucking ground."

He smiled, a wide-open expression that matched his eyes. "Is that right?" He laughed. "It's amazing how you can think you have any chance of keeping this from them. You think they won't come? You think they won't want to open up your guard dog and see what makes him bark?"

Something snapped inside me, and without thought, I shoved his chest as hard as I could, only to stumble back.

He lifted off his feet and flew backward, smashing into the tree with enough force to shake the branches. I stared opened mouthed as he spluttered and gasped, clutched at his chest and fought for air.

My mouth closed, then curved. I lifted my hands and stared at my palms in wonder. I'd done that. I'd been so… powerful. I was stronger than him, a grown man. "Holy shit," I whispered, moving closer to stand over him; down, defeated, weak. "Do I look like I'm fucking scared?"

17
LITTLE FISH

Time passed slower in the swamp. The days were fuller, brighter, and I found myself waking earlier and dreading the time I'd return to sleep. My encounter with Danny had shone a new light on changing, and I didn't want to miss anything. I didn't want it to end. Croc taught me how to move the way he did, how to feel the current and mold my body into it. The water was just as alive as the rest of the Bayou, and I found myself unable to stay away from her for too long.

Croc called her his mother. He said the water raised him, and I'd have never taken him seriously had I not experienced it for myself. She was like a mother. She enveloped, protected, and every time I sunk into her depths, I grew like a baby returned to the womb.

I could hold my breath for an eternity, swim faster than Gator, climb trees with little effort, and jump across the canopy to land among a new set of branches. I was invincible, extraordinary, and all my fears evaporated in the glory of what I could achieve.

Croc didn't break any more rules. He never had a chance to. We were always with the kids or Julia. But his attention never ended. With each new advancement I made, his gaze scorched my skin. I avoided his touch, sure if he so much as brushed against me in passing, I'd disintegrate into ash.

Thankfully, I didn't need his protection as much as I had, and I found moments alone at night. A tree along the edge of the backyard offered the same view Croc had shown me from the roof, and I made it my purpose to climb into its branches whenever the opportunity arose. The quiet beauty cleared my mind.

I slipped out the back door, careful to remain silent. Everyone had gone to bed over an hour before, and I'd waited, making sure they were asleep. I'd been doing it more and more, getting braver as each night passed without incident or discovery. I was better at it. I'd become a part of the swamp, and I could feel it, move with it, from each blade of grass beneath my feet to the grooves and marks that lined each tree.

I lifted my hand and smiled as glowing green fireflies rushed forward to dance around my twirling fingers. My tree beckoned, swaying branches draped in moonlit Spanish moss. Even it was alive. It thrummed, like a note pulled from a string. Each tree had its own unique sound. If I listened close enough, I could hear them all, working together, creating a symphony. A lullaby.

I gripped its trunk, digging in with fingers and toes and pulling myself up to the branch I always occupied. The view took my breath no matter how many times I looked at it. Miles of winding, glittering green. I rested my head back, stretched my legs in front of me, crossed my ankles atop the branch, and watched, listened, absorbing the night. Thinking. Thought travelled farther in this place. It stretched on like the canal, and mine always found the same spot to linger. On the reason I was here. The reason any of this existed in my world: Merle.

"I really wish you were here, old man," I whispered. I'd been forcing myself to come to peace with the fact too much time had passed. He wasn't coming, and I wanted to believe—I needed to believe—that he'd somehow made it. In some form, he was here with us, happy we'd found our way, laughing at Julia's antics and impressed with my new abilities. I preferred it to the alternative. No way could a man like Merle just cease to exist. His spirit burned too bright to ever flicker out.

A twig snapped, and my gaze jerked toward the sound only to find an empty yard. I looked higher, to the roof where Croc slept. The top of his lean-to was the only shadow visible from my position, and I searched the ground on all sides.

A rustle sounded from the tree to my left. My heart skittered, and I lifted, readying myself to make an escape.

Croc pulled himself onto the branch only three feet from mine and crouched, locking eyes with me.

"You scared me." I clutched my heart and sucked in a breath. "You shouldn't sneak up on people."

"I didn't sneak," he said, tone low. "If I'd wanted to sneak, you wouldn't have heard me."

I pursed my lips but nodded, knowing he was telling the truth. "Sorry if I woke you. I couldn't sleep and wanted some air."

"You do that a lot." He moved again, like a cat, arms and legs smoothly working in time. Ready to pounce. The urge to escape crept down my spine, into my legs and feet. I shifted.

Croc's gaze lingered on my reaction, and his breaths sharpened. "You're out here every night."

"It's nice to have time alone." I stepped back, hugging the

trunk of the tree with one arm.

He hummed, a throaty sound that could've been a lasso. It circled my middle, tightening, demanding I come closer. "You shouldn't run."

My heart gave a kick. Who was this man, and what had he done with Croc? This man wasn't innocent. This man ignited my nervous system, and he hadn't even made it close. I took a slow breath and moved another inch. "Why?"

His teeth bared, almost a smile but not quite. Sweet yet aggressive. Playful yet predatory. "Because then I want to chase you."

He lunged, and I jumped back, barely grasping a limb on the next tree. I pulled myself up and spun around.

Croc rumbled a laugh, eyes dancing. "You've been avoiding me."

"I see you every day."

He lunged again, and I did the same, keeping us a tree apart.

"You know that's not what I mean," he murmured. "You don't want to be alone with me." He pulled himself onto a large limb and stood to use it like a bridge to my tree.

I turned, searching for a place to jump, but I'd reached a gap. All the limbs on the next tree were either too flimsy or too high. "Shit!" I ground my teeth, searching. But even as I fought to get away, my body thrummed, matching the trees. Singing for him.

"You better hurry, little fish. Croc's gonna catch you." His tone was light, but I panicked all the same.

With no other options, I jumped back to where I'd been, then kept going, one tree after the next, too quick for my brain to even comprehend which branch I was aiming for.

I made it through six trees, reaching the border of the yard where the cypresses thickened and the moon disappeared.

Before I could reach the darkness, Croc's hand hit the branch next to mine. He swung in front of me, circling my body and caging me to the trunk.

His lips were parted, eyes electric. He leaned forward, pressing his forehead to mine as he gave himself a moment to catch his breath. "You've gotten so slippery," he murmured. "I've been wanting to catch you for weeks."

"I'm not actually a fish, Croc."

His nose touched my hair then lightly traveled down to my neck. "True," he said, "but I still caught you." He cupped my waist, pulling me closer.

I trembled despite his blistering heat. It flooded my chest, pooled into my stomach, warming me up for things I couldn't allow to happen. "You…can't catch a human."

"I know how the rules work," he murmured against my neck. "With humans it has to be mutual. I can't catch a human unless they want to be caught." He gently kissed my skin. "You wanted me to catch you. You want me like this." He pressed closer. "I can smell your arousal." He took another deep breath in through his nose, then released it with a lion's purr. "It's mutual."

I curled my hands into fists, demanding they not reach out and grip him closer. He didn't understand. There were other reasons to not want to get caught. There were plenty of reasons why he shouldn't get involved with me. "I'm not a good catch."

He shook his head. "I'm the hunter. I get to decide that."

His lips pressed against my skin, then again along my jaw. "You're the greatest catch I've ever made."

I lifted my chin and bit the inside of my cheek. "Croc, stop."

He pulled back immediately and stared at me, jaw set and eyes determined. "Why? Why do you think you're not a good catch?"

I blinked away the familiar sting. I'd never told a soul, never said it out loud, and the thought of telling him made bile dance at the base of my throat. He didn't need to know. He didn't need to see that part of me. "There are good reasons. You just have to trust me."

"I don't. Not about this." The words were sharp. "You protected Julia. You saved the babies. You sit next to a man who fills your scent with disgust, yet you don't show an ounce of fear." He gripped my chin between his fingers, forcing my gaze up to his. "You amaze me more than letters. More than words. More than books. You embraced the water, learned the swamp, and it fell in love with you just as hard as I did."

Love. No, not love. He couldn't love me. He didn't even know what it was. He'd never had a chance to learn, not that, not yet. "No, Croc." I shook my head. "Maybe you think you do, and I believe you when you say those things, but you have nobody to compare me to, and there's plenty you don't know."

"Tell me," he demanded. "Tell me what it is so I can tell you it doesn't matter."

"It does matter!" I threw up my hands. "And I…I don't want to tell you."

He stared me down, not giving an inch, and when he spoke again, the words were quieter. "I'll give you anything you want. I'll do whatever you ask. If you want me to stay away, leave you alone, and pretend we don't both feel this way, I will." He held me locked, unblinking, intent. "But I'm not letting you out of this tree until you tell me why."

My eyes turned to slits. He didn't get to demand that. It was my story. My secret, and I'd carried it long before I'd ever met him. "I'm not telling you."

He didn't even flinch. "Then I'm not letting you go."

We squared off, and I wanted to scream at him. Of all the times he could have picked to start behaving like every other stubborn, pig-headed man, this was the worst possible one. He wanted to know. He wanted to see. He wanted to taste the vile, putrid acid that came along anytime I thought of it. It would turn him off, drive him away, change his opinions and alter his view. It would destroy all the things he thought he knew about me.

It was for the best. "Fine," I ground out between my teeth. "You want to know?" My stomach churned, and cool dread filled my lungs, froze my words. He'd never look at me the same. He'd be able to see me, how I truly was, the filth and dirt I kept hidden from the world. "You're not the first," I said.

That wasn't enough. He remained perfectly still, watching, waiting.

"I've been with men before. Lots of men. My body has been used, Croc, over and over again." The more I spoke, the easier it became, and before I could process what was happening, the words poured out like a purge. "I let the aid in the group home do what he wanted because I didn't think I was allowed to say no. I let my first foster father touch me for the same reason. I ran away when I was fifteen and slept with a man in exchange for a place to hide." I swallowed hard. "I let Danny use me how he wanted if he'd lower my doses enough to keep me alive. I'm tarnished, Croc. You think you want me, but—"

Croc pulled away and dropped to the ground below, and it felt as if he'd plunged a knife into every wound I'd just laid open for him.

I looked down, watching him stiffly walk away, only to realize too late where he was headed.

Danny.

18 DEBT

"Croc! Stop!" I ran after him, legs propelling, arms pumping. When I'd resigned myself to telling him the truth, I hadn't anticipated what it would mean. I hadn't thought about how he'd react. The truth was, I didn't blame Danny. Not entirely. I blamed myself far too much for that. I'd made the deal. I'd agreed. If I'd said no, he would have left it at that, and I'd have gotten the same treatment as everyone else. "Croc!" I sped up, pushing myself to my absolute limit, but he didn't listen, and he was too far ahead.

He turned the corner of the house, disappearing from view, and by the time I caught up, he had Danny by the throat, pressed against the tree with his feet dangling a foot above the ground.

"Croc!" I sprinted the final stretch between us. "Stop!"

Danny kicked his legs and clawed at Croc's hand, face red and eyes wide.

I jumped onto Croc's back, successfully knocking his balance enough to lose his grip. We tumbled sideways as he simultaneously regained his footing and maneuvered me safely to my feet.

Danny hit the ground hard, and before Croc could grab him again, I threw myself into his path. "Stop! You'll kill him!"

"I know." He took a step closer. "Go inside."

"No." I held my ground, eyes pleading. "Croc, I

understand, and I appreciate that you care, but you can't kill him. You can't kill people. It's a rule."

His jaw tensed, lips thinned. He shifted his attention back to Danny and sneered. "What will you pay her for the protection she's offering you?" He bared his teeth, waiting for an answer, and when he didn't receive one, he repeated the question in a deafening roar, "What will you pay?"

Danny was silent, and so was I. The world froze over, icy and solid, and Croc was the king of it all. He was a statue, the kind that stood guard over ancient towers. He was terrifying, and no matter what side he was on, I wanted to hide. I wanted to pretend Danny had never arrived and go back to my tree. But I couldn't do that. I couldn't let Croc kill him, no matter what he'd done.

I swallowed hard and took a breath. "I know you're angry—" I paused, needing to be careful with my words. He wasn't himself, and his rage was a fire on the verge of spreading. If I didn't contain him soon, he'd burn us all. "But I'm not blameless. I agreed. It was a deal." Another pause. "It was mutual."

"Mutual?" He shook his head, looking at me as if I'd lost my mind. "I may not know everything about being human, Willow. I may have never left this swamp, but I'm not stupid. I understand what mutual is."

"He wanted something," I said. "I could have said no. I'm sure better women did. He didn't force me to take the deal."

"Did you want to?"

I paused, swallowing back the bile. "I wanted to live."

"That's not what I asked. Did you want to?" he snapped.

I flinched. "I had to…"

"You had to…" His lip curled, and he focused back on Danny. "Did you? Did you have to?" He took a step forward.

I held up a hand. "Croc…"

"He owes me a debt. I've kept him alive. I've given him food. I've offered him protection." Each word was quiet but somehow scarier than the ones he'd shouted. "He needs to pay me."

Danny shifted, then shakily pulled himself upright. "I can. I can give you information. I can tell you about—"

"You'll give me whatever I want!" Croc roared.

Silence fell again. Long and heavy. It deafened the swamp, everything from the smallest creature to the wind stopping to take caution. He pushed past me, ignoring my hands as I gripped his arm and tried to stop him.

I stepped back, breath held. Each move he made was slow, and the tension magnified. The atmosphere charged, and Danny stood like a man who'd stumbled upon a venomous snake.

Croc circled him, eyes blazing electric neon green and muscles coiled and ready to strike. The irony wasn't lost on me. Croc was the embodiment of the chemicals Danny had injected into so many, and despite my objections to his killing anyone, I couldn't help but be in awe of how poetically just it would be if he did.

"Gator!" he commanded. The water stirred, and Gator emerged up the embankment. "Show Danny your teeth."

Gator opened his jaws wide.

Croc motioned with his chin. "Now, put your hand in his mouth."

Danny's eyes widened, and he instinctively pulled his

hands back into himself.

Croc rumbled low in his chest. "I'm not asking."

"Croc…" He couldn't mean it. He couldn't really do that, could he? I met Danny's shining eyes, saw the moisture glinting on his cheeks. His skin was as white as the ghosts he'd created. Pallid. Lifeless. Terrified. I looked into his face, devoid of any mask, for the first time, truthful, honest, and it was a face I'd seen a thousand times before. On the women in my group. On the mothers lined up with their children. On the neighbor, the night they'd forced him to his knees as his wife and daughter were loaded into the back of the truck. It was the face of the fallen, of the conquered, of death.

"He doesn't have to do it. He can choose not to, and I'll just snap his neck."

Danny broke. "I'm sorry! Please, Willow, I'm sorry! I shouldn't have done it. I should have done more to help. I shouldn't have asked you to. God! Just please! I can't do that. I'll never be able to heal. How can a doctor heal without his hand?" His words broke into sobs until I couldn't understand what he was saying.

My chest tightened, stomach clenched. "Croc, that's enough."

"Did you cry like that? When you made your deal?" he asked, unaffected by Danny's pleas. "It's the same deal, isn't it? He wanted your body in exchange for not killing you. I want the hands he used to collect his payment. That's mutual. That's fair."

Danny's sobs dissipated into low moans.

"That's not how it works."

He turned away from me and crouched down, focusing

on Danny. "Isn't it? Is that not how it worked when you had all the power?"

Danny nodded. "It is. I was wrong. I'm sorry. I'll do anything," he choked. "I'll do whatever—"

"I don't care how much you cry. You've got the same options she had. Do you accept my deal?"

Danny looked over at Gator's gaping jaws and gagged, then dry heaved, coughing and fighting to breathe as his wildly shaking hand crept toward its fate.

"No! Danny, don't!" My desperation rose, and I didn't think. All I knew was that I needed to stop it. "Croc, that's not how it works!" I shouted. "Not with us!"

He stood and spun to face me. "Why? Why is it different?"

"Because!" I fisted my hands. "Danny is an asshole! We're not! If we handle it like this, then we're no better than they are!"

"You act like it's my fault if Gator eats his hand."

"It is!" I snapped, flinging a hand toward the scene behind him. "You're the one making him do it!"

"It's the deal," he said. "He accepted it."

"It's a fucked-up deal!"

Croc stared at me as my words echoed in the space between us. It was a bad deal. It wasn't a deal at all. It was coercion. It was forced. My lips parted on a breath, and moisture pricked at the corners of my eyes.

Croc stepped forward, enveloping me in his arms and securing me against his chest. "Exactly," he murmured, the statement for me and me alone to hear. "It wasn't a deal. None of them were deals, and you're not tarnished." He leaned back, just enough to meet my eyes. "That shame isn't yours, Willow.

Your intentions were always pure."

He pulled away then, keeping one arm across my shoulders. "That's enough, Gator."

Gator closed his jaws and heaved a breath. "Oh, sweet baby frogs! For a minute, I thought I was really going to have to do it. Y'all haven't seen the things I have. That man digs in his ass like that's the path to freedom." He shook his head and turned back toward the water. "No, thank you. I'll stick with fish. They're cleaner."

Danny was white faced, sweating, and lethargic as he slumped back against the base of the tree.

"You're okay," Croc told him as he turned to lead me back in the direction we'd come. He squeezed me into his side and kissed my temple. "He's lucky you're human."

19
SHOW ME

Croc led me around back and to the water's edge.

"Where are we going?" My voice sounded foreign to my own ears. I was hollow, empty, unable to make even the simplest decisions. My legs moved where he prompted. My mind followed his direction. The breakthrough he'd forced me to have had overloaded my brain, exhausting my mental abilities. I'd shut down, gone to sleep even while I was wide awake.

Croc released his grip on my shoulders and gently took my fingers in his. "Come with me, into the water."

I stared at him, knowing it was nighttime but not having the presence of mind to be concerned. I nodded, allowing him to pull me down the bank. It was another world, and unlike during the day, each wave our bodies made lit up the depths with glittering green. Croc watched me closely as we waded together toward the center.

"Swim with me," he said, tone the same low, soothing sound he'd used before. "Swim hard and keep up. Don't get left behind." He let go of my hand and dunked down, taking off without giving me a chance to process what he'd asked of me.

I panicked and sunk beneath the surface to follow. The glowing green framed his physique, leaving a trail to guide me. I pushed my body hard, limbs working on memory until I caught up to his side, and we swam. We swam with an intensity we'd never done before. We were one with water, fluid and graceful, dodging rocks and limbs, winding with each curve and bend in the canal.

My mind returned to the present in pieces, relishing the way my body moved, the glittering green, the cool water as it rushed over my skin. I was part of it, the environment, a product of nature, a living being sprung from the breast of a dying mother, and she held me close and whispered encouragement in the form of all the beautiful things she'd birthed. Fish swam alongside of us, glowing just as bright as the swamp itself, before they'd break away to allow new ones to take their place, for once, unafraid of the hunter. Glowing green eyes lit the path, blinking in and out of focus as the gators watched us pass them by like neighbors taking a midnight walk.

I didn't tire. I didn't slow. I expelled no effort and remembered nothing. Danny didn't exist. The world outside didn't exist. The past couldn't follow me, not there, not then. I was safe, washed clean of the shame, submerged in a world that didn't allow room for judgment, not even my own.

We kept going until we reached the place where the water opened into a vast river.

Croc floated to the surface and stared into the horizon. The green faded outwards, diluting into the black water, disappearing like dying stars in an infinite galaxy. "This is the end," he said, tone low. "This is where our world ends, and another begins."

I studied his profile, letting his words wash over me.

He turned to face me. "Who brought you here?"

For a moment, I couldn't answer. I wasn't sure how to. The question was as odd as its answer was obvious. My brow furrowed. "You did…"

"No." He shook his head and swam forward to wade just in front of me. "You did, Willow. You brought yourself here." He took both my hands in his and lifted my arms above the surface. "Your arms." He lowered them back down and let go. "Your legs, your mind, your heart, your body. Yours." He cupped my face, staring into my eyes, drilling the words as deep as they'd go. "No person owns any part of it. Nobody has the power to take it from you. It doesn't matter what happens. It is only yours."

My eyes stung; chest tightened. My throat burned and breaths shuddered. What he'd said went against everything I'd grown to believe. I was defined by simplicities. Get up, eat, stay clean, stay alive. That was it. That was all. My body was just a shell, something I hated but had to have. It wasn't the good part of me. It was tainted and scarred, and I'd hated it for years. I ignored it, keeping it and everything else locked away where I could pretend it didn't affect me. But Croc's light shone too bright, and now that I'd allowed him to see, he wouldn't stop. He highlighted each blemish, demanding it be brought to attention.

I wanted to disappear and pretend the night had never happened. Why couldn't he understand that? "I get it, Croc. I'm a survivor. It wasn't my fault. You made your point." It didn't change anything. I couldn't be fixed. He could show me whatever he wanted. He could prove that I'd been coerced, that I was a victim, and it wouldn't change the way I felt. It wouldn't fix it. "Stop trying to fix me. You can't fix people.

That's not how it works."

"You don't need to be fixed," he said, gaze intensifying. "This wasn't about fixing you. This was about showing you what I see when I look at you." He spoke with passion, demanding I understand. "In the tree, you called yourself tainted. You said you'd given yourself away. That's not true. You're right here. You've been here since the day you arrived, and I've been tearing myself apart ever since, fighting to do whatever necessary to be close to you, if only for a moment."

I looked down, fixing my eyes on the water, rejecting his words the moment they left his mouth. "It doesn't feel like it," I said. "It feels like I've been replaced with something else. I feel like I'm a different person, every time it happens. Like I'm less than I was…" I broke apart, lost control, and a traitorous tear broke free to roll down my cheek. I rubbed it away and clenched my jaw. "I can't get better. I can't heal. There is no medicine, or cure, or way to turn back the clock and make it different. I'm painted in this…this…filth! It doesn't matter what you see, or even if I believe you. Nothing you say or explain or show me will change it. That's not how it works."

He fell silent a long moment, contemplating my words, before he whispered, "That's very sad." He turned away, back to the endless view, and continued in a far-off voice. "If you could have seen yourself, just now, moving through the water like a…like a…" He clenched his jaw and shook his head. "I can't even describe you. If you could see that, see what I see, you would never question your worth." He took a deep inhale, breathing in the night air.

"Croc…I…"

"It's okay." He turned to offer me a soft smile. "I realize

now that this is different. This isn't as simple an answer as I thought it was." He tucked my hair behind my ear. "I'm sorry if I pushed too hard. If I'd known what I do now, I would have gone about this differently." He kept a gap between us, allowing me my distance without even the slightest sign that he intended to attempt anything else. "But," he started, tone more serious, "you don't get to tell me what I want, Willow. You don't get to say how I should feel. I won't view you as less just because you say I should." He tilted his head, forcing my eyes to his. "That's a rule."

I grinned despite myself. "Is it? Did you make that rule?"

"I did." He grinned back.

Even knowing all my secrets, he still wanted me. He meant what he said, in the same way he meant everything when he spoke. Something shifted inside me. Some part of myself acknowledged his view, and for a brief moment, between the situation with Danny and Croc's words, I could almost believe that, maybe, eventually, I wouldn't feel this way. Maybe, someday, I'd be able to love myself again.

I collapsed into him, wrapping my arms around his waist and burying my head against his chest. Safe, secure, and beyond a doubt that he wouldn't expect more. Not Croc. He was different.

He folded his arms around me and leaned back, not expecting anything or demanding a price. He supported me, not just my weight but all the burden that came with it, and we stayed like that as the current slowly carried us back home.

21 SLEEPING MERMAID

Life went on, and my peace returned. Croc kept Danny away from me, and a lot of the flashbacks went with him. He put him to work, cleaning fish, picking vegetables, helping Julia plant and water and pull weeds from the garden while Gator followed close behind, ready to take him out if he so much as sneezed.

Danny's absence wasn't all that changed. The relationship between Croc and I completely evolved. He stopped being a hunter and started being a friend. We were companions, family, and we focused on the children, teaching them books after breakfast and swimming after lunch. We laughed, talked, and worked together.

Eve and Eric grew and thrived. They were normal kids, getting to experience things the way they were intended to, and I was a part of that. It was the greatest accomplishment I'd ever made. It was personal. I was giving them something I'd never had, and I relished the feeling knowing that.

Croc and Eric knelt at the end of the dock, searching for fish worthy of dinner while Eve and I navigated the water further down the canal. I'd been teaching her to swim, focusing on how to feel and move the way Croc had taught me. She was older than Eric—more ready to try—and she took to it like a natural. We moved together, a little more each day, mainly above the surface, but today, I wanted us to do more.

"Are you ready?" I asked her, nervous that I may be moving too fast.

She smiled her snaggle-toothed smile, holding onto a branch with one arm with her feet prepared to kick off as if it were an Olympic race.

I laughed at her seriousness. "Under the water, as far as we can. If you need to breathe, just stop, and we'll take a break before heading back."

She nodded. "Okay, okay. I know that stuff. Can we go?"

Her skin had a glow to it, cheeks rosy and eyes shining with life. Nothing like the girl I'd found, frail and frightened yet still ready to fight to protect her younger brother. Healed. The water, the current, Croc and Gator and plentiful food and freedom had given her the tools she needed to reach her potential, to be this amazingly, determined and tenacious child. It'd given her wings, and I loved watching her fly. "Alright…Ready…Set—"

She kicked off, diving under, and I dipped down to watch her. Her feet became little propellers, and her body waved like a dolphin's, how Croc's did, how mine did. Warmth flooded my chest. She was amazing, doing the things that *I'd* taught her. *I'd* shown her how to do that. My cheeks hurt from smiling as I hurried forward, keeping just behind so I could track her progress and intervene if a problem presented itself.

Eve had no problems. She dodged rocks, maneuvered around logs, and reached out her hands to pet the many fish she zoomed past. She was a little mermaid, and my heart swelled. She made it far, all the way to where Croc had led me, then seeming to know that was as far as was safe, she pulled herself above the surface and turned to find me. "Did you see me?" she shouted the instant I emerged. "Did you see me, Willow? Did you see how good I did?"

"I saw." I laughed. "I almost couldn't keep up."

She sucked in lungful after lungful of air, glowing in the light of her accomplishment, staring out at the horizon. The sun shone onto her face, illuminating her golden curls. An angel. Had I ever been that innocent? Had I ever felt that accomplished? That proud? That happy?

I knew my answer the moment I asked myself the question. I had, just now. In that moment, I felt all those things, because when Eve turned to look at me, she didn't see an orphan or trash or someone less than. She looked at me how Julia looked at Merle; how they all looked at Croc. She'd remember me, this event, years from now, long after I'd gone, and within that memory, I'd be something good, something important, something to smile about.

Eve swam the few feet between us and bobbed in the water before me. "Can I have raspberries when we get back? I earned raspberries."

I grinned and nodded. "I'll make sure Julia understands and gives you all the raspberries you can eat."

Something rumbled in the distance, pulling my attention past her to the massive river beyond. The waves grew, chopping angrily, and almost too late, I figured out what was causing the sound. A glimpse of white traveled beyond the trees.

A boat.

It drifted forward, toward the mouth of the swamp,

where our world ended and another began. Hell had found an opening, a crack to slip through, and all of my tranquility evaporated, leaving me bare and nothing more than the girl I'd been. The girl that needed to survive. The girl that needed to protect Eve.

I snatched her wrist and yanked her into my arms, dunking us both beneath the surface. She clung to me, just as she had that night.

I'd always known fear. When I was a child, fear had taken the place of family. Fear had raised me. Fear had embraced me long before anything else. Fear was my oldest acquaintance, but this wasn't fear. This was different. This was more than that. I pressed a shaking finger to my lips, then let her go enough for us to swim back toward home. I could hear the motor rumbling behind, then the squeal of metal moving against rust. The water clouded with neon green. They were dumping. Why hadn't I remembered what Croc had told me? Why had I let her swim this far?

Chemical clouded around us, blocking my vision. The once cool water turned boiling as the fire found its way inside. It stung my skin, biting, scratching, eating me away as if it'd been waiting for a chance to finish the meal it'd started all those months before. I held onto Eve, using my free hand to feel our way forward, and after minutes that felt like hours, I finally managed to break free of the murk.

I swam harder than I'd ever swam before. Particles and debris rushed past us, creating a vortex, a tunnel. Limbs became demon fingers, digging into flesh, pulling us back. I ignored them and focused on the girl in my arms. She was limp and light, like a little doll that'd been opened up and hollowed out.

When we made it far enough away, I veered toward the bank and pulled us both up onto the mud. "Eve!" I patted her cheek then shook her shoulders. Her skin was deep red, as if she'd been scrubbed down with wire and left to roast in the sun. "Eve!" She wasn't breathing.

I pressed my ear against her chest, listening to the spaced-out thuds of her heart and praying it was because she was preserving her oxygen. It had to be that. She had to be okay. "Hang on, baby!" I opened her mouth and blew a breath in, then pumped both palms into her chest. Nothing changed, and I had no idea if I was doing it wrong, causing more harm, or even wasting time when I could have her in the hands of someone more capable. I needed Julia. I needed Croc. For fuck's sake, I needed Danny.

I pulled her onto my back, linked her arms around my neck, and held her there with one hand by her wrists. I took her with me through the canal, ignoring the cuts and bruises each branch and rock gave as I went. Too quick to focus on anything other than saving her. I'd allowed this. I'd done this. A million failures filled my memory. A million times I hadn't been enough. I'd allowed them all to fade away. I'd pretended I'd changed. That I was different. Better. And I'd let her down.

By the time the dock came into view, I was sobbing. "Croc!"

His head jerked up, and within a second, he was in the water, taking Eve into his arms. "What happened?" he asked, staring down at her as he rushed toward the house.

"I don't know! We swam to the end, and a boat showed up. They dumped the chemicals and she stopped…she stopped…" I couldn't breathe, couldn't speak. My skin was on fire, yet my body shook as if I'd walked through a blizzard to get there. I followed him inside and stood back as he and Julia laid Eve across the couch and looked for the source of the problem.

"Get Danny," Julia said, her own voice lacking any of its usual calm.

Croc didn't object. He sprinted through the open front door, and I fell to my knees next to Eve. She was pale and lifeless when, only a blink before, she'd been shining like the sun.

She had to be okay. She couldn't not be okay, but the chemicals had been so thick, and I'd felt firsthand what half a bag could do to someone. She was so small. She was too little. Had she swallowed it? Had it poisoned her? I wouldn't survive it if she died. She couldn't die. She was too young, too precious. She was mine to protect, since the moment I carried her from that house, and if I lost her now, I'd—

Croc returned with Danny, and I found just enough of my voice to explain everything that had happened.

He checked her heart, her temperature, face set in official script. "She's alive, but she needs to breathe. Her heart is doing its part to preserve what oxygen she has, but it will only last so long." He pulled out a mask connected to a tube with a large plastic ball on the opposite end, then positioned it over her face and pumped the ball in a steady rhythm.

Her chest rose and fell each time, and the atmosphere was frozen, all attention centered on her.

Then, a miracle occurred, performed by the hands of the Devil. Eve sucked in a deep wheezing breath, and so did I, not realizing until then that I'd been holding mine as well.

Julia laughed through her tears, and Croc slumped back against the wall, staring down at Eve's chest as it moved on its own.

I fell apart, bent forward until my forehead touched the floor and thanked whatever god would listen over and over again.

Her eyes were still closed, body deathly still, but she was breathing, and when Danny checked her heart again, it had returned to normal. "She needs to rest," he said. "Dry her and make her comfortable. I have some ointment for the burns. I'm not sure if it will work, but it should at least soothe some of the pain." He looked at me, eyeing my skin. "Willow should apply some as well, and someone should stay close at all times to make sure the girl doesn't stop breathing again."

"I'll stay," I said. "I'll stay with her."

"You're hurt," Croc said.

I looked down at the raw skin. Blood pooled beneath my legs, soaking into the carpet. "They're just cuts. I'm fine. I need to—"

"You're not fine, and Eve is okay for now." Julia waved me off. "I'll watch her while you let Croc help you get cleaned up."

Danny reached inside his bag, pulled out a roll of bandages and a tube of ointment, and handed them to Croc. He paused and stared at the floor. "Would you like for me to stay…with the girl?"

Croc grabbed his arm and hoisted him up. "Stay at your old spot. Gator will watch you, and Julia will call if she needs you inside." He led him to the door, watched him until he'd done as told, then turned toward me. "Go in the bathroom.

I'll heat some water and be there in a minute."

My attention centered on Eve.

"She's fine, Willow," Julia said. "Go get cleaned up. You'll be no good to her if you get an infection."

I nodded and stood on wobbling legs, making my way like a zombie to sit on the side of the tub.

21 TORMENT

Croc joined me a few moments later, carrying a pot of hot water, a rag, and the supplies Danny had given him. Most of my injuries were superficial, minor scratches, but one cut across my knee was deep and by the time he arrived, blood coated the entire top of my leg to my ankle.

Croc shook his head, then gently went about washing the blood away.

"I can do it." I reached for the towel.

He pulled it out of reach and set back to work without comment. The whole while, he wouldn't meet my eyes, and I couldn't say I blamed him. I'd messed up, badly, and the last thing I deserved was Croc's brand of sweet, placating words. I didn't deserve comfort. Not while Eve was still unconscious because of my misjudgment.

We were silent as he cleared the blood, applied the ointment, placed band aids to hold the cut together, then wrapped it all in a thick white bandage. By the time he was finished, the floor around him was a mess.

"I forgot about them. It didn't even cross my mind until I saw the boat." My voice was small. "I shouldn't have let her go so far. I should have never let it happen."

He shook his head as he gathered the scraps of cloth and

trash from the floor. "You made an honest mistake in a place you still don't fully understand." He finally looked up at me. "It's my job to protect you both." His gaze shifted to the gauze he'd applied, and his jaw clenched. "This is my failure." He stood quickly and left the room, closing the door behind him and leaving me there to finish.

I grabbed a towel from under the sink and numbly dried my hair and skin. My clothes were still soaked, but I hadn't brought any new ones with me. I didn't apply the ointment to my skin. I relished the pain, letting it wrap around me. The pain meant that I was still alive, that I'd survived, yet again, and I hoped that meant Eve would, too. She had to. She deserved it so much more. I'd used my nine lives. I'd had my fair share. She was so young, so much better, so much more worthy.

The sun rose and fell until it felt as if it fell first and rose second. Up was down, and left was right, and all was a mess expect for the little girl who slept, too peaceful for the chaos her slumber created.

Julia took care of Eric, assuring him Eve was only tired after her hard swim. He believed her easily, believed us all. He placed his trust in us, the same way Eve had placed her trust in me.

Croc tried to get me to eat and became angry for the first time when I refused. He was an even bigger mess than I was, and the situation was taking a toll on him. He was testy, tense, and spent most of his time the same as I did. Staring at the couch. At her. Waiting.

Julia, once again, proved how much stronger she was than

any of us. She kept to her routine, took care of Eric, and made sure we had everything we needed. She took the hardship like she had undoubtedly taken a hundred others. She met it head on and all but told it to kiss her ass. She kept Eve clean and would occasionally lift her head to try and get her to take water or vegetable broth, and sometimes, she succeeded.

I helped her whenever I could. I made the broth, stroked Eve's hair and offered praise I wasn't sure she could hear. I noted every change. Her healing skin, her returned color. I counted her heartbeats and watched her chest rise and fall. Sometimes, my mind would play tricks on me, and I'd panic for a moment, sure I was imagining the subtle movement. But a hand against her ribs would assure me that wasn't the case, and I'd return to the routine. Watching. Watching. Waiting and thinking.

Every time I closed my eyes, my mind reminded me of who I was and where I'd been. I saw foster siblings I'd long forgotten, scenes I'd blocked out years before. I saw my failures, lined up one by one, presented as evidence of my own guilt.

I'd always known my place. People had a role. Some had nice lives. Others didn't. I hadn't been born to have nice things, a family. I had none of those blood connections, no identity, and my choices had always been poor. Foster siblings had been beaten while I hid and said nothing. People had been dragged away while I fought to get home and save myself. How many hungry children had I passed at the store? How many ration tickets could I have spared? Julia had a garden full of vegetables. I could have done more. I could have helped more, had I been better. Had I been that kind of person. Then Lita, Eve's mother, someone who would have probably protected her far better than I, being dragged away while I sat and watched, unspeaking.

Why had I been spared? Why was I here and not the others? Those were the questions that haunted me. Out of all the injustice, that was the one I couldn't live with. I tossed and turned and begged the images to stop, until Croc pulled me upright and shoved a plate of breakfast into my lap. "You're going to eat that, Willow, even if I have to feed it to you."

I shook my head and sat up to check Eve. "I'm not hungry."

He pushed me back down. "I didn't ask," he said, lifting a raspberry to my lips.

A raspberry. Who was I to have a raspberry when she couldn't? She'd earned it. She'd said so herself, and she'd been right. She deserved to have everything, all the things I'd never had, and I'd robbed her of that. I'd robbed her and so many others. I shoved his hand away. "Stop."

"Dammit, Willow!"

My eyes widened, staring at his tense and worn face. He'd never swore before. He hadn't even attempted to pick up any of the words Julia used so frequently, and the stark shock of hearing him do so was like a bucket of water being dumped onto my face. It woke me up and forced me to the present. He was pale, and the lines around his eyes and mouth seemed deeper, haggard. "Eat," he said. "Please."

I bowed my head, examining the plate, then broke a piece of the fish off between two fingers and numbly shoved it into my mouth. It had no flavor, no substance, but I swallowed it and met his gaze.

He visibly relaxed. "That's good. Eat some more. Here." He lifted it. "Have some more fish."

I couldn't deny him, not when he looked so desperate for me to comply. I finished the fish and pushed the plate away, unable to bring myself to eat any more.

Croc sighed. "Good." He rose, leaning over Eve and pressing his palm against her forehead, then her chest. "She stirred earlier. While you were sleeping."

I shot upright and pushed him away to check for myself. "When? How did she do it? Do you think she's waking up?"

Croc was quiet a moment, then a second later, he draped his arm across my back and drew me away like a child. He settled me into his lap, locked me into a vice like hold, and pressed his chin to the top of my head. "I think she will," he said, words rough. "I think she's going to be okay." He rocked me back and forth, and my first instinct was to pull away. But I didn't, because something told me he wasn't doing it for my comfort, but his own.

I stared at Eve, letting Croc sway us both as I watched for the slightest sign she was lucid. She had to be okay. I needed her to be okay. If she could just wake up now, I'd do whatever I needed to do. I'd give whatever needed to be given, make whatever deal needed to be made. But there were no deals. There was nobody to make one with, and whatever battle Eve was fighting, she was fighting it alone.

As if sensing my panic, Croc shushed me. "She'll be okay," he murmured against my hair. "Danny checked her heart, and he said it's stronger. She hasn't stopped breathing again, and she swallowed the whole bowl of soup this morning. She's okay." Each word he spoke echoed his own relief and soothed my tattered nerves like a balm.

I opened my eyes and realized quickly where I was. Croc still held me, swaying gently like he'd been whenever I'd fallen asleep, but the darkness outside let me know it had to have been hours since I'd blacked out. "How long?" I asked, voice hoarse.

"You were exhausted," he stated, the words echoing his own fatigue.

I peeked up at his face. Shadows clung deeper to the skin beneath his eyes, and he was even more drawn than he'd been that morning.

I tried to sit up, but he held me firm.

"Croc," I said. "You're tired. Get some sleep. I'll watch her for a—"

"No." He pulled me back like a child refusing to relinquish his toy. "Stay here. It's…it's comforting."

I sighed and fell limp, allowing him to scrunch me up like a doll as I studied his expression. His attention stayed glued to Eve.

"I wanted to hold her, too. But Julia said no," he said. "When she wakes up, I'm never going to let her out of my sight again."

My heart ached, and a fresh wave of guilt made my chest tighten and clench. "It isn't your fault, Croc. It's mine. I was supposed to be watching her."

"You saved her," he said.

"From the danger I put her in." I cupped his face and forced him to meet my gaze. He had to understand. I couldn't pretend anymore. I wouldn't do that, not to him, not to Eve, not to all the wonderful things in this place. All this time, I'd been accusing the world of lies. I'd judged Danny's disguise, the officials, the buildings, the government, and all along, I'd been just as bad. I'd been just the same, and I didn't want to lie anymore. I didn't want to pretend. "You don't deserve any of the blame in this. It was all me. My fault. Do you understand?"

He heaved a tired sigh. "I know every danger here, Willow. It didn't start when you arrived, and it hadn't stopped just because I'd grown complacent. I got reckless. It was stupid of me to let you two go off alone, and I'm sorry." He pulled me closer, burying his face into my neck as his breaths shuddered and words broke apart. "I'm so sorry."

I circled my arms around his head and held him tighter, stroking his hair and offering the same comfort he'd offered me. "This isn't my first failure, Croc. It's not your fault." I kissed his temple. "It isn't. Not at all."

We both fell quiet, unmoving, locked together as if we were each the only thing keeping the other from falling apart.

"Willow, are you done?" a small voice whispered. "Can I have my raspberries, now?"

I scrambled away from him, and he was too shocked to stop me. We broke apart, stumbling in our hurry to reach her. Eve was upright. She was awake. She was sitting with the blankets gathered at her waist as if she'd just woken from a nap instead of a five-day coma.

She blinked at us with glowing, neon green eyes.

22
MOTHER JULIA SAYS

Croc gathered Eve into his arms, and no matter who wanted to check her, he wouldn't put her down. He held her like an infant, pacing the living room as he murmured words too low for any of us to hear.

The minute Eve woke up, so did everyone else. Julia cheered and celebrated, forcing Croc to stop for long enough to let her stare into Eve's face before she went outside and got Danny.

He rushed in, checked her vitals as best as he could with Croc not wanting to let him near, then marveled at the new color to her eyes. "Amazing," he breathed.

"What is it? Is she okay?" I gripped his sleeve, unconcerned with who he was or what touching him would usually mean for me. I didn't care. It didn't matter. He needed to fix whatever mess I'd created.

"She's better than okay," Danny said. "Her eyes have mutated, much like Croc's. I couldn't be sure without really looking at his, but this proves my theory." He was practically vibrating with excitement, shaking arms and fumbling hands. "She's developed a tapetum lucidum. It's a reflective layer of tissues found at the back of the retina." He pulled out a small black tool and used it to peer inside her eye. "It's amazing. Tapetum lucidum is iridescent. The colors depend on which minerals make up the crystals, and the angle in which you see them. Hers are the same neon green of chemical 426. It's as if the chemical…mimicked this trait and morphed itself to recreate it." He pulled back and studied the rest of her, ignoring Croc's warning gaze.

"Speak English, Danny. What the hell does that mean? Are her eyes always going to glow like that?" They were brighter than Croc's, blinding in their intensity. "Can she still see properly?"

"She can see better," he said. "It's common in animals." He continued on, speaking slower. "When light enters the eye, it's supposed to hit the photoreceptor. The photoreceptor transfers information to the brain. Sometimes, especially when it's dark, the light doesn't hit it. Think of the tapetum lucidum like a mirror, bouncing it back for a second chance."

I ground my teeth, wanting to hit him in the head until he'd reached my level of understanding. Thankfully, I didn't need to.

"It's for hunting," Croc said. "And protection."

Danny's smile thinned. "Exactly. But her coma is what's most fascinating. I can't be sure without more tests, but my first theory is that she incubated herself while the tissues formed."

"If that's true, then why didn't it do the same thing to me?" I relaxed a fraction, the first blissful bout of relief since the incident had occurred. She was okay. She would be all right, and from then on, I swore to never let her more than twenty feet from the house, and never anywhere without Croc.

"I can't answer that," he said. "It could be that you got less exposed. It could also be that you're more immune, given your history of exposure. Whatever the reason, I'd love to go back there and see how it's effected the environment in that specific area."

My eyes widened. "Are you crazy? What if they came back, or someone else got sick?"

"What if this is the breakthrough needed to save our species?" Danny said. "The goal was always to find a way for humans to withstand the chemical. This is outstanding! When diluted into a natural setting, humans can not only survive it, they transform into nature itself!"

"Which parts of the species, Danny? All of us, or just the *necessary?*" I sneered the word. "Who will be worthy of it? Will I? Will she?" I threw a hand out toward Eve, who was silent throughout the whole exchange. She clung to Croc, head pressed against his chest, both hands gripping one of his.

"That's enough," Croc said, his whispered volume matching none of his tone. He centered his gaze on Danny, daring him to argue. "There'll be no experiments here. You're done. Go back to your spot."

Danny didn't argue, but I could tell he wasn't done. Not by a long shot. This had been the icing on his scientific cake. This was what he wanted, and as he walked away, glancing back at Eve, I saw the wheels turning across his expression. He wouldn't give up, and now, he was more dangerous than ever.

"Watch him," I said. "All the time. He can't leave this place."

"Don't worry," Croc said. He stepped over to the couch and took a seat, still cradling Eve in his arms. "Gator will watch him, and if for any reason he stops, Danny won't survive."

Julia touched my shoulder, then pulled me into a gentle

hug. "She's alright," she said. "Now, eat something substantial and get some real sleep." She patted the back of my head and drew back, then scrunched her nose. "And bathe. You smell like shit."

I drew her back to me, squeezing tight one last time before she patted my shoulder and turned to climb back up into the loft.

Eric settled in beside Croc and Eve, laying his head against Croc's shoulder and shoving his thumb in his mouth. They both went to sleep, and I watched them for a moment, relieved and guilty and grateful all at once.

"She's right, Willow," Croc murmured, breaking the spell.

"That I stink?"

"That you need to take care of yourself. I'm not leaving. Get cleaned up, eat something, rest, and forgive yourself." His voice was low, but too deep to ever be a whisper. "I need you to do those things, because…I need you here with me."

I nodded and blinked hard, then whispered, "I will."

Our daily routine disappeared, replaced by a more cautious version. Croc took over Eve's swimming lessons, and the two traveled the canals together, steering clear of the end. She flourished, bouncing back as if nothing had happened.

I worked more with Eric, staying always at the end of the dock and always with Julia watching. I laughed and enjoyed the time with him, but the fear never subsided, and I didn't trust myself. Julia scolded me several times to let the boy go, let him float, put your hands down, he's fine. Stop hovering!

Still, I was on edge, and every night, when they were tucked into bed and sound asleep, I breathed a sigh of relief.

I wanted to lock them in the house and never let them go anywhere, but I knew that couldn't happen.

As days past, my guard strengthened, and I relied on the others to help ensure nothing happened. But something had changed. I had changed. I no longer felt like part of the swamp. I didn't feel worthy of it. Croc had told me to forgive myself, but I wasn't sure how. There were too many wrongs to forgive. Too many failures to ever right. I put on a show for the children, acting as if everything was fine whenever I spoke or played with them, but the rest of the time, I kept my distance, forfeiting the beauty of the canal in an attempt to protect it all from my natural ability to destroy.

I loathed myself more than I ever had before. All of my faults resurfaced, painting me back the colors I'd always been. Human trash. Poor. Orphaned. Nothing. No one. Just like Danny had said. Perhaps they weren't lies after all, just truths I hadn't wanted to admit. No amount of pretending would change who I was. I'd been so wrapped up in my own fantasy, that I was capable, stronger, more, and it had almost cost Eve her life.

Julia, of course, in all her elderly wisdom, sensed my every emotion and read my every thought. She'd been a mad woman, pestering the shit out of me and trying to force me to participate, pretend again, and forget all about what had happened. We argued daily, which was more her scolding me while blocking my attempts to get away.

I'd just finished gathering a basket full of vegetables from the garden and was headed back toward the house. We didn't need them, but I was limited on excuses to get away and be alone. Twilight emerged, painting the swamp in light blues and grays. Cicadas chirped, bullfrogs croaked, and fireflies slowly awoke, blinking in and out of focus as I cut through the tall grass toward the house.

Croc and Julia stood on the deck, and I paused to watch them. Whatever they were discussing couldn't have been good, not given Julia's tense back and expressive hands. She was scolding him how she did me, something that never happened, and I furrowed my brow as Croc threw his hands up and argued back. Their voices were too low to hear what was said, but whatever it was, it was pissing them both off.

I continued forward, and as I drew closer, Croc's eyes locked on me.

Julia turned, then focused back on him, poking his chest and muttering something else until he stormed inside.

"What was that about?" I asked as I sat the basket on the deck and climbed up to stand beside her.

She took the vegetables and sat them by the door, then faced me with her hands on her hips. I blew out a breath. *Here we go again.* I hesitated, eyeing the path behind me. If I said we needed more corn, would she let me leave again? I wished I hadn't decided to head back so soon.

"Sit down with me." Her tone was calmer than her body language. "Just sit down on the deck and listen to an old woman for once in your damn life."

She didn't wait for me to agree, but, then again, I hadn't really expected her to. It wasn't an actual request. Julia didn't make requests. She made polite demands. She gripped my wrist and pulled me down, taking a seat until we were both side by side with our legs dangling over the ground I'd just climbed up from.

"What now?"

She didn't respond for a long moment. Her face was drawn, gaze focused in the direction of the garden, and she pulled my hand into hers and laid it across her lap, patting it with the other, like a grandmother offering comfort to a grieving child. Her posture and expression made me pause. She looked tired, older. It was easy to forget that Julia was old. She didn't dress old. She didn't carry herself in a way that suggested anything but youth, but, in that moment, she seemed ancient.

"I had a daughter," she said, voice distant.

I stared at her profile, stunned silent. A daughter? No. She couldn't. Her and Merle couldn't have kids. She'd told me that before. When she was twenty-seven, she had an illness that forced her to need a hysterectomy. "You said—"

"Before. When I was young. Merle was still deep into the club. He'd just been handed a three-year sentence, and my parents weren't willing to let me live with them if I kept the baby." She turned to look at me. "The minute she was born, I gave her away. I thought it was best. I figured another family would be able to give her way more than I ever had, surely a better life than Merle and I could provide."

My eyes stung with unshed tears, and I wasn't sure why it affected me as much as it did. Perhaps because of my own mother. Did she look like this when she thought about me? Had she had the same hopes? Had she imagined the same outcome? If she'd have known how my life would be, would it have changed her mind?

"On her eighteenth birthday, I started searching for her. I found the adoption records, and the names of the people who'd taken her." She stopped abruptly and turned away. Her jaw firmed, lips thinned, and her grip on my hand tightened as if she were in physical pain.

A tear rolled down my cheek, and my throat worked convulsively to try and swallow the rest before they could escape. I wiped my nose on my sleeve and took a deep shuddering breath. "Did you find her?"

She nodded. "I did." The words came out broken. "She was killed three days before her fifth birthday by the man who'd adopted her." Her grip tightened further, crunching my fingers together.

I ignored the pain and put my free hand over hers. "I didn't know," was all I could say. There were no words.

She took another deep breath and pulled her hand free to rub her eyes. Her expression shifted, back to the matriarch I knew. The strength I'd relied on so many times since I'd met her.

"I blamed myself for giving her up. I blamed Merle for getting locked up. I hated myself so much. For years, all I did was drink and walk around, pretending I was okay when, in reality, I was dead inside." She heaved a breath. "It took me a long time and a lot of therapy and rehab to place the blame where it belonged: with the man who did it." She took my hand again and shook it, as if begging me to hear her and understand. "Regret doesn't go away, Willow. We all regret. We all have things we wished we'd done differently, but that doesn't mean we can't be worthy of love. That doesn't mean we have to stop living." She cupped my cheek. "I've been a Mama to a lot of different people. I was a Mama to Tex—the man that told Merle about this swamp—until he was twelve years old. But the day you walked into the shop, I knew. *You* were mine. You needed me. You were a place for me to put all that love I never got to give to her."

My dam broke under the mountain of tears, and they burst free, stealing my breath. I wrapped my arms around her, clinging like the child I'd been, desperate for a mother, realizing I finally had one.

Julia held me firm. "I know you hate it when I lecture you. I know you refuse to accept that the guilt you carry is unfounded, but I know. I've carried it. It isn't yours, girl. Merle and I have known that since the day you became ours." Her voice broke. "He was so proud. Both of us have never been anything but proud of how you persevere, how you adapt, how you care for others despite how the world has been for you. You are so fucking strong, Hon."

We crumbled together, forming a pile of broken dreams and missed opportunities. Both of us were damaged, but when combined, we were just enough to be whole, stronger, uniquely shaped and formed by the injuries life had inflicted upon us.

After what felt like an eternity, she pulled away and forced my gaze to hers. "I'm telling you all this so you'll know this isn't your fault. Not one bit of it. I know your heart, girl. You ain't malicious. You ain't the type to hurt anyone, let alone that little girl, and you deserve to be happy."

I heaved a sigh and nodded. She was right. Of course she was. She was Julia, and for the first time in weeks, I let go of my self-loathing and allowed myself an ounce of pride. I loved her. I loved Eve and Eric. I'd give my life to save any one of them. That was a fact even I couldn't deny. I'd made a mistake, and I'd regret that choice for as long as I still drew breath into my lungs. But that didn't make me evil. That didn't make me unworthy. "I see you managed to make even Croc angry," I said, my voice lighter than it had been in weeks.

A wicked grin curved her mouth. "He's another one with a thick damn skull. You'd all be better off if you just listened to me. I may not be perfect, but I've been stupid enough times to know when someone else is doing it."

My eyebrows lifted. "Since when is Croc stupid? I thought he was your golden boy who could do no wrong."

"Answer me a question," she said instead of answering. "And don't even think about lying, because I already know the damn answer. Do you like him? Does he make you feel like the sun shines out of his damn ass? Because if he does—which I've seen you two together, don't try to bullshit me—then you're an idiot for ignoring that. Any damn minute, the greater good could march in here and end all of this. At any moment, our lives could end. You're wasting time and acting like an idiot, and that man is too afraid of scaring you off to make any damn attempts at worming his way past your defenses."

I heaved a sigh, thoroughly chastised. I couldn't argue, not after everything we'd just discussed. She was right. Always infuriatingly right. "Of course I like him, Julia."

"Then *enjoy* him!" She stood and scoffed, shaking her head as she headed toward the front door. "For the love of god, do us all a favor and get fucking laid already."

I rolled my eyes and let her words rush over me as she walked back inside.

23
THE GIVER

I sat like that for a long time, absorbing all Julia had said, what it all meant. All the years I'd wished for a family, I'd failed to realize how lucky I was to have found one. It was more than so many got. Julia and Merle were more than any person could hope for. It didn't matter that they weren't blood. They were mine, and they wanted me. They accepted me.

The story she'd just shared was so similar to my own. I'd always known she was wise. I'd always felt like Julia understood me better than anyone, and now, I knew just how true that was. She did understand, and the fact that she was able to relinquish her guilt meant more than she could ever know. Looking at her, I couldn't imagine that ever being her fault. So, what did that say for me? Did that mean that my failures were just as she'd said? Regrets and nothing more? Had I been needlessly punishing myself for things I couldn't control? The night Croc had forced me to realize my deal with Danny hadn't been a deal at all flashed through my mind. He'd known, even then, yet I was still blaming myself. I was still loathing myself, denying myself joy as self-punishment.

The front door opened, and Croc exited as if Julia had shoved him out. I imagined she had and grinned.

He cleared his throat and shuffled from one foot to the other. "Are you okay?"

I grunted, then stood and turned to get a better look at him. I couldn't deny her logic, not on this. Not with him. All he'd proven himself to be. All he'd done, and all he was still willing to do for not just me, but all of us. "Julia said you two had a disagreement."

His lips pursed. "We did."

"That's out of character. Since when do you argue with Julia?"

He rubbed the back of his neck, a nervous habit I'd noticed long ago. I'd noticed a lot about him. We'd grown closer than I'd ever expected I could be with a man. I knew his favorite foods. How he liked his fish. I knew what time of day he always wanted to swim, and his favorite channels to travel down. I could read his moods, even when he did his best to hide how he was feeling. I knew him like I'd never known anyone before.

"I don't think she's right about this," he said.

"She probably is." The way his eyes widened almost made me laugh. Instead, I focused on the space between us, wanting it to disappear. He was right here. We were right here, right then, and there was no guarantee of tomorrow. "You should." I paused, unsure yet never more certain. "You should probably just do whatever she says."

His Adam's Apple bobbed, and he took one pointed step forward. "You don't mean that. You don't know what it is."

"I do." I stepped toward him as well. An invisible rope tugged, urging us together. It was what was meant to happen. It was the answer to everything, all that had occurred, all the bumps along my road that led me to this place. "She told me what she thinks." I swallowed the lump of nerves clogging my throat. "I…I think she's right."

He stood frozen, stunned. "You do?" Another step forward, his hand extended.

I closed the gap and took his fingers in mine. "I do."

He stared down at me, jaw tight, eyes searching.

I released my demons and guilt. I relinquished my excuses and focused solely on the moment, on what I wanted, on what I'd been denying myself since we'd arrived. He'd single handedly worked his way behind my walls without breaking them. He hadn't forced his way inside. He hadn't taken or demanded. He'd waited by the gate, patient, understanding. He'd patched the holes others had created and replaced the pieces I'd lost along the way.

I reached up and clasped his shoulder, tugging him down to me. Our lips locked, and his parted, soft and pliant, welcoming and submissive. He gave himself, taking nothing, and this time, it was me who explored and learned. I touched his face, memorized his angles, then his neck, his shoulders, his biceps, his hands. I linked my fingers through his and pulled his arms around me.

He held me close, bending his back forward and molding my body into his. Every move we made flowed like the water: cool, natural, fluid.

He lifted my legs around his waist without breaking the contact of our mouths. I clung to him as he scaled the side of the house, glancing between his progress and my eyes, his gaze hooded and dark.

When we reached the top, he laid me beneath him on the pile of worn blankets he called his bed. Then, we just were. No judgements or questions. No second guesses or worries.

He didn't try to press for more. He didn't demand or take the way so many others had in the past.

All the times I'd thought I'd given myself, I hadn't. All the times I thought a man had taken me had been false. I hadn't been there. I'd floated in whatever space I went when I wanted to disappear and hung suspended in a void, out of body, out of mind, distant. But there was no distance with Croc. He covered and surrounded every sense, every nerve, every inch of skin. He followed my direction, only going where I led him with no thought about his own needs. He was beautiful and patient, and I wanted him in a way I'd never wanted anything before.

His hands roamed, going farther than he'd ever gone before, under my shirt, over my breasts, exploring my body without pause or hesitation. He hummed low in his throat, the sound vibrating inside his chest. His fingers moved to my jeans and deftly undid the button, and he broke the kiss to suck in a sharp breath as he pushed them down to my knees. I shivered with need, unable to find the voice needed to beg him to keep going.

He ran the tip of his finger under the waistband of my lilac panties, then met my gaze, questioning, seeking permission. "Tell me to stop, and I will."

I shook my head. "Don't stop."

He groaned and kissed me hard, sliding his hand beneath the fabric and exploring what I kept hidden there. An army of chills marched down my spine, and I arched upward like a cat whose owner had found the perfect place to scratch. I moaned into his mouth, clung to his neck, moved against his hand, and just like with everything else, Croc learned and studied and mastered his task.

When I tried to reach for him, to move further, he stopped me, pinning me to the blankets. "This is different," he murmured against my lips. "I don't want to take from you, little fish. I want to give."

And he did. He gave until my head spun, my thoughts swirled, and all that existed was the feel of his touch, the taste of his mouth, the sound of my cries mingling with his harsh breaths. He lifted me up, high enough to rise above all the pain, all the memories, all the regrets. They were nothing but distant specs, too far away to hold any meaning. Then, when I reached the top, teetering, he held me tight and tipped me over the edge, then kept me locked in his arms as I floated back down to Earth.

I clung to him, shivering and boneless.

Croc whispered against my skin, too soft for me to make out the words but reverent enough for me to know their meaning. He praised me in between each press of his mouth against my neck, my jaw, breaths ragged and sharp. He removed his hand and lifted it to help support his weight.

I pressed my lips to his shoulders and held him closer. "Are you okay?"

He nodded and rolled, pulling me into his chest and holding me close with one arm. "Just let me hold you a while."

I nodded and studied his face, surprised that he'd want to stop but enamored that he did. It was another way in which he differed from what I was used to, and if he wanted to take it slow, I wouldn't be the one to argue. I settled closer and relaxed, allowing the night sounds and cool air to lull me through the contentment he'd created.

24
FEELINGS

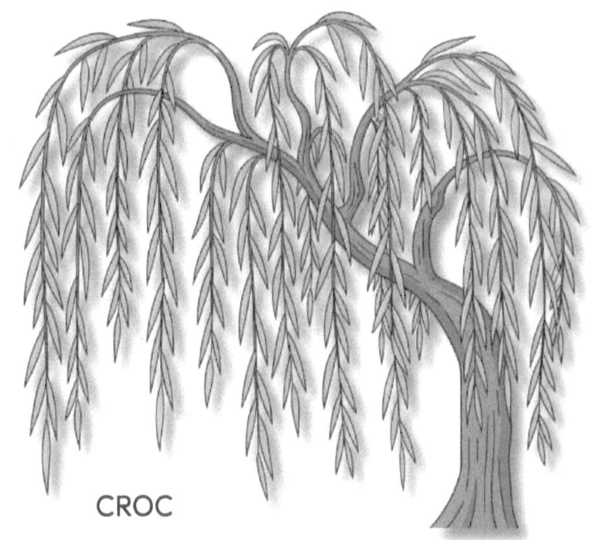

CROC

Her breaths were deep, her heartbeat rhythmic. She was sleeping—in *my* bed, on *my* arm. Her pants were still wrapped around her knees, and her legs were bent. The curve of her hip and the skin of her thighs bare, tempting. She'd let me. She'd asked me to. She'd rocked against my hand and made those little noises that lit my blood on fire. My touch had done that. I had done that. I'd made her come apart, come alive, and I'd never felt stronger, more capable, more skilled. I blew out a breath. She hadn't seemed upset about it after. She'd seemed happy. I'd made her happy. My chest swelled, building pressure until I wanted to crow. I wanted to whoop up into the sky, wake the swamp so it could watch me beat my chest and dance across the roof. But then her hand innocently drifted from my chest to my navel, and I wanted to do something else entirely.

I tensed and held my breath, fighting the urge to roll over and take everything. That wasn't the plan. That wasn't what she needed, and I wouldn't have her comparing me to the men she'd told me about.

I ground my teeth and shifted away, careful not to wake her.

Willow stirred, muttering soft shapeless words as she pulled her knees up tighter and clutched the blanket where I'd been. She was searching for me. She didn't want me to leave, and the urge to return grew. I bit my lip, unsure what to do. She was impossible to read. I couldn't rely on her scent, her expression. They never matched how she really felt.

What would she do if I did? How would she react? Things had been different tonight. If I dropped down, pulled her jeans away, removed that soft purple material she wore under, and buried myself inside her… My jaw clenched, hands fisted, and I shifted uncomfortably on my spot. She'd probably scream. I'd probably scare her half to death, and then I'd be something different to her. I'd be the animal she saw me as when she first arrived, and I'd worked too hard to become a man.

I draped one of the loose blankets over her, immediately mourning the loss of her skin. I had to be patient. I had to wait. She needed to choose to give herself to me, and until she did… I turned away to gaze at the canal below. I needed to swim.

I jumped off the roof, sprinted across the yard, and dove in, pushing my muscles as hard as I could, expelling the tension, creating the distance I needed in order to protect her from the part of myself she couldn't see. But every brush of the water felt like her, and no matter how hard I tried, all I could think about was the fact that she was there, on the roof, in my bed, barely clothed and ready to be caught.

I stopped abruptly and stood, breathing hard and angrily rubbing the water from my face. It wasn't working. Maybe I was an animal. Maybe I wasn't the man I pretended I was.

Maybe I really wasn't any better than the others, and maybe Willow knew more about me than I did myself. If she knew the thoughts I had, the things I imagined doing to her, all the time, when she ate her breakfast, when she made the children laugh, when she just sat and did nothing, just existed.

The urge to go back intensified. I ran a hand through my hair, yanked the strands, then hit my chest, once, twice, same place, letting the pain suck me back to the present. Do not go back there. Not now. Not yet. You're not an animal, and if you act like one, you'll hurt her. I ground my teeth and stood frozen for a long moment, running the words over and over in my head, feeling the water rush past me in the direction I wanted so desperately to go.

"Croc?" Gator hissed.

I opened my eyes and watched him wade toward me. "Who's watching Danny?"

"He's asleep," he said. "But I stay beneath the water most of the time with him, so even if he wakes up, he won't know I'm gone." He stopped a foot away and let his whole back and tail float to the surface. "He's not that smart and even less brave."

I nodded. "Still, if you're going to leave him, you should have another alligator keep watch. Or tell me, and I'll do it."

"Another alligator would eat him." He paused, and his jaws slid into a wide smile. "That's a great idea."

I grinned and shook my head, but his presence eased some of the tension.

"I came to check on you. You're noisy tonight, splashing, grunting, growling, then I finally catch up, and you're beating yourself half to death. I thought the voodoo got you. Did the voodoo get you? I heard some stories about that shit. You don't want no part of it."

I shook my head, remembering all the stories he'd told me as a child and the tension eased more. "No voodoo, Gator. I'm okay."

He heaved a breath. "Oh, good. They make dolls, you know? Make 'em look just like you, then poke and move them around, and you do whatever they're doing. I just assumed, knowing how smart you are, that if you were beating yourself up, it must be because someone was making you." He peered up at me. "Are you sure? You may not even know it."

"I'm sure." I squatted beneath the surface, letting the water reach my chin.

"Oh, okay. Then why? Is this some new human thing you learned? Because I'm thinking this might be one you can choose to skip. It doesn't seem all that smart."

I blew out a breath. "Yeah, okay. You're right. I'm just going to swim for a while."

"You sure?"

"Why wouldn't I be?"

He grinned again. "There's a female in your bed. Don't think I didn't see you carry her up there, and you ain't brought her back down. That's another reason I was sure the voodoo got you. Why else wouldn't you be there? That don't make no sense. It's almost mating season."

My eyes widened. It was. I hadn't thought about it, and I felt ridiculous for not doing so. It made sense and explained why I couldn't seem to gather my control. There'd never been a woman around, not a human, not for me, but now…

"She doesn't want to mate with me," I said, voice quieter.

"I came out here to calm myself."

Gator gave a laugh, then a hoot, then did a roll across the surface as he continued to rumble at my expense. "Oooh! That makes more sense!" He cawed like a giant bird. "You're hitting yourself for…" he trailed off, snickering and shaking his head back and forth. "You—" Again, he couldn't finish.

I pursed my lips and watched him, hands fisted at my sides. "Yes, it's hysterical."

He sobered and rolled upright to study me. "I'm sorry. All you had to do was say something. This is your first season. I can help you."

I smiled but shook my head. "I don't think it works the same for humans as it does with animals."

"It can't be that different," he said. "Just try. What I do is"—he lowered his body until just his head stuck up out of the water—"I get down low like this, then I do this dance that all the ladies love." His neck puffed out as he vibrated, causing the water to splash up at his sides and ripple outward, and a low hum sounded through the depths below. He stopped after a moment. "They hear that and can't get to me fast enough."

I scratched my beard and nodded. "I'll have to try it."

Gator grinned. "If that doesn't work, you can be a bit more blunt." He sucked in a breath, opened his jaws wide and grunted, bellowing loud enough for the entire swamp to hear. "You may need to use a human sound, but that's a go to. She won't be able to resist that."

I didn't know whether to be annoyed or grateful. I was annoyed that I needed help, grateful that receiving mating advice from Gator had oddly put all thoughts of mating out of my head.

I rolled my shoulders, stretching my neck. "I'm better now. Thanks, Gator. Do you want me to go watch Danny or are you going back?"

"I'll go back!" he said. "You need to get over there and try out those tips I gave you."

"Right," I said. "I'll let you know tomorrow how it went."

He swam past, grinning as he went. "You do that." He disappeared beneath the surface, leaving me alone with my thoughts once again.

Mating season. It hadn't even started yet. All the gators would come alive. The swamp would be full of their cries and splashing dances, and I'd be…

I gripped my neck, searching the water for an answer. I felt the pull, had ever since I became a man, but without a female around to mate with, it'd never been a problem. As it stood, I was ready to devour Willow on a normal day, and it took a great amount of effort to be the man she wanted me to be. What would I do when my instincts took over? I wouldn't be a man, not then. I wouldn't have control. It was already starting, I just hadn't realized. On the roof. All the things I'd done to her. It was the furthest I'd ever gone, and while she'd seemed to enjoy it, I wasn't sure how much she'd appreciate it when I inevitably went further.

My body tensed back up at the thought. She needed to sleep inside. As a matter of fact, she needed to stay inside. That's what I'd do. I'd have Julia lock her up, and make her swear not to let me in, no matter how… I groaned and gripped my neck tighter. That wouldn't work. I'd get inside. It would be easy. I'd rip the door right off its hinges. No. I hit my head again, urging my mind to work.

I had to contain myself.

25
BOUND

Croc had awoken something in me, and not just in a physical sense. It was cells and chemistry and DNA. He'd set fire to my nervous system, boiled my blood, melted me down, then left me anticipating when he'd put me back together again. I wanted more. For the first time in my life, I wanted a man. I wanted to give myself, and then that man disappeared.

If we entered the same room, he left it. If I sought him out, he brushed me aside. He was busy hunting, fixing something, checking this, doing that, and he always needed to be alone. For weeks, I barely saw him, then, I stopped seeing him at all. It was as if he'd never existed, and the only indication I had that he was even still alive was Julia. Each time we ate, she made him a plate then ventured off unannounced to deliver it to him. She refused to let me follow, ignored my questions, told me all was fine, said Croc had his reasons, and for the first time since I'd known her, her lips were sealed.

I paced the floor every time she left, tossed and turned through sleepless nights, and with each day that passed, my frustration festered like a wound. The need became tangible–a living, breathing entity that clawed me from the inside out and left my skin raw, sensitive, and far too tight.

My hormones were on high alert and ready to take the plunge, but the tall glass of water they'd chosen to dive into was nowhere to be found.

I lay in bed, wide awake, staring at the ceiling as if it were everything I'd ever hated. My teeth bared a little more each time an alligator started screeching. They'd been doing it more and more, especially at night, and something about the sound inflamed my irritation, because I wanted to ask him why, and he wasn't there to tell me.

He didn't get to do that. He didn't get to ingrain himself into my life then silently slip out of it. It wasn't fair. If I'd upset him, he could at least explain. Nothing made any sense, and I couldn't take it anymore.

I kicked my way out of the blanket and smacked my fists against the cushions on either side of me. My teeth clenched tighter, forming a barrier between my scream and the peacefully sleeping children in the next room. It wasn't working. It wouldn't stop. He'd done this. He'd done something, and I'd be damned if I was going to go one more minute without him fixing it.

I rolled from the couch, threw on my shoes, and stormed out the back door with no direction or thought. It was later than sin, and the swamp was alive with bellowing gators. Grunts sounded from the east, a low hum drifted from the west, then silence fell for a period of time before the harmony repeated itself from a new direction. I didn't understand what was happening, not without Croc to explain it, but I knew it was somehow connected, and I was determined to understand before the sun rose.

I trudged through the grass, following my instincts,

smelling the air and praying I'd be able to sense him the way he could me. An internal compass urged me into the thick trees, over roots and through the mud. I ignored each scratch from a limb and gave little thought to what dangers may lurk within the darkness.

My stomach clenched and held as his scent hit my senses. Earthy and masculine and raw. I picked up my pace, following the smell until I could hear his harsh breaths, then I saw him.

I pressed both hands against a cypress and peeked around it.

Croc sat against a tree, his head hung forward. Thick chains cut across his chest. He was locked in place, banded to the trunk. His hands were behind his back, and his legs were stretched out flat, ankles bound with thin rope. I stared, shocked to see him that way; hair disheveled, glinting with sweat. Red marked the skin where he was bound as if he'd been fighting to break free. Had Julia done this? Why?

I took a step forward, and a twig snapped beneath my foot.

Croc's head shot up, and he sniffed the air hard. A deep, masculine laugh rumbled from his chest, then like a star caught behind a cloud, he darkened and jerked savagely against the restraint.

I jolted back a step. "Croc?"

"Come here," he said, but the rough tone to his voice didn't sound like him at all. It was aggressive, guttural, and as his muscles bulged and strained to no avail. His anger mounted. He jerked again, baring his teeth and fighting against the rope until a trickle of blood rolled down his stomach. He groaned and slumped forward, focusing his steady gaze on me. "Willow." The clouds gathered around him, building a storm. "Untie me."

I hesitated, caught between common sense and senseless need. "Why are you tied?" I took another small step, reassured that he couldn't free himself, then slowly filled the gap between my hiding spot and his feet.

He stared up at me, breathing harder, lips curved as he twisted deftly against whatever held his wrists behind him. "Help me with the rope, Willow."

"I don't know if I should." I peeked around him, checking where the thin twine was wrapped tightly around his wrists.

It put us close, and I sucked in a breath as he darted forward and bit the waistband of my jeans.

I jerked back and stared down at him. Something wasn't right. He wasn't himself. "Why are you tied?"

He hung forward, stretched toward me, eyes locked on my middle for a full minute before he cut a look up at my face. "It's mating season." His voice was low and slow. "You can feel it, can't you, little fish? That's why you're here. That's how you found me." He shifted his left shoulder, tugging hard to one side. "If you untie me, I'll take care of you."

Something carnal beckoned me closer, but under it was a clear warning. There was a reason he was restrained. He'd chosen it. No way could anyone have tied him like that if he hadn't let them, and judging by the amount of chain and rope he'd made them use, he'd been deadly serious about keeping himself contained. "I don't think I should. If you let yourself be tied like this, there had to be a reason."

"The reason doesn't matter." He jerked again, then

clenched his jaw and viciously wrenched back and forth, kicking his feet against the ground before he fell still again. His whole body stiffened as he glared at the ground and caught his breath. "You're here," he said, returning to the calm. Like Jekyll and Hyde, he flipped, animal to man, rabid to serene. "You came here. I can smell that you're ready for me. You want me inside you." He thrust his hips upwards and bit his lip. "Untie me, Willow."

My eyes widened, but a dull ache throbbed between my thighs. I could barely breathe. He wasn't himself. Croc would have never acted that way, spoken that way. It was different, and I would have been a liar if I said I wasn't excited. His need for me was intoxicating. It wasn't the same as the others. He'd tied himself to protect me. He'd been strapped to this tree for who knows how long just so he wouldn't push me into anything. Men had been pushing me into things for as long as I could remember. They never paused to do so, and I'd never had a leg to stand on against them. But not then. Not that night. Not this man. Raw power radiated from him, unparalleled strength. He was the strongest man I'd ever known, the first one I'd ever loved, and he was completely under my control. The irony was beautiful.

Croc must have sensed the change in my thoughts; his eyes narrowed, and his body stilled. "Willow," he murmured. "Untie me."

I shifted my weight. "I don't think I will," I said. "This is a new situation that I find very interesting."

He jerked again to no avail, then rumbled low in his chest. "Do you?"

"I do." I stepped forward and lowered myself in front of

him. "If you think about it, you're completely at my mercy."

He leaned closer, fighting to reach me. "Then give me mercy."

I studied his eyes, the sharp angles of his face, then pulled back.

Croc growled, jerked, and fought harder, then sagged again, breathing heavily.

The tension thickened, and whatever atmospheric phenomenon that had taken over the swamp made me bold. I leaned over him, straddling his lap, then pressed a kiss against his chest. "Is this okay?" I asked, mimicking the words he'd said to me.

He moved his hips, thrusting upwards hard enough to bounce my whole body.

I gasped and clung to his shoulders.

He smiled. "Untie me, and you won't have to ask."

I swallowed hard and sucked in a breath. "I don't mind asking." My hands pressed against his shoulders, leveraging my weight as I formed a gap between our bodies and focused on his face. I kissed his jaw, the corner of his lips.

Croc turned his head and captured my mouth like a man starved. He kissed me deeply, urgently, stealing control even when he was completely contained.

I could have broken free, but I didn't. I savored the feeling and sat back down, moving against him.

He bit my lip and groaned. "I'm yours, Willow. Every part of me."

"I thought a person couldn't take a body," I breathed as I continued. Our clothes were too thick. The barrier was offensive. The need clawed harder, and I knew I'd die if I didn't do what my body was urging me toward.

He watched as I moved against him, eyes hooded, face darkening once again. "I can give it." He pulled at the ropes, wiggling his shoulders as he stretched back and forth in an attempt to free himself. "I want to give it to you. All of it." His jaw clenched, neck strained. "Untie me, and I'll show you."

"I don't think you'd be telling me to untie you if you were yourself right now," I whispered, but I didn't stop. This is what I'd needed. I needed this friction, this man. I needed to feel his shoulders, arms, chest. My hands ran over him, memorizing each inch of his skin. I'd been slowly burning alive, and he was like rain on a fiery blacktop. Together, we produced enough steam to build a sauna, and I wanted to sweat. I wanted to leave him revived and renewed, healthier, clean.

"Willow?"

The tone of his voice caught my attention. I locked eyes with him, and for that brief moment, he was Croc. Sweet, lovable, endearing Croc. He shook his head. "You should go."

"You want me to go?"

"I want you to be safe, and you're right. I did this for a reason. Go back to the house, and I'll be back once this is over."

"How long is that?" My voice came out shrill, outraged. He was asking me to leave, and every part of me was furious at the request. Couldn't he see that I needed him? Couldn't he see that I was suffering? Didn't he want me? He'd wanted me bad five seconds before.

"Another month." He grimaced and clenched his eyes shut. A war played across his face. "You need to go. Now."

"I don't want to go."

His nostrils flared. “Willow.” My name was a warning. “I’ve almost got my wrists loose.”

My heart skipped and stuttered. The anticipation grew. If he’d meant to scare me away, it wasn’t working. “That’s exciting.”

He groaned. “You don’t want me like this. My control is slipping, and I won’t be gentle. I won’t be… I won’t be a man.” His eyes cut into me, demanding I listen and understand.

I caressed his cheek, his hair, gently ran my fingers over his ear, then back up over his scalp again. When had this happened? When had he become so precious to me? I’d pay any price for him, give any part of myself for him. “I’ve never liked men, Croc,” I whispered gently. “But I love you.”

26
HEAT

CROC

She was in my lap, her little breaths sharp and quick, grinding herself against me. Each time she did, I throbbed, and I wanted to grab her. I wanted to rip every ounce of cloth from her skin and give her what she was searching for. I wanted to see her eyes widen as I filled her up, hear her cry out each time I moved.

The rope unraveled a fraction, finally worn too thin, but the chain was thick, and I knew I'd never be able to break past it.

"I thought a person couldn't take a body," she whispered, throwing my words back at me.

Couldn't she see she was torturing me? My insides boiled at the chains, at my inability to act. "I can give it." I tugged at the rope again, working it left to right as the frayed threads cut into my flesh. "I want to give it to you. All of it." And I would. I would sink so deep into her body she wouldn't know where I ended and she began. I'd mark her as mine, make it so she'd never doubt my feelings again. "Untie me, and I'll show you."

"I don't think you'd be telling me that if you were yourself right now." Her pace increased, movements deepened. She ground her body tight against mine, back bowed and nails digging into my shoulders, unaware that her words had been like a dagger to my heart.

I watched her, small and precious, delicate. She had no idea what she was asking for. She wouldn't want this, and all my imaginings suddenly seemed cruel and sick. I was a monster. "Willow?"

She paused and drew back to meet my gaze.

I ground my teeth against the words I needed to say. They wouldn't come. The animal I was didn't care if she was hurt. He didn't care if she never looked at him the same way again. That wasn't his concern. "You should go," I ground out.

Her lips parted. "You want me to go?"

No. The rage grew hotter, more insistent. If she walked away then, I'd live in hell for the remainder of the season, replaying the feel of her grinding against me, wanting me, begging me. I'd fight and claw and kick until I passed out from exhaustion, then I'd wake to live another day full of regret. But none of that mattered. She mattered. I couldn't lose her. "I want you to be safe, and you're right. I did this for a reason." The words tasted foul. "Go back to the house, and I'll be back once this is over."

Her scent soured. I'd upset her, but it was nothing compared to how she'd see me if I allowed myself to…

"How long is that," she snapped.

"Another month." I shut my eyes, and bit down hard on my tongue. Despite my desire to protect her, the other part of myself continued to desperately work the rope, fighting to break free and stop me before it was too late. "You need to go. Now."

"I don't want to go," she said.

My stomach clenched, muscles pulsed. If she knew the images I had as she said that, she wouldn't be so eager to stay. The rope loosened, and I almost gave in. She wanted to stay. She wanted this. No. She didn't understand. She didn't know what she was asking for. "Willow," I warned. "I've almost got my wrists loose."

She sucked in a breath, and bit her lip. "That's exciting."

I groaned. She needed to hear me. She needed to listen. "You don't want me like this. My control is slipping, and I won't be gentle. I won't be." I paused, hating myself even more for not being what she needed. "I won't be a man."

The soft skin of her palm ran over my cheek, then up into my hair, over my neck. I held my breath and fought against the urge to tug at the rope. I'd snap it. I'd free my hands and she wouldn't get away. I wouldn't let her go. I'd take her right there. Chained and all.

"I've never liked men, Croc," she whispered, too gentle for the violence building up inside me. "But I love you."

I froze as her words washed over me, warm and inviting, permissive, accepting. Control fled. I gave up. A weak man was no match against my true nature. I couldn't save her. Not from myself. "Say it again," I growled.

"I love you." She kissed my shoulder and rocked her hips again.

I held my breath, clenched my jaw, fisted my hands, and felt the moment I lost the battle. The rope snapped. She was mine.

She gasped as my arms circled her, gripping and pulling and tearing at her clothes. I held her with one arm, locked in place as I unwrapped her skin. She was mine. My female. Her scent was sweet, heavy with arousal, and I throbbed harder with the need to feel her.

I gripped the center of the thick covering she wore under her shirt and jerked, breaking the clasp and tossing it aside. Her skin was paler there, creamy and silver, reflecting the moonlight. I tasted each breast, and her scent made my manhood push harder against my jeans. I gripped and bit at her flesh, relishing each small sound I earned in return.

The fear never came. I'd expected it, almost needed it to force me to stop. Instead, her desire stole my breath, heady and thick. Her fingers curled into my hair and yanked me closer.

I groaned and trailed my palms down her sides to the last barrier between us. I jerked at her waistband, needing it gone more than I needed air.

Willow drew back and threw her hands over mine. "Wait."

I froze, fingers clamped, muscles twitching with the desire to continue.

"I don't want to walk back completely naked," she breathed. "Just let me take them off."

She wanted me to let her go, and I didn't think I could do that, not anymore.

"Croc..." She cupped my cheek. Her eyes were so soft, just like the rest of her, and it calmed me. I could have sunk into them, floated for an eternity, and never needed to return to the canal again. "I want this. I won't leave."

It took all my effort to release her, and I had to grip my thighs to keep from pulling her back.

She stood and stepped back to where my feet lay, and I

stared. Her hair hung loose, heavy and dark against the pale skin of her chest. She was liquid moonlight, shimmering silver, and the delicate curves of her body reminded me of the water. When she didn't remove her jeans but instead circled around me, I panicked. "Willow," I growled, jerking once again at the chains.

"Wait," she whispered, tone soothing. "I'm going to unchain you."

I froze. *Tell her to stop*, my mind shouted. *Tell her to leave.* But I didn't say it—couldn't say it. The chains wiggled and loosened one by one, and my control went with them. There was nothing stopping me now. Nothing to stop this. As soon as they fell around my lap, I reached forward, snapped the rope that bound my ankles and jumped to my feet.

I turned to find her completely bare, soft, and delicate, perfect. I sucked in a breath that shuddered in my chest, then stiffened as she walked forward and reached down to undo my jeans.

"I don't like you tied up," she whispered. Her eyes held mine, never leaving me as her soft hand reached inside and curled around my length.

I groaned and startled her as I dropped down, captured her thighs, and pinned her firmly against the tree.

She cried out and clung to my shoulders, and I swallowed the sound into my mouth, kissing her hard, moving my hips, finding the place where my body could fit into hers and slowly pressing forward.

She stiffened, and I broke away to watch her face. Her eyes widened. I wanted to see that. I wanted to watch her and remember every detail. I pushed again, another inch, then paused and studied the part of her lips, the tilt of her head as she arched her spine and offered herself to me.

My breath hissed as I fought for control, but she was so warm, so perfect, and the rest of the world faded away. My focus centered to only her. I pushed again, then groaned as she met my movement, rolling herself down to take all of me into her.

I pinned her tighter against the tree and held her still as the sensation washed over me. Her scent clouded my senses. Her hands gently caressed my arms, like water rushing over my skin or a cool breeze when the swamp grew too hot to bear. She was the feeling of waking up, knowing I wasn't alone. She was the nights I fell asleep, remembering the day I'd had with her. She was the feeling I had when I was a boy, and Pappy was still around to tuck me in. She was peace. She was comfort. She was home.

I rocked again, long and slow, and those soft hands curled and gripped. She whimpered, and my heart thundered, blood raced. "Is this okay?" I asked, but my words echoed none of the care I was fighting to take. I wanted to let go, forget my name and lose myself in hers.

She nuzzled my neck and answered me with her hips, rolling her spine. My knees buckled, and I caught myself by one hand against the tree. My breaths grew harsh, audible, and I couldn't move. Not when she did that. Not when she clung to me, hands on my shoulders, elbows on my chest, legs locked and body grinding to create the sweetest friction. Her mewling cries into my ear were almost too much. I grunted and groaned, sounding almost pained as I gripped the tree harder and crashed through each wave she created.

Then I felt her, just like I had that night on the roof. The smell of her sex grew stronger, her movements more eager, and the building pressure made her body clench tighter around mine.

I pressed her to the tree again, stopping her movements.

She whimpered. "Croc."

"No." I wanted to give her that. I wanted her to come apart because of me. I wanted to feel her crumble and pulse and know that I was the cause of it.

I drew back and thrust hard, relishing the cry she gave, floating in the euphoria of knowing she was mine, we were connected, and she wanted me just as desperately as I did her. I gave her all of it, the good and the bad, the man and the monster. I squeezed her hips and lifted her higher, then watched her face morph, her eyes squeeze shut, her lips part around my name as she repeated it over and over. It was the most beautiful thing I'd ever seen, and I forgot to think. There were no rules.

I was a hunter, unchained, unhindered. She'd slipped away a hundred times, and now I'd finally caught her. I drove harder, taking until my body soared, and my focus narrowed. Her slick heat, her harsh breaths, her soft skin, her small cries. I nuzzled into her, kissing and tasting and sliding and whispering soft praise and gratitude against her skin.

She was the greatest thing to ever happen to me, and I knew, no matter what happened, I wasn't going to let her go.

27 DISAPPEARANCES

WILLOW

The storm I'd watched cloud his aura darkened and morphed into a winding twister. He sucked me in and spun my thoughts until the only direction I could decipher was toward him. It was different. It was incomparable.

He touched me here, kissed me there, tangled my limbs around him tighter, and drove into me so completely, I didn't know where he ended and I began. All I could do was drift, be tossed and rocked in the waves his chaos created. But, inside this storm, there was calm. Croc kept my face above the surface, carried me with him, breathing a better life into my lungs each time he sunk deeper.

He was rough but not careless. Demanding yet tender. He took until I cried out, but he gave it all back with an intensity that made my legs tremble.

And when the waves began to crash, my body convulsed and lungs expanded. His name erupted from my lips like the final crack of thunder before the world settled.

He kissed me more gently, caressed me softer, then gathered me into him and carried us both through the trees and into the water.

He waded into the canal, then stopped and held me with

one arm, alternating back and forth as his hands cupped the water and drizzled it over my shoulders, my neck, my chest.

I gazed up at his face, absorbing the tenderness of his touch, and my throat clogged. My eyes burned.

When his eyes met mine, his lips pursed. He cupped the water again and lifted his hand to let it gently drip over my forehead, then he took his thumb and wiped my temple, my cheek. "Did I hurt you, Willow?" he asked, words rough.

I placed my hand over his and held it there. "No." I turned my face, kissed his palm. "You didn't."

"You're crying."

I lifted my other hand and felt the moisture on my cheeks, but I couldn't be sure if it was from me or the canal. "I'm not."

"You are," he bent forward and hoisted me up, pressing our foreheads together, "I'm sorry. I should have made you go."

"You tried to make me go. I didn't want to. I still don't." I feathered my lips against his. "If I'm crying, it's because I've never been as happy as I am right now."

He drew a breath that shuddered in his chest, then pulled me into a crushing embrace.

I let him hold me and used my hands to cup the water up and over his back, his shoulders, his arms, washing away the dirt, sweat, and blood that coated his skin. My chest ached more with each new cut I uncovered. He'd done that. He'd bound himself and suffered, all to protect me.

He was right. He wasn't a man. I'd dealt with men. I'd lived in a world full of them, and apart from Merle, not one had ever caused me anything but grief. Croc was perfect, inside and out, and he cherished *me*. For the first time in my life, I felt lucky. I felt blessed, and those were things that didn't exist in the current world unless you were born with them.

"You're a gift," I whispered, both to myself and him.

He loosened his arms, allowing me access to cup the water over his chest, his stomach.

I focused on my work, but I felt his eyes on me, watching, intent. "I'm not used to having someone take care of me." I flattened my palm over his chest, running it down to the V of his stomach. His muscles shook under my touch. "I guess I got overwhelmed." I glanced up at him. "It was beautiful, Croc."

He nodded, acknowledging my words, but he didn't speak. His face was shuttered, his eyes fire, and the bone in his jaw jumped in time with the knot in his throat.

"Are you okay?" I asked.

He grunted, and his lip twitched at one side. "You're asking if I'm okay?"

"You look tense." My lips curved. He had no idea. He was God's gift to women, designed specifically for me, and he was worried that I'd have some complaint. It was absurd. It would be like winning the lottery and complaining about how to spend it. What would he do if he knew how perfect he was? Would it change him? I didn't think it would.

"I'm a little tense," he admitted as he lowered me backwards and continued his washing. He bent his legs and rested me there, letting the top half of my body float out in front of him as he gently ran his hands over my skin.

I watched him, completely content with giving him control. His hands were rough, but the water softened his touch. He massaged as he went, avoiding my more intimate areas. I tilted my head. "Why are you tense?"

"Why do you think?" He met my eyes for a brief second and arched a brow before returning his focus to his hands. "I'm nowhere near finished with you, Willow."

When the sun had just started to wake and paint the air in hazy blue light, Croc carried me home on his back. My arms over his shoulders, hands clasped loosely at his chest. His grip gentle yet sure on my legs. I kissed his neck the whole way home until he climbed onto the roof and laid us both atop his blankets, side by side on our backs, where we stayed for a long time. Quiet. Companionable. Croc held my hand up in the air above us, absently rubbing my fingers, studying their size and shape and comparing them to his own.

Now that the night between us had passed and my mind had time to clear, the thought of birth control and protection came crashing down on me like the aftershocks of an almighty earthquake. I watched him, torn between total contentment and full-blown panic. My mind wouldn't stop. I didn't regret being with him. Not at all. What I regretted was how I'd been so stupid as to risk bringing another child into a world that was absolutely fucked. Not just any child, *my* child. A mother. I didn't know how to be a mother. I'd never had one, and didn't history always repeat itself? Shitty parents beget shitty parents? Abuse and neglect leads to more abuse and neglect? I'd tried to pretend with Eve, and she'd almost died.

There had to be a plant or berry or bark. Some form of nature I could use as birth control. Danny's bag. My mind locked on the idea. The chances of him carrying around contraceptives weren't the slimmest I'd encountered by a long shot. He'd given me a pill after more than one deal was done. The idea of asking him for it, however, made me want to crawl inside a hole and rot.

Croc linked our fingers and dropped our joined hands to rest between us. "What's wrong?"

"Nothing."

He turned to look at me. "It's not nothing."

I almost laughed. "I'm pretty sure you're the only man in existence to actually know that for a fact."

"I can smell it," he said, not understanding my joke.

I blew out a breath and shifted onto my side. I'd been reluctant to voice my concerns with him since the moment they entered my mind. I didn't want to ruin the moment, and I was afraid he'd take it the wrong way. But there was no hiding it, and if I wanted to have any chance of finding a solution, I'd rather it be with his help. I bit my lip and stared at his face for a long moment, procrastinating the inevitable.

"What is it?" He flipped to match my position and cupped my cheek, caressed my temple, and held my gaze with a look soft enough to break me more than any man ever could.

"I don't want babies." The words flew out in one blunt jumble of syllables, and my chest ached at the loss of them.

His eyebrows lifted, then lowered as his gaze averted. He scanned the blanket, thoughtful for a long, drawn out pause. "You said that," he murmured. "In the beginning." His lips pursed. "Never-ever-ever-ever–"

For fuck's sake. He was breaking my heart. I cut him off. "Yes. That hasn't changed, Croc. You understand that, right?"

He nodded, still not meeting my gaze. "I understand."

I bit my lip again. Why did he have to look so sad? Why

did he have to make me feel like I'd just massacred every puppy on earth? "If things were different, I would."

He looked up. "If what was different?"

I sighed and shook my head. No doubt he thought he could devise a plan to fix whatever was in his way. Our laying side by side even having the conversation was proof that he was capable. Hadn't that been what he'd done? He'd made every effort to demolish my reasonings as to why we couldn't be together, and there we were. Together. This wasn't as simple, though, and no man, not even Croc, could fix it. "The world, Croc. If the world was different. But it's not, and I don't want to subject a baby, especially ours, to the way things are."

He studied my face. "But we're in the swamp," he said. "It's different here. I can protect you—our baby."

"For now. But how long until that changes? How long before they accomplish something in those experiments and send people in here, or anywhere like here, and discover what this stuff can do." He needed to understand. It wasn't him. It wasn't about commitment or a lack of faith. It was logic and bad luck, and there was nothing either of us could do about it. "All it takes is one hint for everything to fall apart. There may come a day when we need to run, and I can't live with the idea of having an infant when that happens." I squeezed his hand. "We still have Eve and Eric. They're like ours, right? We're a family here, aren't we?"

An argument brewed in the lines of his face before he finally blew out a heavy breath and flopped back onto his back.

I tilted my head back. His hands were clasped over his

chest, face tense, staring up into the early morning sky.

"What can I do?" he asked. "It's already happened."

My heart broke for him. It wasn't fair. Maybe I wasn't cut out to be a mother, but if anyone deserved to be a father, it was Croc. He'd be excellent at it, probably even good enough to make up for what I lacked. That didn't change what he couldn't control, though, and no matter how amazing he was, he was no match for *the greater good.*

"I need Danny's bag," I said in a soft voice. "He may have something in there that can…fix it."

"Fix it?" His gaze jerked back to me, fully alert. "What does fix it mean?"

"It will stop me from being pregnant." I retrieved his hand and pulled it close, holding it in both of mine. "It will stop it before it can start. If he even has it. I don't know. But I need the bag, Croc. I don't want to have to ask him for it."

He released a breath that lifted his whole chest and rumbled on the way out. "Okay," he said as he rolled off the blankets and stood. "I'll go get the bag. Don't move."

I watched him go with the ridiculous urge to tell him to stop. It didn't matter. We'd do whatever made him happy. It was outrageous. It was a baby, not a choice of dinner or sleeping arrangements or what to watch at a Saturday night movie. A baby, and as much as I wanted him to have one, it wasn't me that made it impossible. I hadn't made the world the way it was. I hadn't started the movement that put Josef Arogander in power.

The sun was visible now, just peeking over the canal, and I marveled over how different the day was to the one before it; how much could change in an instant. Time had morphed my life, over and over again. I was like a butterfly, constantly evolving and reshaping, but today, I noticed it more. Today was different. Today, it felt like I'd finally grown wings.

I watched the sun go from deep orange to bright yellow, steadily rising until it was high enough to blind me, then I gave up on being patient and crawled to the edge to search for Croc. It shouldn't have been taking near as long as it was. Had he run away, determined to hide until a baby was ready to pop out?

Then, I saw him cut through the trees into the yard at a brisk pace.

My stomach soured. Something was wrong. "What happened?" I called down to him.

He looked up sharply then shook his head. "I'll get you a shirt, then I'll carry you down." He quickly closed the gap and climbed up the side, then grabbed a button down he'd had hanging off the corner of the lean-to.

I watched him closely as he pulled it on me and started doing up the buttons.

"Croc?"

He focused on his task.

"Where's the bag?"

His shoulders slumped, hands stilled. The bone in his jaw jumped, and his eyes finally rose up to mine. "He's gone, Willow. He left, and Gator didn't notice because he was," his jaw clenched, "distracted."

"Gone?" It couldn't— He couldn't— A million scenarios played out like nightmares through my mind. Officials taking the kids. Then rounding us up. Killing Julia. Taking Croc to be tested and poked and prodded until he wilted away. "What do you mean 'gone'? Did something…did the gators…" Please let the gators have eaten him. Let him have drowned. Anything that kept him from reaching the outside.

"I don't know," he said, "but I'm going to take you inside where you can keep an eye on Julia and the kids while I go find him."

I nodded and swallowed hard against the lump in my throat. What if he made it out? What if he made it back and convinced the officials about what he'd found here? What if he brought them back?

It was all the fears I'd just voiced to Croc as to why we shouldn't have a child. I'd spoken them out loud and brought them to life.

Croc pulled me into his arms and started down. When we landed on the deck outside the front door, he gave me a tight hug. "I'll find him," he murmured, then drew back to look at me. "And if I don't, it's because he didn't make it far."

I searched his gaze, willing myself to believe. He was right. I'd seen it myself firsthand. I'd seen how quick the gators could sniff someone out, how soon they'd arrive in numbers to hunt that someone down. "Okay," I said, taking his hand in mine and pressing a kiss to the side of it. "Be careful."

He snorted, then tilted my chin up to press his mouth to mine. "I'm not worried," he murmured against my lips. "I'm just mad I had to put a shirt on you and leave."

I smiled into the kiss and relinquished my stress. If nothing else, I trusted Croc to handle it. Danny was one man and not exactly a pioneer. Croc was right, he wouldn't make it far.

He reluctantly pulled away and opened the door for me. "I'll be back," he said, even though he still didn't move to let me inside. "Don't change your mind about anything while I'm gone."

I grinned despite my lingering unease. "About what?"

"Anything." He tugged me into his arms and kissed me again, harder, rougher, until my toes curled and my heart raced, then he pulled back and groaned low in his throat. "Stay just like this until I get back."

I nodded and bit back a whimper as he released me.

He paused twice before he shook his head and started to walk away. Halfway across the yard he froze and turned back as if he'd forgotten something. "Willow?"

"Yeah?"

"Is it okay to kill him now?"

I would have laughed, had he been joking, but he wasn't. He asked the question as if he were checking to see if we needed milk from the store. I shook my head. "No."

He grimaced, nodded, and turned away, shaking his head and muttering beneath his breath until he dove into the canal and disappeared.

28
ARMY

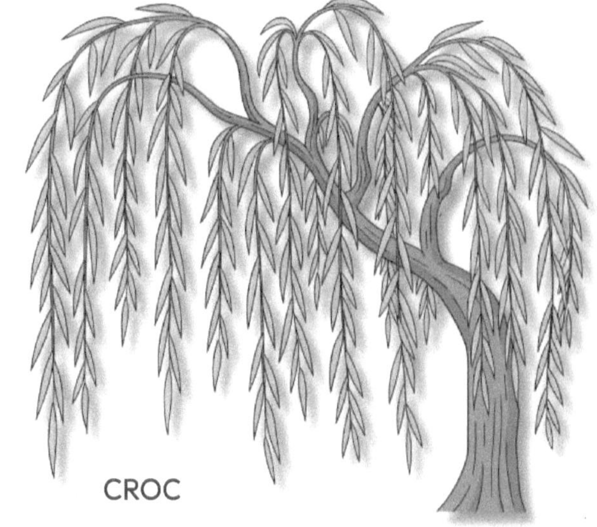

CROC

He was gone.

I tracked him all the way to the end. He'd ran. He'd ran and fallen over himself, moving clumsily through the trees, breaking branches and leaving a trail. He'd made it easy, but I'd been too preoccupied, and so had every alligator in the swamp.

I stared out at the big water, searching, even though I knew he wasn't anywhere near. His scent was faint, mingling with the smell of the sludge. Dump day had been three days ago, and he'd been waiting for them. He'd planned it. He'd succeeded.

Willow's words echoed through my mind. She'd said this would happen. She'd said she couldn't have my child because there would be no protecting it. I let out a roar and threw my knuckles into the closest tree. It cracked and splintered, but it didn't break because it was stronger than I was, and so were the many men who would undoubtedly come.

They wanted her. They wanted my babies. They wanted Julia.

I stood back and straightened, taking a deep breath in and turning back toward home. This was my world. This was the world I'd been born from. The canal was my mother. The gators were my brothers and sisters. The house, the garden, and everything that I owned had been built by Pappy.

Willow was wrong. She had to be. I had to prove it. I had to protect. I opened my mouth and released the call, pulling it from my lungs, deeper and louder than I'd ever done before. I called to all of them. Every gator, every frog, every bird and creature, no matter its size. Snakes slithered across the earth. Insects swarmed. Answering me. Answering the sound that'd been ingrained into my lungs since childhood. They knew this wasn't the same. This wasn't a skinned knee, a scared boy, a child in a tree too small to get down. They'd helped me grow into a man, and now my deep rumbling echoed that change; insistent, urging, demanding, and they answered quicker than they ever had before.

They arrived in droves and followed me as I went, multiplying until I stood in the yard surrounded by an army. Croaks and bellows, buzzing and hisses all mixed into one deafening sound. Gator broke through the crowd and stopped just in front of me, head up, eyes intent, and I met his stare briefly before addressing them all.

"Men are coming," I shouted.

Silence fell. Attention on me. I stared out at them, every set of green eyes, every flutter of wings, ancient gators to newborns. Every shape and size. It was the world I knew; the world I'd grown up in and survived and learned, and I'd protect it.

WILLOW

I heard him. His haunting call pierced the walls of my subconscious and lifted me out of a dead sleep. My insides twisted, eyes opened wide, and the urge to answer him made me sit up and turn toward the door.

Julia sat in a chair she'd dragged into the living room, a book loosely held in her lap and her attention fixed in the same direction. "What is that?" She stood.

I did the same, moving past her to reach the door first. Croc's cries echoed across the swamp and grew louder, and the swamp answered him. Julia forced herself beside me and froze at the sight of him breaking through the trees. Birds flew overhead, frogs and gators and snakes and bugs and every creature we'd come to recognize flocked around him. He was formidable to watch. His eyes were brighter, glowing even in the daylight, and he looked different. Somehow larger. Somehow stronger. He stood straighter. His face more solemn. His jaw set. Gaze determined.

He was regal, like a king calling his subjects to war, and when his voice echoed out, silencing the masses, I realized with stunned horror that he was.

"Men are coming," he bellowed out, then he slowly moved, pacing back and forth. "They want to cut us open and see what's inside. They want to take the swamp and use it for themselves. They want what's ours, and I can't fight them alone."

He stopped walking, and when he spoke again, the words were low, dark. "Will we let them?"

An uproar resounded, splitting my ears like dead air on a radio. I covered my ears, scanned the masses. It was an army. An army Croc could control.

He turned, and the look in his eyes made my heart give an extra beat. He was more than I'd imagined. Not human.

Not animal. Godly. Otherworldly. Something else entirely; something formidable and thunderous.

He turned back to the flock. "Watch for them. When they come, give the call, then we'll show them how nature feels about their behavior."

Another uproar sounded behind him as he turned away and closed the space between us. Julia stared at his face in a mix of wonder and pride. He hugged her tight, then let go and engulfed me in his arms. "I can," he murmured into my ear, crushing me against him. "I will protect."

"He's gone?" I breathed against him, mind racing. It felt like a dream. It felt unreal. He felt unreal. But it wasn't. It was happening, and the perfect world I'd grown so accustomed to was imploding.

"His scent ran out at the dump site," he released me to address Julia, too. "He went with them."

She nodded, and the words seemed to age her. The lines of her face drew tight, deepened, and paled. Her attention centered on the kids sitting quietly in the middle of the floor. They'd ventured out and huddled together, like ghosts of the children I'd found the first night. They knew who was coming. They knew what that meant, and no army Croc could conjure would ever be enough. He didn't know. He didn't understand.

"We need to leave," I said.

Croc stiffened. "Why? You saw. The swamp will stop them. We will stop them."

"It's not that simple," I said, though the words broke on their way out. A sob formed in my throat. Another home lost. A wonderful home that I'd allowed myself to grow attached to. "They have guns, Croc. They have guns and bombs and firepower. One man could take down a third of those animals in less than a minute." I blinked rapidly, then squared my shoulders and swallowed the despair. The dream was over, and it was once again time to survive.

I turned away. "Julia, pack Merle's bags. If we go now, maybe we can get deeper into the woods and hide until we can find a better plan."

"We can't run, girl," Julia said, voice tight.

I turned to stare at her. "We can't not run."

"Where will we go?" she snapped. "You'd have to swim for days to reach the other site, and the children won't make that. They're too small. There's nowhere else to go."

I shook my head, but she was right. The children couldn't swim it, and neither could she. Any other direction would lead us to them, without an army and a swamp to back us up. We were trapped. We were condemned. This was the end. I ground my teeth and gripped my hair. "We have to hide the children." I turned back to Croc. "Where can we hide the children?"

"The children can stay with you and Julia on the roof until it's over." His tone was dark.

It wasn't good enough. "Julia can take them to the garden and hide in the old shed." I looked at her. "Cover yourselves in mud, that way if you hear them, you'll be able to run into the woods and hide."

She held my gaze a long moment, then pulled me into her arms and squeezed with all her strength. "I wish things were different," she whispered hoarsely. "If I could give you my youth, I would, in a heartbeat, Little Bit."

Her use of Merle's nickname broke the last thread that held me together, and I choked, clinging her tighter, memorizing the smell and feel of her hug, knowing it could be the last time I ever felt it.

She pulled back and wiped her eyes, then set to work packing a bag to take with her and the kids. "If this is going to happen," she said, meeting my gaze, "We won't make it easy for them."

I nodded and turned back to Croc. "We need a plan. We need to set up traps, build weapons, do whatever we can before they arrive."

He gripped my arm and pulled me outside, shutting the door and pinning me to it. "You act as if we've already lost," he hissed at me. "Why? Why do you always doubt me?"

"You don't know what's coming, Croc." I cupped his cheek. "We'll be fighting fire with sticks, and the best thing any of us can do is hope we die before we're taken." I held his gaze, keeping the words as soft as I could manage. "The alternative is much worse."

His eyes blazed. "Trust me," he said, holding me locked with those shimmering irises. "Believe in me, in the swamp, and I will prove it to you, Willow. I will."

I wanted to. I wished it were possible. I'd never wanted to believe anything more. I studied his fiery expression. It was what he'd always wanted from me, and if these were the last days, hours, minutes of our lives together, I'd give him everything I could. "I believe you," I said, "and I'll follow you wherever you go."

He kissed me then, rough and demanding, sealing my words into law. Then, he pulled back and took my hand, leading me behind him toward the trees.

"Where are we going?" I asked, glancing back to the house where Julia and the kids remained and not wanting to leave them alone just yet.

"To get ready. To prove it." He turned and saw where my focus laid. "They won't sneak up on us, Willow. We'll know the minute they come within a mile of this place."

I nodded, and I followed, and I tried to believe.

WILLOW

29 THE GLUE

We had a plan that wouldn't succeed, but the time for running had ended. If we ran, they'd catch us. If they caught us, the deals began. I was done making deals. I was done bargaining for my life. Too much had changed. I'd changed. The life I had with Croc was mine and mine alone, and I wouldn't give a single ounce of it. I'd rather die in the swamp, commit my body to the place where my favorite memories lingered.

We'd gathered every kitchen knife and connected them to our waistbands. A stack of sticks lay in a pile, sharpened into points on both ends, and Croc worked hard to jam them all upright inside the many holes he'd dug along the tree line. He covered each one with leaves and moss before moving to the next, working at a pace that made me dizzy.

It wasn't enough.

Julia and the kids coated themselves in mud and left with a duffle bag to go to the garden, and Croc became a man determined to make this what it could never be. He wanted to prove it, just like he had everything else. He'd proven that he was different. He'd proven that I wasn't tarnished. He'd proven that my body was mine and mine alone, and he'd proven that being with a man could be something profound.

But he couldn't prove that we could win, and each time he looked at me, I had to swallow back the sob that so desperately wanted to break free. Julia and the kids were as safe as they could be. They had a slim chance. But Croc and I...we needed to die. "When they show up," I started when he finally stopped to sit beside me. We were on the ground at the tree line, and Croc grabbed a stick and started helping me with the pile I was working on.

"We'll kill them." He dug his knife into the wood.

I laid mine down and gave him a look. "When they show up, we can't be caught."

He paused and tilted his face toward me. "What are you saying?" His voice was tight, as if he already knew the answer.

"If— When the time comes, we have to end it. Ourselves." I swallowed hard. "Each other."

"No." The words shot out of him like a crack of thunder. "You will not die."

"I have to die," I whispered. "And so do you." My voice broke. "If they capture us, we'll die anyway, just much slower, and trust me—" I forced his eyes to meet mine "—you don't want to experience being a test. I'd rather be dead than go back."

This wasn't a fight for survival. It was my last fuck-the-government. For Merle. For Lita. For the kids that had their mother stolen and for the people who'd been killed. For the world murdered under the guise of salvation. "I just want to kill as many of them as we can before that happens."

Croc gripped my hand tight, then jerked me into a crushing embrace. "I want to make a deal," he rumbled against my hair.

I sucked in a deep, shuddering breath. "A deal?"

"A deal." He loosened his grip to hold me at arm's length. "Will you make one with me?"

My lip trembled, but I nodded. I'd have done anything for him.

Croc settled his forehead against mine, fingers digging into my arms.

I swallowed the pain and waited. Each of my muscles tensed, from my jaw to my toes, as I fought to hold myself together. At any moment, I'd break apart, and I couldn't afford that, not yet, not until it was over. I'd be broken soon enough.

"When I manage this," he finally spoke, "when I show you, when we beat them, then I want you to promise me something in return."

And there it was. Another deal. A piece of my soul in exchange for survival, but for once, it wasn't me on the bad side of the arrangement. It was him. He was bargaining for something he already had. My soul was at his disposal. I'd have given him any part he wanted, free of charge. "Whatever you want." I kissed his mouth once, then sucked in a breath and stared into his eyes as I fought to swallow my emotion. "Whatever you want, Croc."

He touched my hair, then pulled my head tighter to his and squeezed his eyes shut. "When this is over," he rumbled, "I want a day."

"A day?" I studied his shuttered expression. A day. I'd give him a thousand. I'd give him every one I had left.

He opened his eyes, and the emotion he'd been containing spilled out. The neon green shimmered, endless, raw, searing my thoughts and branding their image into my memory. For however long I had left, I knew, I'd remember this moment. This sight. When my last breath left my body, it would be his eyes that sent me off to whatever place came next.

"A day." His fingers curled against my scalp. "An entire day for me to tell you how amazing you are, and you not only have to believe me, you've got to accept it. All of it. Every word. Can you do that?"

His words liberated the last thread, and I unraveled. My vision blurred, tears sprung free, and my breaths broke apart inside my chest, rattling my bones, shaking my spine. I clung to him, buried into his embrace, and let his scent flood my senses. "Don't you get it?" Sobs slipped through each gap my words created, mingling into the syllables, dragging out the sounds. "I already do."

Croc rocked me back and forth and stroked my hair. He murmured soft words against my ear. He comforted and healed and kept my pieces safe, together, whole. I'd never been more whole, and it wasn't because he completed me. Croc hadn't filled the gaps my life had created. He'd given back every part I'd lost. He'd found them in plain sight then shown me where they'd been all along.

He'd made me love myself, so that I could love him.

I sucked in a breath, then another, calming myself just enough to raise up and capture his lips with mine. Two people, separate and whole, molding together to form the purest form of intimacy. It wasn't one sided or misguided. It wasn't half measured or deceitful. It wasn't about flesh or lust or a means to an end. It was sacred and spiritual. It was beauty in its most natural state, and it was everything I wanted before I left this world.

We made love, neither giving, neither taking. We shared and memorized and sunk into each other atop the soft marsh, under the canopied sky, amidst the world that'd joined us together, and it was bittersweet.

It was I love you, I need you, I accept you, and I'll never forget you, all wrapped up into a beautiful goodbye that made us both move slowly and fight to savor each second.

It was what we both deserved, and it was the last time we'd ever have it.

30
WAR

It started as a whisper, a distant cry that multiplied as every species joined together one by one to give the call. Treetops shook as birds took flight, and Croc cawed to them, matching the ear-splitting clamor of the flock. Cranes, herons, cardinals, and crows all bled into one, building a twister. I gaped at the sky, then at him. He walked sideways, hand outstretched, closing the few feet between us without looking my direction. His attention remained skyward, on the birds, on himself as he cried out to the mother. To the brothers and sisters. His voice shifted in and out of character, one animal to the next, hammering out instructions on the frontline of a war. This was a war. He ducked as he hissed, drawing snakes from the water, the branches. They slithered across the yard, down the bank, past our feet. He croaked, and frogs hopped after them. He conjured a plague, like Moses against the Pharoah, performing miracles.

When he reached my side, his hand rested on my back, but he still didn't look at me. "We're okay." He followed the words with a series of grunts, and monstrous, squealing rats sprinted out of hiding places.

"You sound just like them." I didn't sound like me. My

voice was too small, as if I were a mere mortal speaking to a god. He was impossible, but impossible was our reality. One central government was impossible, until it wasn't. Mass killing citizens was impossible, until it wasn't. Things ever getting any better was impossible.

Until it wasn't.

Croc's fingers slid to my shoulder. "Watch this."

He roared at the sky, and the mass of birds darkened, thickened, dove.

Screams erupted. Then gunfire. Bullets became fishhooks, yanking feathers from the sky. Hell had found a crack. Hell was on its way. I watched the formation struggle, migrating closer, knowing what that meant. The Greater Good was here, and they were coming for us. It was only a matter of time. An icy chill settled over me. They wouldn't bother with IVs, not now. They'd have bigger tests for us. Horrible tests. The thought of Croc strapped to one of those chairs, alone and suffering and surrounded by lies.

He cried out as if he already were, and the sound broke me like the world never could. His eyes, crazed eyes. Like the women in my group. Like the people at the store. Like the men who cleaned the trash-coated streets. Like Lita on the day this all began. They were killing his family, forcing him to watch.

I wanted to block his view. I wanted to pick him up and run. Croc wasn't like the rest of us. Croc was still human. The last human on Earth.

Croc gripped my forearm. "New plan!" He dragged me with him to the trees, threw me over his shoulder, then jumped. I squeaked, clinging on as he raced through the branches.

He deposited me behind a curtain of moss, then pulled one of the kitchen knives from my belt and slid the handle into my palm. My fingers curled around it; his curled around mine. "If you stay here, those things can't get you."

Those things. He'd barely listened when I tried to prepare him, too caught up in offensive strategy. He squeezed my hand, and for a blessed final moment, I had his full attention. Croc studied my face. I memorized his.

I couldn't lie to him. I wouldn't paint our fate. He needed to know, and better he hear it from me than learn the hard way. "They're too big, Croc. They can get us no matter where we hide, and I—"

He palmed the sides of my face, and his look said it all. Don't question. Don't doubt. He needed me to believe in him, and I couldn't take that away. I leaned in, brushing my nose against his, breathing him in for the last time. I'd give him everything I had. Everything that was left.

Croc took my mouth as if it belonged to him, making promises he couldn't keep. I let him. I melted into him. For a split second, I slipped away. This could be the last of our broken rules, and I wouldn't waste a single second on worry.

He leaned back, holding me still when I tried to follow. "Throw the knives, Willow. Like I showed you." He yanked one off his belt, then nodded for my agreement. "Don't let them see you."

I nodded, and he left me, moving three trees over to crow insistently at the sky.

I parted the moss and watched the din answer. Swirl up, dive. Swirl up, dive.

This was happening. My heart slammed against my

ribcage, then stopped beating altogether as the first wave of clinical white scrambled from the trees. Bodies swung and bent as the ground swallowed them. Croc's traps were like hungry mouths that had never found a greater good. I stared, trying to get an idea of their numbers. They seemed endless. How long could we keep them back? How long before they inevitably made it closer. Already, they were regrouping. The pits were all uncovered. Too easily passed. Had we had more time, we could have dug a trench. We could have built a moat. Had we had more time, I could have convinced him to leave. I could have made a better plan.

We could have had a life.

Had we had more time.

Croc threw three knives, each hitting a target. A spine. A throat. A back. He straightened and drew in air, filled his chest like an iron hive, then heaved out a swarm. Insects burst from the trees, gathered like droplets, building a tsunami. Croc's volume built with them. His muscles strained as his arms lifted, and a wall of buzzing black rose between us and our deaths. It took my breath away, then gave it back. For the first time since Croc said Danny was gone, I breathed. I hoped. I imagined.

Croc dropped his arms, and the wave crashed. Chaos exploded. Officials became ghosts, shadows scrambling for light, ducked bodies and flailing arms. It was working. Croc directed the bugs; the bugs directed the men, driving them closer to the water.

But Hell had smoke.

Thick grey puffs rolled into existence, driving back the horde. As the view cleared, my vision blurred. Nose, throat, and lungs burned. Tear gas. I held my breath and squinted at Croc. "Cover your—"

Croc bellowed, and alligators darted from the canal, jaws clamping around legs, arms, and thighs before dragging their prey back into the murk. Officials wailed. Officials fell. An incessant crack of machine gunfire. Gators piled up like big-game trophies. So many. Too many. They were painting our world red: the ground, the dock, the bank. A basecoat of blood to start their new reality.

"No!" I wrenched my knives free, flinging them with little thought, desperate to reverse it. Fix it. Turn back time. But if Croc wasn't enough to stop them, what chance did I have? I was useless. Powerless. The same as I'd always been. The same as we all were.

My new world was falling to the same ruin the last one had. Only, this one had been so much more. I had belonged. I was part of it, and I was crumbling.

Croc thundered, an explosive, booming growl. It lifted all the little hairs on the back of my neck. The gators slid back into the water, out of sight. The officials paused, slowed, looked around with lifted guns and skittish movements.

Croc crouched, breathing harsh, gripping the branch with a force that made me pity the tree. He pulled the last knife from his belt. "Willow," he said without looking in my direction. "They need me."

I swallowed hard, already shaking my head. "You'll be no good to them if you're dead."

"I'll be no good at all if I stay here."

Without him, what good was there? My vision swam, and not just from lingering fumes. It was too soon. "Then I'll go with you."

"No." It was instant and rough, and before the words could pass his lips, his gaze whipped to mine. "They need *me*. The babies need *you*."

The babies. His babies. Our babies. He knew the truth now. That this was over before it started. That we could never win. I swallowed convulsively, pursed my lips, demanding myself to keep it together. I couldn't fall apart. Not yet. Not when he needed me most. "They need you more than they've ever needed me."

I looked away from him and counted. Ten. Twenty. Twenty-five. Thirty. Fifty. Still too many. Force hadn't worked. It wouldn't. Not when they were all armed with semi-automatic weapons. All strapped down with bullets draped over their shoulders and chests. Their commander turned to give more orders, waving the rest toward the dock.

Then, I saw them, our babies, and what little hope I still possessed disintegrated.

Julia yanked her arms, fighting to free herself from the men pulling her forward. They had her. They had the children, and they seemed so much smaller. Crouched. Slumped. Scared. Little mice amongst the filth. Mud coated their skin, like it had the day we arrived, blocking their colors, dulling their joy.

An official holding a loudspeaker stepped over and took Eric's arm, yanking him in forward. The speaker gave a high-pitched screech as the man turned it on. Then he swung it to his face as if it were a prop, nonchalant, boastful. "Didn't I tell you, Willow?"

Danny.

It was over. It was worse than I could have ever imagined. I couldn't watch. Not this. Not them. I gasped and choked, fighting for air, for calm, for the ability to think, but no option seemed plausible. No answer existed.

I emptied, collapsed, slumping onto my branch as I stared at that tiny, cherub face. His downy brown curls. His sorrowful eyes, too aware for his age.

"Croc?" I needed him. I needed him to hold me together because I didn't think I could anymore.

But Croc didn't answer.

Croc was gone.

I scrambled to my feet and raced after him. "Croc! No!" He was too far ahead, swinging through the trees, sprinting across limbs. I moved faster than I ever had, eyes frantically shifting whenever I'd lose sight of him. I couldn't lose sight of him. If I did, I may never find him again.

Croc leapt from the trees and sprinted across the yard, much like he had the night he saved me from the alligators. Guns lifted, pointed, and I forgot how to think. All I did was move. Move faster. Move, move, move.

He ducked, then spun, shoving one official back while simultaneously snatching his weapon. He held it by the barrel, bashing it into the skull of the next man in his path.

The first dart hit Croc's shoulder; the second his arm. He yanked them out as he pushed forward, colliding full force with the scrambling Danny. The intercom chimed as it hit the dirt.

Danny screamed.

Croc smashed his skull into the ground, silencing him once and for all.

More darts hit Croc's back, too many to count. He pushed to his feet and spun in a circle, roaring murder, daring them to come closer. "You should never have come here!"

Three darts pierced his stomach. Two more in his chest. He grunted, stumbled.

"No, no, no, no, no." The words rattled out of me, and I missed my grip on the next branch. I slipped, fell, body smacking limbs on my way down. I landed back first, and my lungs deflated, locked.

I looked around, stunned, broken, done. Gaps in the trees offered a front row seat I didn't want. Croc was limp as they flipped him over. Men cuffed his wrists, then his ankles, tying it all together like a pig they would roast slowly. They'd hurt him. They'd kill him, then make him live with it. A corpse, already gone, forced to sit day after day and feel himself decay. It was a fate worse than death, and I couldn't do anything about it. Nobody could do anything to stop it.

I turned away from the sight, gasping like a fish left to die on the bank. We hadn't done it, but I'd known we wouldn't. I was tired. Tired of fighting, of suffering, of losing. I was tired of trying, of failing, myself, the people relying on me. I wanted to close my eyes to all of it, never wake up. It didn't matter where we went or if we went anywhere at all. How could I exist after this? How could I stay awake, watching, as the children fell to the same fate? The fate I'd barely managed to save them from the last time.

Then the intercom sounded again, and a small, mechanical voice announced, "I think I can."

My head whipped over, finding Eric bent with his mouth pressed against the device. He was too small to lift it, forced to rest it on the ground. He pulled the trigger, and his voice crackled again, "I think I can."

"I think I can!" Eve's voice rang up. "I think I can!"

"I know I goddamn can!" Julia stomped the foot of one of her captors. He jolted enough to lose his grip, and she elbowed him in the face before another man could restrain her. That strange chaotic harmony we'd created that night returned, magnified. "I think I can. I think I can." It grew, croaking, crowing, hissing, bellowed, "I think I can." It rose all around us, building momentum like the happy train chugging up its hill.

"I think I can," I rasped, pushing past the pain and to my feet. "I—" I heaved a breath "—think I can." I stumbled, then stepped, then ran. "I think I can."

"I think I can! I think I can!" A battle cry. Our battle cry.

Screaming officials and snarling beasts fought to intercept me. A man covered in cottonmouths fell backward in my path. Another landed as if thrown, legs missing and face ash. I skirted around and over, moving with the obstacles how I moved with the canal. I'd grown. I wasn't a coward making dark deals in the shadows of society. I was a protector. I'd been chosen by the Earth herself, made strong by her hands, and I would fight until the last breath left my lungs.

My lips curled around a snarl as I pushed my muscles to the limit, racing toward my family. Devils sprouted as I went. Tranquilizer and stun guns lifted, but I was too fast. Too powerful. Too awake.

I threw one man who stood in my way and then snapped the neck of another. Tranquilizer darts hit my skin, but they were nothing compared to the chemicals I'd endured. In the back of my mind, I awaited my death. I waited for the moment my vision would fade. When they'd get me down. But the thoughts couldn't make it past my subconscious. I couldn't hear them over the menacing roar of our army. "I think I can! I think I can!"

The longer I remained on my feet, the louder I became. The more I believed I could. We could. The swamp moved with me; the wildlife aided me. Then I was back in the moment that started all of this, gathering two children into my arms and promising to protect them. "Inside!" I called to Julia, not knowing where else to take them. We rushed through the chaos, and I pushed them into the worn shack, knowing it wasn't enough.

"Just stay here, I'll—" I couldn't finish. I couldn't lie. "I love you. All of you." My voice broke, and I closed the door, turning back to the fray. My eyes scanned wildly until I found Croc. I sprinted toward him.

The so-called Greater Good wasn't looking so great. With each second that passed, we made them fall. Fifteen. Ten. Maybe we would win. Maybe it was possible.

But no sooner had the words entered my mind, the world arrived to laugh at them.

A boat drifted into view, loaded down with fully armed men.

A new wave, worse than the last. The man at the wheel took one look at the sight and called up a sharp, "We've got suits! Take 'em down, boys!"

I threw myself over Croc just before the guns went off. *Crack, crack, crack, crack, crack*. I covered my head, muscles tensed, and aching in anticipation of a hit. I focused on the steady rise and fall of Croc's lungs, telling him goodbye inside my mind, thankful to have had him for a little while.

Gators circled us, forming a wall of protection. Then, all at once, the world fell silent. No pain. No pinch. No darkness come to swallow me. I lifted my head.

The remaining officials were full of holes, covered in blood, scattered with arms and legs bent at awkward angles. I peeked up at the boat. It'd stopped, and the men on board stood still, waiting for a new command. That's when I noticed their clothes. Worn jeans and T-shirts, leather jackets and tattooed skin. Not officials. They weren't officials. This army of giants was on our side.

"That's a lot of gators you've got there," the same man at the wheel called with a grin. "I don't suppose you can stop them from eating us."

I ignored him and checked Croc's face, felt his pulse, patted his cheek and shook his shoulder. He coughed, groaned, before his eyelids opened the smallest of cracks..

"Are you okay?" I ran a hand over his forehead, then quickly broke his bindings.

He nodded and tried to sit up, only to flop back down and clutch his head. "The world is spinning," he said. "But I'm okay." He looked around, taking in the gators around us, then seeming to remember our situation, pulled me against his chest.

"It's alright," I said. "We won." My voice broke and lifted, "We won, Croc! We did it!"

His eyes opened fully, and, this time, he finally managed to pull himself into a sitting position. I kissed his lips, reassured with the fact that he was alright, then stood and stared in horror at the devastation surrounding us. So many dead. Too many gone. A part of myself, a part of us, lay lifeless upon the ground. I swallowed the lump building inside my throat and blinked hard to clear the moisture clouding my vision. "Gator!" I cried out, voice high and shaking. "Where's Gator?"

"I'm right here," he said. He'd been right beside me, the first one to curl around to shield us.

I dropped down and hugged him, my cheek against his back, my grip tight. "I thought you were dead."

He laughed low. "I already told you. I'm fast. Real fast."

Croc reached over and laid his hand on Gator's head, his body bowing in obvious relief as his other arm circled my shoulders. I choked on a laugh that sounded more like a sob and burrowed deeper against the scales, ignoring the men still waiting for a response, or gratitude, or some acknowledgement. I didn't know who they were, but they'd helped us.

"Little Bit?"

31
BAYOU SUNSET

My eyes widened, heart lurched, and I jumped up and spun around to see him standing at the front of the boat, gripping the rail with both hands. "Merle!" I ran forward, watching him swing himself over the side and down the ladder. We met halfway, and I jumped into his arms, knocking us both down into a crushing hug. "You're alive!"

His hands shook against my head as he patted my hair. "So are you, girl."

I lifted up and looked at his face, then back over to the boat. "So that's…"

"Tex," the man greeted with a nod.

"Without the map, I couldn't find this place, so I went to his spot along the river." The whole time he spoke, his eyes strayed to Croc. The wild man still surrounded by alligators.

My breath shook at his expression, because it was the same he always got when impatient for answers. He was here, alive, and able to look that way. A million stories filled my mind at once. "I have the wildest shit to tell you."

Merle smiled. "You ain't the only one."

The front door banged open, and Julia rushed out with a hand shaking over her mouth. She looked like a walking swamp thing, covered in dried mud from head to toe, but Merle didn't seem to care.

He strode away from me, heaved her up into his arms, then held her like she was the only thing holding him to the ground. Julia sobbed into his neck, gripping his shirt with one hand while the other half-heartedly smacked his arm.

He held her pinned to his chest and supported her weight until she'd calmed. Then, as if they'd never been separated, he said, "I see you dolled up for me."

She smacked his arm harder and gave a high cackling laugh. "You asshole! I was worried to death!"

He rumbled. "Dammit, woman! I went as fast as I could. I'm not a young man anymore."

She craned her head back. "So, you like this look?"

Her smile was watery, but it wasn't diluted. Not like the ones she'd given since he disappeared from view that night. Julia was so good at pretending to be okay, it was easy to believe her. But seeing her now, it was obvious she hadn't been. She hadn't looked like this.

Merle dipped her back and kissed her hard, and a chorus of hoots and catcalls echoed from the boat. He pulled back, grinning like a cat. "You could cover yourself in cow shit and still be the hottest damn thing on God's green earth."

"I'm glad you think so. Just wait until you see your car."

His smile fell, eyes narrowed. "What about my car?"

My chest tightened. They were both alive. The kids slowly emerged, pulling all of our attention, and I dropped down and opened my arms wide. My family.

They ran forward, collapsing into me, and I lifted them both like I had the first night we'd met. Only this time, we were safe. We had help. We had hope, and we had a real chance.

Tex's men set forward with a plan to dispose of the officials. They sent the half-eaten ones floating down the canal, and the ones hit by bullets were buried deep within the woods. When the stain of the greater good was cleansed from the swamp, Croc mourned. He mourned each animal individually, saying his goodbyes, murmuring his gratitude. Giant men helped him give each its own grave. We stood on the bank of the canal, looking at row upon row of upset earth.

Then, Croc sang. Just as he had that night. Only this song wasn't joyous. It had no words. It was long and low and haunting, composed of a language he'd built, and the surviving animals joined in to mimic each rise and fall, each echo and sorrowful moan.

I bit my lip and swallowed my tears, but they were too many. My nose ran. My eyes blurred. My breaths shallowed. The swamp was forever changed. It would never be the same again, and even the canal mourned the loss of what had been.

The men stood just behind us, feet shoulder width apart and heads bowed in respect, but the minute the swamp awoke to join Croc, eyes lifted and widened, taking it all in and glancing amongst themselves.

I didn't blame them. I'd felt the same way. I'd experienced the same awe, and I'd been blessed to be accepted as a part of it.

When Croc finished, he turned and found me, wrapping me in a tight embrace before moving to do the same to Julia. He'd released them into the hands of the mother, and I could feel her. Hear her in that silent language saying everything was going to be okay. They weren't gone because death was not the end. She was us, and we were her, and she was immortal.

The thought comforted, then Croc comforted. His arm draped around my shoulders, tucking me into his side as he led the way home.

Julia and I made a feast large enough to feed an army. Nothing about Croc could be considered small, yet Tex and his men made him look that way. They were almost as bulky as they were tall, and not one of them entered the house without having to duck beneath the doorframe.

It felt like sardines packed into a can, but we made it work. Everyone piled in, sitting wherever they could. Eve and Eric referred to Merle as Papa, and that was all it took to melt his heart. He and the men teased and played with them, tossing them back and forth across the living room as they squealed in delight.

Julia and I made fish and rice with the raspberry sauce she'd conjured the first night, and I'd never thought we'd need to make more than one ear of corn, but that day, we cooked ten.

Croc watched it all at a distance, smiling whenever Eve or Eric called to him, but otherwise, he kept to himself. Except for occasionally…

I was laying food out on the table, when he gently took my arm and placed his lips close to me ear. "You're beautiful."

I blushed and grinned, turning back to Julia and the stove.

When the table was set and men lined up single file to get a plate, he appeared behind me again and whispered, "You're stronger than all those men."

I glanced at him, then pretended I didn't hear and continued handing out plates. I knew what he was doing. It was the deal. It was his payment. We'd pulled it off and now I had to accept all he said. But if he was going to claim I was stronger than fee-fi-fo-fum and all his brothers, he was pushing it a bit far.

When everyone had their plates, I sat on the floor close to Merle and took a bite of fish.

Croc sat down beside me with his own plate, then leaned over and whispered, "You'd make an amazing mother."

I choked and spluttered, and he focused on his plate with a grin.

Merle raised an eyebrow at me. "You alright there, Little Bit?"

I nodded and took a big gulp from my glass of water. "I'm fine. Guess I just went a bit *too fast.*" I glanced at Croc, eyes narrowing.

He didn't look ashamed.

Talk turned more serious as Tex relayed everything he knew.

"Government made the green to deal with the trash and ended up with a jacked up witch's brew." He took a huge bite of fish. "Shit ended up being so toxic, motherfuckers can't even stand close to it. I don't know about you, but it seems to me the obvious answer would be to stop using it. But *no*. They keep making the shit until there ain't no-damn-where to put it. Start dumping it anywhere they think the sun don't shine. Doing all these failing tests to try and fix there stupid."

"How do you know all this?" I asked. He talked about it

as if he'd been there. Or, perhaps they had their own Danny to squeeze information from.

His eyes met mine. "Different ways. A bit here. A bit there. A buddy of mine got a gig working out at the plants when they were still containing it in silos. It didn't matter what type of gear they wore, the workers dropped like flies. People caught wind, stopped taking the job." He readjusted his legs, shifting his weight. "Word now is they're making people who've been listed do the work."

Julia stepped over and plopped another fish onto Tex's plate before taking the seat next to Merle.

Tex licked his fingers and grunted his appreciation. "It's been too long since I had one of your meals." He smiled, and his whole face changed with the expression. He was far too young to be an old friend of Merle's, but he looked the part. His head was shaved on both sides, and one long tangle of thick braids started at his forehead and hung long and heavy down his back. Tattoos covered his neck, curled around his temples, disappearing beneath the collar of his shirt. He devoured the offering then sat back against the wall with a sigh. "I was told they marked these sites not long after they started using the chemical, all remote locations. My guess is they knew from the beginning there'd be too much to contain any other way. I count four so far in North America. No doubt they have more."

Croc straightened and leaned closer. "Danny said there are six. You think they're all like the swamp?"

"Six?" Tex's eyes glinted as they shifted over, studying, inspecting. "I don't know about the other two, but the four we've found seem to be. Ours is, so it only makes sense. More people like you. More animals like your gators." His lips curved. "That's what we've been searching for."

"Enough to build a bigger army?" Croc asked, and I knew the tone. He was planning, only this time, it wasn't just about me. He wanted to avenge his animals, his family, and his intentions couldn't have been any plainer if he'd flat out said them.

Tex's smile widened. "That's the plan." He glanced at Merle, then Julia. "The way I see it, this swamp isn't safe anymore. They'll come back, maybe not for a while given the message we floated down to them, but don't be mistaken. They're coming back here, if only to see what the hell they're dealing with."

Croc sat back with a slow nod. "What do you suggest?"

Tex straightened like a salesman about to move the best car on the lot. "We have a large camp, right on the river, and enough men to defend it should they decide to check us out. Your gators could follow us all the way there and have enough water and space to be comfortable."

Croc looked around the shack, lingering on the pictures of Pappy hanging on the wall.

I took his hand and squeezed, knowing what leaving would mean for him, but unwillingly to vote against it. I'd come too close to losing him, and I wouldn't be able to rest here, knowing what the future would bring us.

He met and held my gaze for a long moment before turning back to Tex. "We'll go with you."

Tex could have been a cat that just got its claws in a turkey. "That's exactly what I wanted to hear." He turned to his men. "You hear that, boys! We've got gators."

A burst of hoots and rough sounds sparked to life, and the house shook with the force of pounding fists and stomping feet.

I stared at the hoard, half amazement and half trepidation. They were building an army. They were planning a war. A war against Josef Arogander, an attack on the greater good, and we'd just signed up for it.

Croc squeezed the hand still holding mine and pressed his lips back to my ear. "No matter what happens," he murmured, "Croc will always protect Willow."

I met his eyes, shimmering pools of neon green and truth, and I believed him. I accepted it. Because that was the new deal, and I loved it.

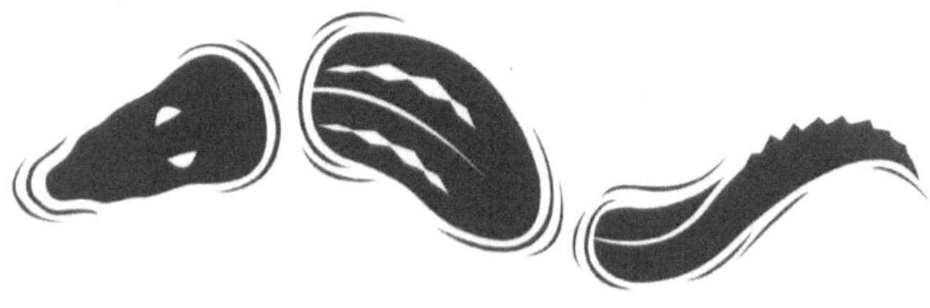

Coming Soon to the Human Nature Series

#2 Boondocks
#3 Badlands
#4 Boulevard

About the Author

Wendy Mae Mansell grew up in a trailer park in Alabama. She's been hungry, cold, and wanting more than once. Her vocabulary was expanded by the patrons of the truck stop her mama worked at as a cook, and the friends who've mostly all since either died or gone to jail. She moved away when she was seventeen, and has since built a stable life with her husband and children. She still drinks her coffee out of whichever cup is clean, and may or may not be wearing raccoon pajamas as she writes this. Her goal is to create character-driven stories that shine a light on the issues she is passionate about.

www.ingramcontent.com/pod-product-compliance
Lightning Source LLC
LaVergne TN
LVHW100523110826
845146LV00002B/752

* 9 7 9 8 9 9 5 4 5 0 3 0 6 *